RUNNING SCARED

BY

KEN DOUGLAS

A BOOTLEG BOOK

A BOOTLEG BOOK
Published by
Bootleg Press
2431 NE Halsey, Suite A
Portland, Oregon 97232

Bootleg Books may be purchased for educational, business, or sales promotional use. For information please e-mail, Kelly Irish at: kellyirish@bootlegpress.com.

Second Bootleg Press Trade Paperback Edition.

September 2005

10 9 7 6 5 4 3 2

ISBN: 0974524654

Bootleg Press is a registered trademark.

Cover by Compass Graphics

Printed in the United States of America

This Book is Dedicated to the Pirates in the Night

Death took some of us.
The law stopped others.
Some of us were captured.
Some of us got away.
A few of us are pirates still.

I may have moved on,
but I remember you all.
It was a hell of a life.

I would like to offer my grateful thanks to Ruth Lund off the South African flagged Sailing Vessel *Dignity* for her valuable insight into Joey and the pages she contributed to the manuscript.

And I would also like to say many thanks to Dianne Nilsen off the South African flagged Sailing Vessel *Vula* for giving me Nina.

Running
Scared

CHAPTER
ONE

JOEY SAPPHIRE WAS SHAKEN from a deep sleep to a splitting headache, a howling wind and cold chills. She hadn't had the nightmare about her father in years. Harold Vanderveer, policeman, racist, murderer. She clenched her fists against the memory of him. He'd bragged about the blacks he'd killed, filling his home with venom. He'd driven his wife to an affair and the happiest day of Joey's life was when her mother had told her they were going to live in Scotland with her new father. She'd been twelve years old, had hated apartheid since she could remember. She had been glad to go.

The boat was rocking and that didn't make sense, because they'd tied it up at the Marina till Mick got back from visiting his parents in the States. It had to be storming something fierce outside to jerk *Satisfaction* around in the slip. It was storming that night in Scotland when she'd learned her father had taken his life back in South Africa. Shot himself in the head with his own gun. He couldn't adjust to majority rule. He'd rather kill himself than answer to a black man. Maybe he wasn't evil, but he was pretty damned close. Joey didn't mourn him.

She scrunched her eyes tight, shutting him from her memory. She knew she should check the boat, but she was too tired to get up. Besides, *Satisfaction* was safely secured. There was no reason for her to check anything. She tried to nod back to sleep when something tickled her breast. Mosquito? She scratched, felt something sticky. What? And she was nude. She never slept that way.

A fly buzzed her, landed on her stomach. She slapped at it. Her hand squished in the sticky stuff. What was it? She was in a fog. She smelled something strange, like the meat section of the outdoor market in Port of Spain. She didn't eat meat, never had it on the boat. Something was wrong.

She pulled herself out of the dream fog, opened her eyes. She was on her back, staring skyward through the overhead hatch. The night was clear. Countless stars dotted the heavens. She sighed at the sight, then a cold shiver shimmied up her spine. *Satisfaction* didn't have an overhead hatch above the master berth.

She gasped. She wasn't on board her boat.

There were no clouds. No rain. And the boat wasn't in a slip. It was at anchor somewhere. That explained the movement.

She moved her hand, felt someone next to her, snapped the hand away. His skin was cold. She shivered herself. That's what happened when you fell asleep naked with open hatches on a breezy night.

Oh, my God, the thought raced through her, stabbed her soul. Who had she gone home with? She tried to think back to the party up at the hotel. Obviously she'd overdone the Christmas cheer. How could she ever face Mick?

She couldn't tell him.

"Shit," she muttered. "I'm in trouble." She sat up, knuckled the sleep out of her eyes. Her head throbbed. She must have had a lot more eggnog than she'd thought. How could that have happened? She never drank too much.

She had to pee. She started to get out of the berth when she felt something move in her lap. Instinctively she reached for it, picked it up. "What?" She cut her palm. "Ouch." It was a knife. She threw it aside, jumped out of the berth. The cut was deep, the pain took her mind away from the hangover. Feet on the deck, she turned to the man she'd gone home with and screamed.

He was big, nude, pasty white under the starlight. His long hair was splayed about his shoulders. It was covered in blood.

Joey couldn't suck air fast enough. In and out, in and out. She was hyperventilating.

Dead.

The man was dead.

Gasping air, she staggered backward, slammed into the bulkhead, sunk to the deck. Think, think! She couldn't. Her mind was spinning out of control. She was dizzy, vertigo was overcoming her. She was about to pass out.

Gotta stop it.

She grabbed a deep breath, clamped her mouth closed, held it as long as she could, maybe ten seconds, then exhaled and did it again. A little longer this time. And again, and again, and again, till she was breathing normally.

She didn't want to look, but she had to look. She pushed herself up. On her feet, she moved toward the dead man. He was even bigger than she'd first thought. A giant of a man. A cow. She saw what he had between his legs, no, a bull. She felt between her own legs, she wasn't sore, a man like that would make any woman tender the morning after. So she hadn't had sex. At least that was something.

Still struggling for air, she forced her eyes up to his face and stifled another scream. The Bull's throat had been sliced open. It was as if he were wearing a grisly smile under his chin and the blood that had flowed from it looked like a long black beard that had oozed around the body, strangling it, suffocating it.

"Come on, Joey," she said. "Snap out of it."

She should call the Coast Guard. She backed away, turned and made her way to the salon. She found an overhead light, turned it on. The radio was in the nav station. She picked up the mike, turned to channel sixteen, pushed the talk button. "Trinidad and Tobago Coast Guard, Trinidad and Tobago Coast Guard, this is Sailing Vessel—" She paused. Sailing Vessel what?

It didn't matter. All she had to do was give her location, they'd find her. But she didn't even know that. She dropped the mike. Looked around the boat, saw nothing with the vessel's name on it. But even if she learned it, she was still going to have to tell them where she was. The companionway was open to the outside, not locked up tight, the way Mick kept their hatches when they were on board at night. Apparently the Bull wasn't as paranoid as her American husband. She shuddered. Apparently he should've been.

The air was brisk when she stepped out into the cockpit. She knew right away were she was. The boat was anchored off the heliport, near the small military museum. As for the name of the vessel, she hadn't a clue. She looked over the boat. A steel ketch, but she didn't know it.

She drew in a deep breath of fresh air. Outside she realized how cloying it had been below, with the coppery smell of blood, the fresh meat smell of death. She didn't want to go back down there, was about to shout out for help when she realized she was still nude.

Then a horrible thought tumbled through her. They hang murderers in Trinidad. Only two weeks ago they'd hung nine men for the same crime. Three grisly hangings, three grisly days in a row. And they left the bodies twisting from the gallows all day long. She wrapped her arms around her breasts, hugged herself. Her fingerprints were on the knife. She couldn't call the Coast Guard or the police, they'd arrest her, hang her. Fear shot up her spine. She didn't want to die.

She looked down, eyes roaming over her body. Blood was smeared all over herself. How come she hadn't noticed it before? Shock? Then she realized she had. The sticky stuff. Sure, the sticky stuff. Amidships she spotted a swim ladder. First order of business, get the blood off. Then she'd worry about the dead man. She stepped over the lifelines, climbed down the ladder, lowered herself into the dark water and scrubbed with a vengeance till there was no trace of the blood left.

She climbed back on board, cold, frightened, but thinking clearly now and dripping seawater over the deck. Normally she wouldn't go below deck wet, but this captain wasn't going to care. She studied the radio as she passed the nav station. No, she wouldn't be calling the Coast Guard. She found her clothes on the settee, started to put them on, but stopped herself. She had a lot of work to do first.

Back in the forward cabin, she forced herself to climb up onto the berth. She reached over the body, grabbed a fistful of sheet and pulled it from the mattress, draping it over the Bull. In seconds, that seemed like hours, she had the body wrapped in the bloody shroud. She found more sheets in a cabinet opposite the bed, took two of them and wrapped them around the body till no blood soaked through.

She was so scared, but she had to go on, so she searched the boat, found some line and duct tape. An idea formed as she wrapped the gray tape around her palm, sealing her wound. Her original plan had been to drag the body up on deck, roll it over the side and hope the current took it out to sea, where it would disappear forever. Then she'd be safe. But she couldn't count on that. What if someone found it? They'd identify him, someone might remember that he'd left the party with her.

Joey put her hands to her neck. She imagined the hangman's noose. She couldn't just drop him overboard. She had to sink him and make sure he stayed sunk.

She went back on deck to study the ground tackle. Please God, let the boat have two anchors. It did. She needed pliers and she found them in a tool box.

Back at the body, she wrapped it with the duct tape. Satisfied the shroud was secure, she tried to drag the Bull out of the rack. Couldn't. He wasn't a bull, he was an elephant. She'd never be able to drag him through the length of the boat and pull him up through the companionway.

For a few seconds she was stumped, but the thought of a noose around her neck stimulated her thinking. She took a long length of line and tied the rope around the body's feet, then she climbed out through the overhead hatch. On deck she took the windlass handle out of a holster that was attached to the mast. She went to the windlass, dropped to her rear, used the handle to disengage the chain gypsy. That done, she wrapped the rope around the drum. Now, instead of pulling up the anchor, the anchor winch would pull up the body.

She pushed the deck button, the windlass came to life, the rope tightened and she saw the ghostly shrouded feet come up through the hatch. She kept her hand on the button, heard the legs break as the force of the windlass bent them back. She pulled her hand off the button as if it'd been burnt.

Holy God, that snapping sound ricocheted through the night. Surely someone had heard. She held her breath, but no one popped out of the other boats. No one shined a megawatt light at her. If they did, she'd be discovered. She had to hurry.

She pushed the button again. More bones cracked as the body rose, bent and broke as the anchor winch pulled it through. Then all of a sudden she heard a ripping sound, somehow the sheets had gotten caught on the hatch lever. Now there was a gaping hole in the shroud and the Bull's head poked through it. His eyes, open wide in death, seemed to be staring up at her. Not at her, through her.

God, she couldn't take it. She scooted to the lifelines, pulled herself up to her knees, stuck her head over the side and vomited into the sea. She couldn't stop it and she couldn't be quiet about it. Gut wrenching spasm after spasm, until she had nothing more to come up. She was out of breath, sucking air again. She fought it, brought herself back under control. Any second she expected to be discovered, but still nobody poked a head up. Nobody shouted over to see what was wrong.

"You can do this," she mumbled.

She used the pliers to unshackle the anchor from the chain. Then she dropped the chain back in the chain locker, cringing at the sound it made as it clattered on down. Marley's ghost couldn't have been any louder.

She took a deep breath. Still the bay slept.

Time to finish it. She took the line off the windlass

and tied it to the second anchor with a bowline, then she pushed the body under the lifelines feet first till it was hanging over the deck, folded at the waist.

"I'm so sorry," she said, "but I don't know what else to do." She pushed the anchor out of the bow roller, jumped back when it splashed into the sea and cried out when the head thumped against the deck as the anchor pulled the body on down.

The body gone, she thought about her father again. Was that why she had the nightmare, because subconsciously she knew she was sleeping next to a dead man? Then she remembered one night when she was a little girl. He'd bragged about tossing a black man into the sea. She had just done that, tossed a body to the sea. That didn't make her any better than him.

"Stop it, Joey," she muttered. "Don't think like that." She'd spent her whole life trying to atone for him. She'd taken her mother's maiden name, Ryder, as her own, so that when she went back to South Africa she wouldn't be burdened with the hated Vanderveer name. She swam for her native country in the Sydney Olympics, bringing them two golds on her twenty-sixth birthday, rather than swim for Scotland. She'd worked as a social worker in the townships right up till she got married. She'd spent her weekends working with battered women and had given a good part of her income to charities that benefited abused kids. She'd done enough, she deserved to be free of him.

She went below, straight to the forward cabin, where she picked up the knife. She flung it through the hatch, heard it splash. Then, fighting to keep herself from gagging, she flipped the mattress over, hiding the blood.

She made up the bed with clean sheets, then went to the galley where she found dishwashing liquid. She filled a bowl with water and washed down everything she might have touched.

Once the boat was scrubbed down, she took a trash bag from the galley, stuffed her clothes into it along with a bath towel she'd stolen from the head. She did a quick walk through and was satisfied that all appeared normal. She didn't know who the Bull was, didn't know how soon he'd be missed, but she hoped it would be a long time, long enough for anyone who may have seen her with him to have forgotten.

Now there was nothing left for her to do, save get away, get back to *Satisfaction* in the marina and pretend none of this had ever happened. She clutched the trash bag in a firm grip as she again went down the swim ladder and slipped into the sea. She made it to shore with ease, toweled off, got into her clothes, then started along the road to the marina about a half mile away.

She looked to the sky. The stars seemed so peaceful. She imagined God up there, frowning down at what she'd done. Chills shivered through her, tears welled up.

What had she done?

She couldn't have killed him.

She was sure of that.

So who had?

And she couldn't have, wouldn't have, climbed into the sack with a dead man, no matter how drunk she'd been. That meant that whoever had killed the Bull had done it while she'd slept next to him. Her stomach spasmed. She bent to her knees, went through a series of wracking dry heaves. She had nothing left to come up, but her body tried to empty her stomach anyway. And all through the stomach clenching pain, one thought kept pounding her brain.

The murderer knew. He knew about her.

CHAPTER TWO

NINA BRAVA WOKE with the first slivers of sunlight that streamed into the room. She sat up, stretched, and smiled, no morning sickness today. Then she jumped out of bed, crossed over to Joana's bed and shook her.

"Wake up, it's my day."

"*Bom Dia*," Joana do Campo said.

"English, Joana, you promised." Sometimes Joana slipped into Portuguese, but Nina was always quick to remind her that if they truly wanted to learn English, they had to live it, especially among themselves. She wouldn't be happy till she spoke as well as Tom Cruise.

"Yes, yes, Good morning, Nina, happy birthday. And happy Christmas Eve." Joana was Nina's best friend in all the world. They were so alike many thought they were sisters. Both tanned, hazel-eyed woman with dark hair that flowed over their shoulders.

"Not just any birthday. I'm twenty-one." She hugged herself.

"Just another birthday."

"Not if you're an American." Nina loved the Americans. "Twenty-one is a big deal. It means you can go to a bar and drink."

"You've been drinking since you were eleven years old," Joana said and Nina sighed, that was true. Nina first met Joana in the whorehouse the day she lost her virginity, ten years ago. She'd been sick afterwards and Joana introduced her to rum. If you drank enough, you forgot about the men.

"But I'm thinking like an American now. I'm twenty-one and I've got my whole life ahead of me." She twirled between the beds and hugged herself again. "We've come so far together, you and me, and we have a long way to go."

"And we're going to get there, wherever that is."

Together, Nina and Joana owned half of *The Connection*, the internet cafe at the Bay View Hotel in Fortaleza. It was a four star beach front hotel with a large outside entertainment area, pool, bar, restaurant and its own marina, which accommodated foreign yachts. *The Connection* had a good location, overlooking the marina, sported ten Apple Mac computers, served coffee, tea and pastries and even beer and mixed drinks after 5:00. It was the in place for both the yachties and the locals to hang out and send their e-mail.

Captain da Silva, the port captain, was their silent partner in *The Connection* and owned controlling interest in the hotel. Nobody outside of Nina and Joana knew that, but then he was the only man they'd been with from the bad days who knew who they really were and where they were now. He'd come to the whores because he was an old widower who wanted a young girl one more time before he died. That one more time turned out to be once a week for two years.

Now he had prostate cancer and would do anything for them. Three years ago, when his illness was diagnosed, he bought the girls from the whorehouse, set them up with a room at the hotel at no charge and gave them their half interest in the internet cafe with only three instructions, never cheat, treat the customers like family and tell no one of his interest in the business, and he meant absolutely no one.

Although Nina loved the old man, she knew him for what he was, a criminal who used his position at the port to enrich himself. Cocaine floated into Fortaleza unobstructed, then found it's way onto the captain's planes bound for who knew where. But that was none of Nina's business. If stupid people wanted to take drugs, then that was their own affair, she had no regard for them. If she and Joana could come from the kind of life they had and not even smoke cigarettes, then she didn't feel sorry for those people with a purse full of money that got themselves addicted to the white powder.

The captain had no children, no family, save for Nina and Joana. In a funny kind of way he looked upon the girls as his daughters and like kids everywhere, they yearned to leave the nest. Though the captain loved them, trusted them, confided in them. Though he'd saved them, sheltered them, protected them. And though their lives were certainly very much better now then they were before, they still felt owned.

The captain knew this, knew they were saving to buy him out of *The Connection* and encouraged it. He wanted them to be free, to fly away on their own. To that end he'd assisted in their education and training and set them up in the business, but the final step was theirs. He wanted them to earn their freedom and Nina and Joana were determined not to let him down. The wanted to make him proud.

"Want to play a set before work?" Nina asked. To stay fit, Nina and Joana played tennis on the hotel courts every evening and many mornings. Joana had developed a wicked serve and Nina had been working furiously to counter it, something she really wanted to do before she had to give up the game for the baby's sake.

"Sorry, I can't." Joana pushed herself out of bed. "I have to get ready for the tour group, remember?" Joana and Nina both worked as tour guides on their days off. This, Captain da Silva frowned upon as he didn't like anything that took their time away from *The Connection*, but every little bit helped, the sooner they bought him out, the sooner they'd feel free. "It's an all day tour, so I won't be home till late."

"Be nice to the tourists and answer all their

questions," Nina said. "In English."

Joana loved the tourists as much as she herself loved the foreign yachties. Especially the Americans. America fascinated her so much so that she surfed the net at least an hour a day, studying up on the United States, reading about its fabulous cities. Someday she and Joana were going to save enough money to move there and open a Brazilian restaurant somewhere near Hollywood. It was their dream.

"Oh, Nina, we've become such brown nosers, we should be so ashamed." Joana was fighting a smile. Nina didn't like it when Joana learned words first.

"I don't know that word."

"What, *ashamed*?"

"Oh, you." Nina grabbed her pillow, threw it at her friend. "What does it mean, *brown noser*?"

"Ass kisser," Joana said.

"I don't understand."

"It means somebody has his nose so far up someone's asshole, it's turned brown."

"Yuck." Then, "We're not brown nosers." True, Nina liked helping the yachties any way she could. She helped them clear in through Customs and Immigration and advised them where to go for groceries, fuel and cooking gas. She liked doing it, it wasn't brown nosing.

Besides, the Customs and Immigration officials were glad to have her help because it saved them the aggravation of having to deal with impossible foreigners, who were always telling them how their country should be run. She was providing a service, it wasn't brown nosing. It wasn't.

"Find something to do," Joana said. "I have to get ready."

"Okay, I guess I'll go walk some laps in the shallow end of the pool." It was Saturday, *The Connection* was closed and Nina didn't have a tour. It was that rare day when she didn't have anything to do. And it was her birthday, too. She was looking forward to a special day, a day she could just hang out and do as little as she pleased. She didn't get many of those.

"You can go a morning without exercise," Joana said. "You won't get fat."

"Yes I will," Nina said as she slipped into her skimpy bikini. Her stomach was still flat and she was glad of that. She wondered how much longer it would be before everyone knew. She still hadn't told the captain, was dreading the moment when she'd have to. He wouldn't understand, he'd think she'd been stupid. Well, maybe she had been, but she'd been in love, was still, and wanted the baby more than anything.

She hummed the Beatles' 'Yesterday' to herself as she approached the pool. Then she saw him swimming laps and the tune was caught in her throat. Mick was back. She rubbed her stomach. What would he say when she told him? She hoped he'd be happy, but she didn't see how he could be. He was married. She closed her eyes, hugged herself, but he'd come back. That had to mean something.

She watched him for a few minutes as she used to watch him jogging barefoot in the early mornings. He had tough feet, a dazzling tan and rippling muscles. But now the tan was fading away. She frowned. That was one of the things that had attracted her to him, his healthy outdoor look. And he had trimmed his hair. She didn't like that at all. She'd loved his thick blond hair, the way it touched his shoulders, the way it felt when she ran her hands through it.

He stopped swimming, stood in about a meter of water. She was standing with the sun at her back and he put his hand to his eyes to shield them against it.

"Who's there?" He must have felt her eyes on him.

"It's me." She stepped forward.

"Nina?" He smiled and her heart skipped a beat. He had the most beautiful smile, almost like the baby Jesus in the painting over at the church. Then, for an instant, an arrogant look flashed across his handsome face. Maybe he could smile like the baby Jesus, but sometimes the devil peeked out of his eyes.

"It's me, who else?" She came forward, sat by the edge of the pool, dangled her legs in the water. He looked so good, good enough to eat. All of a sudden she felt all squishy inside.

"I missed you," he said and her heart took off. She felt it thumping in her chest, racing out of control. Just a few words and she was melting before him. But what words. He'd missed her. He'd missed her.

"I missed you, too." She tried to sound casual. She didn't want him to think she was a lovesick girl who'd been moping her life away because he'd left in the middle of the night without even saying goodbye.

"I got the divorce," he said as he shuffled through the water toward her.

"What?" Her ears were on fire. She couldn't believe

what she was hearing. It was so wonderful, too wonderful to be true. She'd wanted him so much, dreamed of him so much, now he was here. Wait till she told Joana.

"It's why I had to leave so suddenly. Joey was starting to suspect and I couldn't take a chance she might find out, because if she thought there was another woman, she never would have let me go. She would have hung on like Christ on the Cross."

"That's not a nice thing to say."

"What?"

"What you said about Jesus."

"Oh, sorry."

"Can't anybody get a divorce in America?"

"Yeah, but I didn't want to hurt her. Besides, I wanted to keep some of my money. If she would've hated me, she'd've taken it all."

"So what did you tell her?"

"I said I liked men."

"What? You said you were gay?" Nina thought about his friend David, who had come down when Joey had flown to Scotland to visit her parents. Mick had promised to spend the time with her, but instead he was with his handsome friend. She'd thought maybe they had spent a little too much time together.

"Yeah, that's what I said. She was hurt, but she said she understood. The divorce wasn't final till last week or I would've been here sooner."

"You could have called. I was so worried."

"I'm sorry. I should've, but I'm here now." He smiled that innocent smile.

"You didn't even check out." Nina knew that because

that was her job, handling the yachtie's Customs forms.

"We checked out at Belem." He moved right up to her now. "I love you, Nina." He put his hands on her hips, lifted her up, pulled her into the pool.

"Mick!" She hit the water with a splash. It chilled her as she went under and the water washed all her doubts away. She loved him, he loved her. She pushed up from the bottom, shot through the surface and he grabbed her in a strong hug.

"I really, really missed you." He covered her lips with his own and she was lost in the magic of his kiss. She was in heaven. Almost. She had to tell him about the baby. Better to do it now, while he was in such a good mood. She pushed against his shoulders, broke the kiss.

"I'm pregnant," she said.

"What?" he pushed her away.

"I'm sorry." She didn't know what else to say. She'd been in love with him. He'd told her he was getting a divorce. He'd promised to marry her. Still it was stupid to stop taking precautions, she knew how babies were made, after all.

"Sorry?" he said.

"Yeah." Her heart fell.

"What for? That's wonderful news."

"It is?" She felt the tears welling up.

"We'll get married ASAP."

"ASAP, what is this ASAP?" She rubbed her eyes.

"It means, as soon as possible," he said. "ASAP, get it?"

"Yes," she said, though she didn't understand. Then, she got it. "Really, ASAP?" Now the dam burst. She tasted the tears on her lips. Salty, like sweat. "I'm so happy."

"Me too, sweetie." He pulled her into another kiss. She didn't like him calling her Sweetie, because he called Joey that. But under the circumstances, it was okay. Married. She couldn't believe it.

This time he broke the kiss. His face was centimeters away. "I mean it, let's do it as quick as possible." His smile lit up his face. She looked into his sea green eyes to see if he meant it. He met her stare straight on without blinking.

"We can get married this afternoon," she said still looking into his gaze.

"Doesn't it take a couple days to get the papers?"

"This is Brazil," she said. "You can do anything you want if you know the right people. Captain da Silva at the port can fix it up."

"Do we have time to go to my room first?" he said and she caught a quick wink.

"Yes, silly. The captain doesn't even get in till after ten."

"Great." He took her hand, led her out of the pool. Nina couldn't believe it, he'd divorced Joey, wanted to marry her and was happy about the baby. She shook with joy. She was truly the luckiest woman in the world.

Chapter Three

Paul Snelling sighed, went to the curtain and looked down at *Satisfaction*, lying peacefully in her berth. Joey Sapphire was aboard now, probably sleeping the sleep of the just. He closed the curtain, looked at the digital camera on the nightstand. He had the photos now. Two sets and that was a problem.

The bastards.

He reached for a cigarette, lit it with a Zippo. David Atwood, the American Ambassador's son, had borrowed the use of a friend's boat to fuck another friend's wife.

Was about to do it last night when interrupted. Atwood, so intent on what he was doing, hadn't heard the Zodiac's outboard when Snelling approached the sailboat.

"Come on, I want you in me," Snelling heard Joey Sapphire say as he'd crept aboard. "I want you to fuck me. I want to be fucked. Hurry up!"

"Just a couple more pictures," Atwood said and Snelling had seen the flash.

"Stop playing around and let's do it," she'd said as Snelling lowered himself through the companionway. He saw through the boat to the forward berth. It was dark where he was, the forward cabin was lit up. Joey Sapphire was nude. David Atwood was positioning her for another picture.

"Spread your legs apart and put a couple fingers in." Atwood was standing in front of the berth.

"You want me to play with myself?" Joey Sapphire moved to face Atwood and himself behind the young man with the camera. She spread her legs apart, started masturbating. "Like this? Is it getting you excited?" She giggled. She sounded like a little girl. It made Snelling feel like a pedophile. He was disgusted.

"That's it, perfect." Atwood started snapping pictures as Snelling stopped at the galley.

"No more." Joey Sapphire took her fingers out of herself. "I want to fuck. Now!"

"What the lady wants, the lady gets." Atwood tossed the camera on a settee next to the berth as Joey Sapphire lay back, legs still wide apart.

Snelling grabbed a serrated steak knife from a wooden knife block, tested it with his thumb, plenty sharp. He stuffed it in a hip pocket of his Levi's, blade first, then put on the ski mask, black with a white ring around the eyes and mouth. He'd seen his reflection in the mask, knew what he looked like. Like a black ghost, a terrorist, a serial killer, all of the above.

"There's a masked man behind you," Joey Sapphire said to Atwood, his penis inches from penetration.

"Stop now!" Snelling said.

"What?" Atwood went limp in an instant. Christ the guy had been hung like a horse. Snelling fisted his hand in Atwood's full head of hair, pulled him away from the drugged woman he was about to mount. Atwood tried to cover himself when he saw the gun.

"Forget about your dick and think about the pictures you took. You come up with them real quick and you can live," Snelling lied.

"What pictures?" Atwood said.

"Don't be stupid with me."

"All right, all right, I know what you want."

"Hey, what about me?" Joey Sapphire was still on her back, starting to rise.

"Put your head on the pillow, close your eyes and go to sleep," Snelling said.

"No sex for Joey?" she'd said.

"Not tonight," Snelling said.

"Okay." She closed her eyes.

"The pictures, son," Snelling said.

"Got 'em right here." Atwood grabbed a camera case from the settee, took out a couple tiny SmartMedia flashcards. "They're on these." He handed over the cards. "It wasn't my idea, honest."

"Honest?" Snelling had said. "What are you a fucking child?"

"It was all Mick. He made me."

"Mick?" Snelling had said, though he knew all about Mick Sapphire. Only a few questions a week ago around the marina and he'd gotten both their names, had learned Sapphire was in San Antonio and that David was in England not due back for a couple days. So he'd decided to do Sapphire first rather than wait around in Trinidad, but when he got to Texas he hadn't been able to get Sapphire away from his famous father.

"Yeah, Mick Sapphire," he's in Texas, but he'll be back any day," Atwood had said, but Snelling knew better, because when Sapphire had finally broken away from daddy and gone to the mall, he'd somehow sensed that he was being followed and disappeared. How it had happened, Snelling didn't know, but it had. Luckily a check on his VISA card told Snelling Sapphire had purchased a full fare ticket to Rio. If the man wanted to disappear, he shouldn't have used his credit card. Not knowing where in Brazil Sapphire was going to wind up, Snelling came back to Trinidad, just in time, it seemed, to save the bastard's wife from being fucked by his friend.

Atwood had been afraid. Snelling had expected that. Had blamed the whole thing on Mick Sapphire, he'd expected that too. But what he hadn't expected was the boy's frightening good looks. Why on God's green earth would a boy that looked like he'd just walked off a movie screen have to resort to drugs to get a woman in bed?

Snelling was pushing sixty, didn't regard himself as suave or attractive to women, yet he didn't have any trouble in the lady department. However, here was a boy, rock star handsome, who had to cheat to get laid. It made no sense, but then most of what went on in the world made no sense to him.

Catholics and Protestants in Ireland, Jews and Moslems in the Middle East, Blacks and Whites in America, stupid, all of it. Cheating husbands, wayward wives, a nine to five job you hate, kids out of control, what was the world coming to? Snelling longed for a simpler time. A time when you could fix your own car, take the tubes out of your television and check them in the tester down at the supermarket, a time when there was a two cent deposit on Coke bottles.

"Get up on the bed." Snelling stuffed his gun into the shoulder holster he wore under his loose fitting batik shirt.

"Yes, sir." Atwood hopped up on the bed, eager to please and obviously relieved that Snelling had put the gun away, but his relief was short lived, because quick as a rattlesnake strike, Snelling pulled the blade from his hip pocket and slit the boy's throat. Then he fisted a hand in Atwood's hair, thumped his head onto a pillow and ran the knife around the jaw line as Atwood kicked his feet in vain.

He held the head in place until the life had gone out of the boy and there was no sound on the boat, other than the rhythmic breathing of Joey Sapphire, now deep in a drugged sleep.

Any other professional in Snelling's position would have cut the girl's throat, too. But in his long career he had never killed a woman and he wasn't about to start at his career's end, not unless he had to.

He spent four restless hours on shore with the night vision glasses, waiting till he saw her come on deck. He watched as she hauled the body from below and dropped it overboard. He watched her swim to shore, watched her dress, then watched her walk away, long hair, wet on her shoulders, swaying back and forth as she moved away from him.

She was resourceful.

He respected that.

He wondered if she'd wiped the boat down, got rid of the blood, removed her fingerprints, then concluded she probably had, as she'd taken her own sweet time on the boat. She hadn't panicked.

Once she was out of sight, he turned on the camera, checked the LCD and saw Joey Sapphire, blonde and nude, legs wide apart. She had small, child like breasts, but then she was a swimmer, and legs that wouldn't quit, also good for a swimmer.

He turned off the camera, took out the SmartMedia card, melted it with the Zippo, then lit a cigarette as his cell phone vibrated.

"Snelling."

"It's me," Clay Clayton had said. Snelling and a few others called him Claymore, because of his penchant for blowing things up.

"What'cha got?"

"Another hit on Sapphire's VISA card. He's staying at the Bay View Hotel in Fortaleza."

"You find out what he's doing in Brazil yet?" Snelling said.

"No, but I'm on it."

"Don't do anything to spook him, just sit tight till I get there." Snelling hadn't given much thought to the fact that the photos were on flashcards, digital media, until he'd viewed them on the back of David Atwood's camera and saw that the two cards were identical. They'd made a backup, maybe more than one. He couldn't let Clayton do away with Mick Sapphire until he had a chance to question him. If there were more copies, he had to know, had to get them.

"Why the change in plans?" Clayton asked.

"I'll tell you when I see you." But of course he wouldn't. Nobody could ever know about the photos, not even Clayton who he trusted with his life.

"You're the boss."

"If he moves, stay on him."

"I won't lose him."

"Keep me posted." Snelling punched the end button, snapped the phone closed.

Dragging his mind back to the present, he looked down at Joey Sappaires's boat again. Then he reached into his pocket, took out the bottles he'd taken from David Atwood's coat pocket. One was labeled, LUDES, the other GHB. Quaaludes to get them to party down, GHB to make them compliant and to forget afterwards. Probably mixed the drugs with alcohol. Judging from the way Joey Sapphire zonked right out at his suggestion, It was a wonder they weren't killing the women they drugged. He tightened his grip on the plastic bottles. Plenty of women had died at the hands of GHB, gamma-hydroxy-butyrate, the date rape drug. A couple drops could knock 'em out, a few more put 'em in a coma some didn't wake up from.

If there was one thing Paul Snelling couldn't abide, it was a man that abused women. Angry now, he pocketed the pills again. Maybe he'd give Mick Sapphire a taste of his own medicine when he got a hold of him.

* * *

In the early morning, sitting in the cockpit, Joey hugged a strong cup of coffee and watched the marina come to life with the rising sun. Pirogues returning with their fish rippled the smooth water. Workmen trudging past with boat parts and spray guns shouted a cheery "Morning, Skip," to yachtsmen puttering about their decks in various degrees of consciousness. Crew lugged laundry, garbage and provisions up and down the quay under the beady eyes of a pelican perched on a pylon. Was it only yesterday that this had all been a grand adventure in a tropical paradise?

The horror of the night came flooding back. Like the sudden darkness before a thundering squall. She had stumbled through the night to the marina numb with fear and shock, her only goal to reach the safety of *Satisfaction*, the ketch which had been her cruising home for the last year. A scalding shower had not been able to stop her violent shivering, but surprisingly, after a long drink to slack her raging thirst, she had collapsed onto her bunk and fallen into a fitful sleep, waking as the early morning light streamed in the port windows.

Her first thought on getting up had been to phone Mick. He had the ability to cut through her more emotional responses to stressful situations with an enviable, calm practicality. But what could she say to him standing in the very public phone booth at the end of the marina? "Hi there, by the way, I ended up on another man's boat last night." She couldn't explain it to herself, let alone Mick. No, better to wait until he was back in Trinidad in three days time. Face to face she would find the courage. He would be hurt, but he would be on her side.

All through the eight am Trinidad Cruisers' Net on VHF radio she held her breath, waiting for the moment when someone would report that a gruesome murder had taken place last night or, at the very least, that someone was missing. But when the net controller called for any *emergency, priority, or medical matters*, nothing was reported.

A loud thump on the foredeck had her almost jumping out of her skin.

"Morning, Joey, what happened to you last night?" It was Sven. He was a Danish singlehander they'd met in Cape Town, preparing for the Southern Atlantic leg of his circumnavigation. She felt herself flush hot and cold. How on earth could she answer that question? Who would believe her if she said, "I slept with a dead man."? She opened her mouth, fishlike, to stutter some meaningless thing when she realized there was no need to, as Sven went on, "One minute you were dancing like a crazy woman and the next you were gone."

"I guess I had too much too drink. Fortunately I made it back without falling in the water."

"I saw you with a cigarette. Gotta watch it or you'll

start smoking again." He laughed, waved, then was off down the dock, getting about his day's business.

"For crying out loud, Joey, smoking?" she muttered to herself. She hadn't had a cigarette in over a month. The last thing she wanted to do was start back up again.

Then she thought about the sheer unbelievable enormity of what she'd been through last night and it overwhelmed her. All of a sudden her heart started thumping, slamming into her rib cage. She closed her eyes, took a deep breath, slowed it to a manageable pace. Thank God Sven didn't seem to think anything untoward had happened last night. Maybe none of the others that had been there did either.

She tried to remember the details of an evening that had begun with rum spiked Christmas eggnog and dancing. But she had no memory of meeting the man whose body she'd consigned to the deep, and she had absolutely no idea how she'd ended up on his boat. Could her drink have been doctored?

She shivered with the thought of it. She wanted to talk to Mick. She decided to phone him anyway, just to hear the reassuring sound of his voice. Dialing his parents number in San Antonio, she focused on making her tone light and casual. But instead of getting Mick's mother or father on the line she got a recording.

"I'm sorry you've missed us," Catherine Sapphire's voice said, "Old Harry and I decided at the last minute to spend Christmas in Hawaii, so the two of us just took off like newlyweds yesterday." A man's laughter in the background. Mick's father. "We'll be back on the Twenty-eighth. Leave a message when you hear the beep.

Oh, and Merry Christmas."

Joey hung up,

What was that all about? Just the two of them? And they were spending Christmas in Hawaii? That didn't make sense, not unless Mick had cut his visit short. But then why hadn't he called, told her when he was coming back?

She shivered. The bottom line was he wasn't with his parents. Had he been and gone early or had he lied to her?

She felt a chill that reached right down into the pit of her stomach, like she'd just dropped twelve stories in a fast elevator. What on earth was going on? It was as if a giant hammer had smashed into the crystal glass of her life, shattering its beauty and light, scattering senseless shards which bore no resemblance to its previous shape.

Where was Mick?

Again she felt the sticky blood on her fingers and the cold, dead weight of the body. Nothing was the same as it had been and even Mick was acting strange. Could he possibly have seen her last night? Was he part of this terrible mess? Could he be missing? Perhaps even murdered? Did she dare go to the police about it?

Never had she felt so alone.

With the slow realization that Mick was not going to bail her out, she found herself clenching her fists in white knuckled fear and growing anger. It reminded her of the time when fifty knots of rain heavy wind had blasted their yacht away from the South African coast. Gripping the wheel, she had focused her stinging eyes on a small break in the lowering clouds, determined not to wake Mick during his much-needed off watch, she'd made up her to get through the storm by herself.

And she would have to do the same now.

CHAPTER
FOUR

CLAY CLAYTON HAD HIS EYES PRESSED tight into the binoculars as he stared from the second floor at the Brazilian beauty clutching onto Mick Sapphire. She was the kind of golden brown that suggested some kind of Indian ancestry mixed with a healthy dose of the tropical sun. He felt a stirring between his legs. That babe had the tightest ass he'd ever seen in a thong bikini and her tits jiggled, trying to bust out of that tiny top with every move she made. He could see her nipples. The girl might as well be naked.

He felt himself getting hard, couldn't help, who could? He dropped a hand between his legs, squeezed. Two bits of yellow string, that's all she had on. She was small, with a mane of dark hair running down her back. She had the ass, tits and perfect legs. Some guys had all the luck.

He pulled the binoculars from his eyes, backed away from the curtain. He wasn't able to get all they'd said as he'd only had a side view of their faces, but he was able to read enough from their lips to know the girl was pregnant with Sapphire's kid and that they were getting married.

Clayton's stomach growled as he moved away from the window. He tossed the binoculars on the bed. The guy already had a wife and yet he was about to marry that Latin honey down there. He grabbed himself between the legs again, squeezed again. Then he picked up the phone and ordered an English breakfast.

Snelling wanted the Sapphire guy watched, but not touched. It didn't make sense. No way was the guy into anything like national security. He wasn't a spy. He wasn't a traitor. He wasn't even political. So what was it? Who was Snelling working for and why had he been so quiet on this one? Always before when Snelling sent him on a job, Clayton knew what was what. On this one he knew squat.

He was still turning over the variables in his head when room service knocked on the door with his breakfast. He let the girl in, watched her setup the table, then wolfed his breakfast down.

What was it about?

Had to be money, otherwise Snelling would've said

something. He was doing this on his own. He was onto a score and he was using his old friend Claymore Clayton, but he wasn't cutting him in.

"Not right," Clayton mumbled as he scratched his beard. Something about the humidity made it itch. He hated the tropics. In no time at all the sun turned his face even redder than his hair. His skin wouldn't take a tan, his private curse.

He pushed his chair from the table, went back to the curtain. Sapphire had a room on the other side of the courtyard. The blinds were closed. If he had himself a piece like that, he'd close the blinds, too. For a second he thought about going over, banging on the door and roughing Sapphire up while he was in the middle of getting his rocks off. That way he'd get a look at the girl. She had big tits for a girl her size.

But as much as he'd like to get a look at her naked, maybe grab a feel, he knew it would be a bad idea. Snelling wanted Sapphire watched, not messed with. It made Clayton angry. He fisted his hands. There had to be a way. There was money here. He could smell it. And his nose was never wrong.

An hour later the girl left the room across the courtyard. Clayton grabbed the binoculars. She might as well have been naked, that, combined with the knowledge of what they'd been doing, made him hard. He kept the binoculars trained on her as she sashayed along the open hallway and took the stairs down to the pool.

Clayton sighed. He'd had good looking women in his time, but never any that he hadn't paid for. That Mick Sapphire must be some kind of stud. Clayton didn't know what his wife looked like, but if she was anywhere near as hot as the babe he'd just finished with, Sapphire was one lucky guy.

Twenty minutes later the girl came back. The bathing suit was gone now, replaced with a simple white summer dress. It was cut low, showed lots of leg. She glowed in it and Clayton found himself getting hard again. Very unprofessional.

She knocked and Sapphire met her at the door. They left, holding hands as they made their way to the stairs. Clayton watched from his room as they crossed by the pool and made their way to the lobby. For a second he thought about following, but he knew they'd be back. Besides, his nose was still itching with that money smell.

Snelling said to watch only. Searching the guy's room came under watching as far as Clayton was concerned. The lock was child's play, in seconds he was in. Sapphire had unpacked, putting his clothes in the bureau drawers under the television. A duffel bag had been folded and stowed in the top of the closet. It looked like he was planning on staying awhile.

Hidden underneath the duffel bag, Clayton found a small leather grip, the kind one would wear over the shoulder. He took it out, opened it. It was lined and inside he found a digital camera, some of those miniature flashcards for storing pictures, a copy of Jack Priest's latest horror novel and lots of money. Three banded stacks of hundred dollar bills. Thirty thousand dollars.

What the fuck, was the guy stupid? Anybody could break in here and take it. Clayton was tempted to take it himself. But didn't. Instead he pulled apart the Velcro that held the bag's lining in place, was about to drop in the tiny transmitter when he saw the flashcard.

What was it doing there? Probably pictures Sapphire didn't want anyone to see, maybe even shots of that babe without her yellow thong, Clayton thought as he slid the transmitter—a hostage tracking system, an inch and a half square with the diameter of a dime—under the lining on the bottom of the grip. He almost took the card, but then Sapphire would know someone had been in his room, might even find the transmitter, so he left it in place and sealed up the Velcro. Obviously Sapphire used the grip like a purse, else he wouldn't have had the money in it, so it was a safe bet he'd keep it with him when he traveled. It was a good place for the transmitter.

Clayton took a look around the room. For a second he thought about sitting Sapphire down and finding out what it was he was into, where the money was. But he threw the thought away almost as fast as it entered his head. Nobody went against Snelling and lived. He'd killed more men than the Pope had saved. When you worked for him, you did your job or you died.

At the door, Clayton took a look back, checked to make sure everything was as he'd left it. It was. He closed the door and again thought about working over Sapphire for what he knew. He was a good interrogator, after all. One of the best.

So how come Snelling didn't trust him to question the man? How come he wanted to do it himself? It didn't make sense. Then all of a sudden it did. There was only one explanation. It was about so much money that Snelling thought Clayton would double cross him if he knew.

He was dreaming about dollar signs as he slipped back into his room. He was going to have to sit Sapphire down and have words with him before Snelling arrived, then he was going to have to kill him in such a way that Snelling wouldn't suspect. Make it look like a robbery. Muggings and murder happened down here all the time.

* * *

Married. Nina couldn't believe it. They were sitting at the hotel restaurant overlooking the marina. Mick had a far away look in his eyes and for a second that worried Nina. She was afraid he wasn't happy about the quick marriage.

"You're not sorry, are you? About, you know, getting married?"

"No, no," he said, "not that. I've got some other problems I'm trying to work out, that's all."

"What kind of problems?"

"Just stuff. It doesn't concern you."

"Everything about you concerns me. We're married now, remember?"

"How could I forget." He smiled when he said it, but it seemed forced.

"Don't say it like that," she said.

"I'm sorry. I just need some rest before I get on with my life."

"Is that why you came back, to rest?"

"No," he said it fast. "I came for you. I was going to take you back to Trinidad, to the boat, but now that I'm here, I'm remembering how nice it is. Would you mind if we stayed awhile?"

"If that's what you want, but I'd like the baby born in America."

"What?"

"I got a passport."

"Really?"

"Yeah, I was going to go to America to have the baby. I wanted her to be an American citizen like her father." Somehow she just knew the baby was going to be a girl.

"Nina, you never coulda done that." Mick laughed. "You could never get a visa."

"Sure I could, I've got some friends in the right places, but that's not a problem now that we're married."

"Let me see the passport." He leaned over his food as he said it, eyes boring into her.

"I don't have it on me."

"Where is it?"

"Up in my room."

"I keep mine with me all the time." He reached into his inside coat pocket, pulled out a wallet, the kind you can keep money in without folding it. His passport was inside. "See. That way no one can break into my room and steal it. I'll keep yours here, too."

"But it's my passport."

"It's safer with me and you won't have to worry about it. Besides, we're gonna be doing all of our traveling together from now on."

"Okay," she said. But it didn't sound right. It was her passport. "I'll give it to you later on."

"Good girl." He took a sip of his wine.

"Are we going to stay at the hotel?" she said.

"That's no way to start our life together, living in a hotel." He shook his head, set his glass on the table. "I thought we'd get an apartment someplace where it'll only be you and me, all day long, all night long."

"But I have my business." She didn't know why she'd brought it up. If he'd wanted to leave for Miami tomorrow, she'd have gone in a flash, but somehow it didn't seem right, leaving Joana with all the work if she was still going to be living here..

"Honey, I've got plenty of cash, you don't have to work anymore." And as if to prove his point, he pulled that wallet out again and took out his credit card to pay for the dinner, but not before she saw that he had a lot of US green money.

"Do you always carry around so much?" she said.

"Babe, I never go anywhere without a couple thousand dollars and another five or ten close by, just in case. You don't ever have to worry about money again." He signaled the waitress and Nina held her tongue till Mick handed over his card.

"I wasn't worried about money," she said. But she had been. She'd grown up without it, been jealous of others that had it all her life. She was very worried about it. "I just didn't want to let Joana down."

"Believe me, babe, she'll be happy when she hears you're giving her your share of the business," Mick said.

"I'm not doing that," Nina said. What was he talking about? No way would she walk out on Joana. They were a team, forever and always, married or not. Once she got to America, she'd figure out a way to earn money and send it to her. And as soon as they'd paid off Captain da Silva for his half of the business, they could sell *The Connection*. Then Joana could come to America and they could open their restaurant. She loved Mick, but no marriage was going to stop that.

She looked at him, tried to reach into his eyes, see into him, but he just smiled, then said. "Maybe you're right. Yeah, you are, you shouldn't give up what's yours, you never know what could happen."

She was about to get angry, but the waitress came back with the credit slip for him to sign. It was probably a good thing, because she was curling her toes, something she did to keep from losing her temper. The last thing she wanted to do was fight with him on her special day, her twenty-first birthday, Christmas Eve and her wedding day all rolled into one.

Yes, her birthday, in all the excitement she'd forgotten.

"Today's my birthday," she said as they got up from the table.

"Congratulations." He kissed her cheek, took her hand. "Let's go upstairs and celebrate. And afterwards we'll celebrate Christmas."

"All right." Nina sighed. He hadn't asked how old she was. Twenty-one was supposed to be special for Americans and he hadn't asked.

Mick keyed the door, pushed it open.

"You're supposed to pick me up and carry me over the doorway."

"The what?"

"You know, what just married people do in the movies."

"Oh, the threshold. You want me to carry you over the threshold?"

"Please."

"Sure." He picked her up. "You're heavier than you look."

"I am not."

"I was just kidding." He laughed.

Then all of a sudden she was falling. She hit the floor on her back and rolled to her side. For a second she thought Mick had dropped her, but then she saw the wild man as she started to get up. He had Mick in a headlock and he was hitting him in the stomach. Again and again and again. And Mick jerked with every blow. The man was killing him.

Nina jumped on the big man's back, raking his face with her fingernails. The man dropped Mick, grabbed a hold of her arm and flung her over his shoulder as if she weighed nothing at all. She hit the sofa with a thud and her breath was knocked away.

She gasped, fighting for air, struggled to see how Mick was and, even though she was having a hard time catching her breath, she couldn't believe what she was seeing.

Apparently she had given him all the time he needed to get on out of there. He jumped to his feet, ran out the door, leapt over the balcony. Nina heard him crash into the garden below.

The big man started after him, stopped at the doorway, glared at Nina and for a second she was afraid. She'd been with a lot of men and knew that look. This one liked to hurt his women. But instead of coming for her, he turned and jumped over the balcony as Mick had done.

And then she was alone.

Chapter Five

JOEY HAULED HERSELF OUT of the cockpit. She was down, depressed as she'd never been before. Sweat trickled under her arms, her head screamed, her mouth was dry, her tongue thick. It stuck to the top of her mouth as if it were made of Velcro. She craved water.

"God, Joey," she muttered, "just how much did you drink last night?" She looked up into the morning sun, put a hand to her eyes to shield them against it.

"What's wrong with me?" She was standing at the shrouds, didn't remember how she'd gotten there. Only three or four steps from the cockpit, she must have done it, but God help her she couldn't remember. Her head felt like it was going to explode. She was bathed in sweat, despite the fact that a cool breeze washed over the deck.

Oh, Lord. She was falling, her knees hit the lifelines as she tumbled forward. She threw a hand out in a desperate attempt to grab at the shrouds. Missed and went over the side head first. Her feet caught on the lifelines, her head thumped into the side of the boat with a painful smash that ricocheted through her body. Then she slipped into the water.

Somehow she managed to grab a breath before she went under. Reflex took over. Dazed and disoriented, she struck out for the surface, broke through and swam to the finger pier. She grabbed the end of it and pain shot through her right hand as she pulled herself out of the water. On the dock she sat with her legs over the end, feet barely touching the water as she inspected the knife wound from the night before. There was a little blood on her palm, she'd opened it up.

Satisfied the wound was okay, she looked around the marina. Had anybody seen her uncoordinated fall? That would be hard to explain. She looked around. That pelican was still there, still watching. He took off, eyes wide as he dove into the water. He shook his head, splashing as he swallowed the fish. Joey had the mother of all hangovers. She felt like that fish.

"What happened to you?" It was Jimmy Kay the dockmaster's assistant. He was a sixty-something West Indian with no teeth, no hair and no sense of humor.

"I raced that pelican over there for a fish."

"Who won?"

"Are you actually playing along with a joke? Because I don't think I could take it if you were. My world's upside down right now. I need at least one thing to be as it should be."

"And me being boring is what you pick? I'm flattered." His lips were twitching, she saw gums. His eyes twinkled, the wrinkles in his forehead started to spread out.

"You're not gonna smile? You never smile."

"I saw the pelican get the fish, you lost." He busted out into a gum flapping laugh. It came from deep in his belly, like an erupting volcano. He sprayed spittle, bent at the waist, grabbed his knees. "You lost," he said again.

"It's not that funny."

"You wanna swim, you're supposed to use the pool. 'Gainst the rules to dive off the boat." He straightened up. He was a tall man, thin and wiry. Every fiber of his being seemed to be rippling with laughter. He started swaying, moving at the hips.

"You stop that!" Joey couldn't help herself, she started to laugh, too.

"I'd dry off if I was you." He stopped laughing and Joey wondered if it'd be another fifty or sixty years before he cracked another smile. Was it a once in a lifetime thing?

"Right." She pushed herself to her feet. Her head hurt, but strangely the nausea was gone. She must have been drugged last night. That was the only explanation, and the drug was still wrecking havoc with her body.

Back on board she drank a glass of cold water,

KEN DOUGLAS

savoring every drop. That went a long way toward
making her feel better. Then she checked the knife wound
again, ran the hand under cold water, a tiny bit of red
blood washed down the drain, the bleeding had stopped.
She washed the hand with disinfectant soap, then put a
bandage on it. The wound was in an awkward place, but
it would probably be okay in a day, two at the most.

That taken care of she went to her cabin, changed
into a bathing suit, wrapped herself with a towel. One
sure way to cure a hangover was a good workout. She
went to the pool, dove in and started swimming laps. Free
style, breast stroke, back stroke, butterfly. She swam
through the pain in her head and kept it up till her arms
ached, then she flopped over onto her back and leisurely
floated in the cool water.

The headache gone now, she swam to the side and
winced when she grabbed onto the ladder to climb out.
That knife wound still hurt and she'd lost the bandage in
the pool. A quick check of the hand, no bleeding.

All of a sudden the hairs on the back of her neck
tingled. She felt as if she were in a graveyard in the middle
of the night. No, she felt like there were eyes on her, like
she was being watched. Still in the water, still holding
onto the ladder, she looked around the pool. A young
couple were sitting on lounge chairs, talking. An older
guy was standing in the shallow end, playing with a little
girl. Some people were having breakfast under an
umbrella covered table. Nobody looked threatening.

Maybe she was just being paranoid. She climbed out
of the pool, looked around again, she couldn't shake the
feeling. But then she was scared and felt guilty, so maybe

48

paranoia was natural.

She wrapped her towel around herself and went back to the boat where she changed into yellow shorts and a matching halter top. Then she ate a bowl of Cheerios before climbing into her berth with her clothes on. Just for a few minutes, she told herself, but she quickly fell into a deep sleep.

She came awake hours later, covered in sweat, to a dream of vultures circling the spot where she'd dumped the body into the water. Too bad for the corbeau birds, he was fish food now. She shivered in her hot berth when she thought of him down there, shrimp and crabs busily feasting on that handsome face.

In her mind's eye she tried to picture that face as it would have been in life. She took herself back to the Christmas party at the hotel. She'd danced with Sven. She remembered that. She remembered moving through the buffet line with him in front, the American Ambassador behind. The ambassador's wife had been interested in South Africa, peppering Joey with a million and one questions. When she found out Joey lived on a boat, the questions increased, but by then Joey had figured out the woman was an airhead. The questions were a way of moving through a conversation without revealing anything about herself. A politician's trick, something her husband must have taught her.

She remembered a hand at her shoulder. She remembered turning into the most beautiful emerald eyes.

"You have to watch yourself around my mother. She's like a cop when it comes to conversation," the man had said. He had a face like Michelangelo's David. She remembered how his arms rippled under his short sleeved white shirt. He wore a silly tie, it had a hula dancer on it. His smile was irresistible. He was a big man, the kind of person women left their husbands for. "My name's David," he'd said.

"How fitting," Joey had joked.

"I'm a friend of your husband's," he'd said.

"Really? How come I don't know you?"

"You do now," he'd said, then she jerked her mind back to the present as a horrible truth tortured her. David, with the face chiseled by a master, was the American Ambassador's son, the Bull, the dead man.

"Oh, Lord!" She opened her eyes, was breathing fast. She held her breath, slowed it down. She tried to cast her mind back to what happened after she'd met him, but it wouldn't go. Sven had said she'd danced like a wild woman. She had no memory of it.

She turned her thoughts to her husband. All her life she'd dated nice guys, was a nice girl herself, then she'd met Mick, the wild American who'd sailed his boat into Cape Town with his even wilder girlfriend, the hot new Mexican actress Katie Ortega.

Joey had been staying with a friend near the marina where Mick and Katie were living aboard *Satisfaction*. They were the most fun. Parties every night where they sat around, drank rum and coke and talked about life on the sea, politics, religion, everything. They knew so much, had been everywhere. Joey had been swept off her feet by them, reveled in their company, then all of a sudden Katie was gone, back to America to do a movie with Harrison Ford, her year long sabbatical over.

And then the unexpected happened, Mick started lavishing attention on her and she was thrilled. She couldn't believe he preferred her to the actress everybody was talking about, but he did. They were married a month later and two weeks following the wedding she was at sea.

It was a new life for Joey. And for reasons she didn't understand, being in love with Mick freed her from the dark shadow of her father. No longer did she feel like she had to atone for what he'd done. It was time for her to live her own life and to live it for herself. And she started doing just that. She rapidly fell in love with the sea, *Satisfaction* and the lifestyle. Mick had her sailing like a pro in a matter of weeks. She spent every possible moment at the helm, getting the feel of the boat. Mick had said she was a born natural and she had to agree, she loved it so.

Mick, she thought, where was he? What was he up to? No good, she'd bet. No damn good. Stop it, think positive thoughts, she told herself. He was her husband, dammit. But dammit where was he? If he wasn't spending Christmas with his folks, he should be spending it with her. She got out of bed, went to the galley, drank almost a whole bottle of Gatorade, never had she been so thirsty.

She looked out a port window. The sun was setting, darkness fell fast in the Caribbean. She'd slept the day away. She'd never done that before. Ever.

She shucked her sweaty clothes, stepped into the shower. Afterwards she pulled on her sleep shirt, ate a light meal of left over macaroni and cheese and gulped down more Gatorade. Then she went back to the forward berth, climbed in and closed her eyes. Sleep wouldn't come and she didn't expect it. She tried to bury her thoughts.

Twice she crawled out of the rack to pee. The light from the dock lights outside streamed through the port windows, giving the inside of the boat a surreal feel to it. She'd never noticed it before, but now on her short trips to the head, she felt like she was living in kind of a ghostly horror story. After doing her business in the bathroom she couldn't get back to her bed fast enough.

She was on the toilet for a third time when she heard someone move on deck. Mick, was her first thought, but an inner voice told her not to shout out. How come she hadn't heard him step onto the boat? How come she wasn't hearing footfalls across the deck? Whoever was up there was being stealthy, walking like he didn't want to wake anyone on board.

Joey didn't know what to do. She started to get off the toilet, but stopped herself. Maybe she'd imagined it. She strained her ears, heard a squeak. He was coming through the companionway. She shivered. The door to the head was open, no need to close it with nobody else on board. She saw a beam of light coming from the salon. He was shining it into the forward cabin. Thank God she hadn't been in bed.

She fought a gasp as she heard him moving around, heard a drawer in the galley open, close. What was he looking for? It couldn't be money or jewelry, not in her silverware drawer.

She needed a weapon. She dashed her eyes over everything in sight, saw nothing she could use. She took shallow breaths. What if he didn't find whatever it was he was after? What would he do when he discovered he wasn't alone? She felt panic rising, fought it down.

She was tempted to bend forward, take a peek, but she was afraid. Then she saw her handheld mirror next to the hairspray. She seldom used either, but she'd sprayed her hair before the party yesterday and used the mirror to check that every hair was in place. She hadn't put them away.

More noise, now he was in the salon. She inhaled a quiet breath, held it and picked up the mirror. Please God, don't let him see. She eased the mirror out the door, just a fraction, craned her head to see what it reflected.

Gun!

He was wearing a black ski mask, a wraith moving through the boat, a terrorist. Who had a ski mask in Trinidad where it was usually hot as hell? Only the worst kind of criminal. And he had a gun.

She watched as he opened a cabinet, rifled through her belongings, then went on to another. He was being thorough. Soon he would be at the head. Soon he would discover her. She set the mirror down, picked up the hairspray. Not much of a weapon, but better than nothing.

The boat went quiet. He'd quit searching. Had he found what he'd been looking for? Joey willed her heart to be quiet as she struggled to hear.

Not a sound.

Nothing.

He must have heard her set the mirror down. She put her finger on the spray nozzle. She sensed him moving, though she heard no sound. God himself would be hard put to hear him.

Then he was there, glaring down at her on the toilet. She shoved the can forward, sprayed his fiery eyes as he was bringing the gun to bear. He screamed as she flew from the toilet, smashing into him. "Yeoh," he yelled as his head thudded into the opposite bulkhead.

She kneed him in the groin, sunk her teeth into his neck, chomped down. He screamed in an effort to get her off as she pummeled him with closed fists even as she tasted his salty blood.

He grabbed a fistful of her hair, tried to jerk her off, but she held on, teeth clenched, ripping into his flesh as he finally pulled her away. She spit blood. She still had the spray can in her other hand. She smashed it into the mask, where his nose should be, was about to hit him again when he smashed a fist into her stomach. She lost her breath with a whoosh. He pushed her away, stumbled back and by the time she caught her breath, he was gone.

CHAPTER SIX

NINA RAN TO THE DOOR, saw the man run along the side of the pool below even as she heard a car roar out of the parking lot. That had to be Mick. She didn't know he had a car. The wild man stopped at the gate. His quarry had been lost. He turned, looked up at her and for a second Nina thought he was going to come back.

She stared down at his bushy beard as he was captured under the outside lights. He stared back, unafraid, as if he knew Nina wasn't going to shout out. She wouldn't, all her life she'd dreaded the police, but he couldn't know that. He took a step forward and Nina's heart skipped a beat. He laughed. He knew the effect he was having on her. Knew it and enjoyed it.

He blew her a kiss that chilled her. Then he turned, stepped through the gate and vanished into the night.

She backed into Mick's room and closed the door. He had one of the expensive corner rooms with a view of both the pool and the sea beyond. She went to the phone and called her room in the employee's quarters over on the other side of the hotel. Joana picked up on the first ring.

"Where are you?" Joana said. "The party's already started."

"Thank God you're back!" Then, "What party?"

"Your birthday party, stupid." Joana was speaking English, good she hadn't had too much to drink yet. "It's supposed to be a surprise."

"Listen, this is important. Send everybody home, then get over to 213 as fast as you can. I'm in trouble."

"Okay." Joana hung up. Five minutes later she was at the door. "What's wrong?"

"I got married this afternoon."

"No!" Then, "To who?"

"Mick."

"The baby's father?"

"Yeah. I'm sorry you weren't there. It all happened so fast."

"It's okay, I know you love him. Congratulations."

"Maybe not." Nina told her everything.

"He ran away and left you?"

"He must have had a good reason."

"There is no such thing as a good reason for a man to

run away and leave his woman behind, especially if she's pregnant."

"There must be." Nina felt like a black cloud was enveloping her, stealing away her joy. It was dark now and getting darker, both the day and it seemed, her life. She looked around the room, then said, "I think the man with the red beard who broke in here was American."

"You can't be right. That's never happened before."

"I know. It's crazy. Unless—"

"Unless he didn't pick this room by chance, unless he was after Mick."

"Yeah."

"You think he's coming back?" Joana said.

"Who, Red Beard or Mick?"

"Either one, both."

"Mick, I hope so," Nina said. "Red Beard, I don't know."

"You really think he was American, the man with the red beard?"

"He didn't talk and it all happened so fast, but yes, I think he was. And you know what else? He had a look in his eyes, he wasn't afraid."

"What do you mean?"

"He reminded me of those officers we used to have to, you know, sleep with. They weren't afraid of anything because they knew nothing could ever hurt them. Red Beard was like that. He wasn't afraid of Mick or the police. He wasn't afraid of anything.

"We should get out of here."

"I can't, I have to wait in case Mick comes back."

"There's a vacant room on the other side of the

courtyard. We can use one of the maid's pass keys and watch from there. That way if he comes back, you'll be waiting, but if Red Beard comes, you won't be home."

"Good idea, let's go."

Four hours later Nina had to accept the fact that Mick wasn't returning. That dark cloud that had been hovering over her had turned to a shroud. She felt like she was suffocating. She loved him so much. How could he leave her like that, run away? "Come on," she said. "You can help me pack up his stuff."

"What for?"

"For when he does come back," Nina said.

"Nina?"

"He'll come back."

"Okay, let's go over there and do it," Joana said.

They'd been together so long, they almost functioned as one. Joana went to the bureau, Nina to the closet. Joana opened the drawers, Nina pulled down the duffel bag from the top of the closet, tossed it on the bed as Joana pulled underwear, T-shirts, shorts and socks out of the bureau. Nina pulled a corduroy jacket off a hanger, folded it, dropped it on the bed and was going back for the slacks when she saw the leather bag on the top shelf. It had been buried under the duffel bag. She pulled it out, opened it.

"Whoa!"

"What?"

"This!" Nina held up a fist full of money.

"Oh my!" Joana sat down on the edge of the bed.

"Come on." Nina put the money back in the bag, zipped it up. "Let's get out of here."

"We're gone." Joana hopped off the bed, started for the door as Nina slung the leather camera bag over her shoulder and they left room 213.

Now she knew Mick wasn't coming back, but it wasn't so bad. He'd told her he'd planned on taking her to Trinidad where his boat was. Apparently Red Beard had interfered with his plans, but Mick had told her about his extra money. Obviously he wanted her to find it so she could afford to follow him there.

She sighed.

He loved her.

He did.

The money proved it.

In their room Nina tossed the camera bag on the center of her bed. She grabbed a breath, held it to slow her beating heart, but it didn't work. Never had she seen so much money.

"Is it real?" Joana said.

"It must be." Nina felt a dazzling ray of white piercing the black that had been smothering her. It was going to be all right. Mick loved her.

They stood at the foot of the bed and stared at the bag. Neither moved for the longest while, it was almost as if they were afraid they'd wake up and the dream would be over or the spell broken.

"You want to count it?" Nina said.

"It'll burn my fingers," Joana said.

"It won't." Nina laughed.

"It will, I know it will."

"It won't, I promise."

Joana pulled her blouse off, unsnapped her bra, kicked

off her shoes, started to work on her jeans.

"What are you doing?" Nina thought her friend was acting crazy.

"I'm getting naked."

"What for?"

"I want you to cover me in money." She pulled her jeans and panties down, stepped out of them, then jumped on the bed. "Come on, cover me up."

"Don't you want to count it first?" Nina laughed again.

"No, cover me up. Bury me in it."

Nina picked up the bag, opened it and took out a banded roll of US hundred dollar bills.

"Hurry, I'm getting all excited."

Nina pulled off the rubber band, sprinkled the money over her friend. "How's that?"

"More, I want it all over me."

"What my best friend wants, my best friend gets." Nina opened the other two stacks and splashed the money over Joana.

"Oh, it feels so good. I could close my eyes and sleep forever."

"Come on, get up and get dressed."

"Why?"

"Because it's my turn." Nina pulled her dress off and in seconds she was rolling around in the money with her friend.

They laughed and giggled as if they were ten years old. As if they hadn't spent almost half their lives in a whorehouse. They laughed as if they were free.

"Maybe we should count it now," Joana said when

they were all laughed out. She got off the bed, started to dress.

"Yeah." Nina got up, put her clothes on.

"Thirty thousand dollars exactly," Joana said fifteen minutes later as she fingered the last hundred dollar bill. Then she said. "What are you going to do?"

"I'm going to Trinidad. He'll be waiting for me on his boat. That's why he left the money."

"You think?"

"He told me about it. He wouldn't have done that if he didn't want me to find it."

"What if Mr. Red Beard caught him. You should call Captain da Silva—"

"And see if Mick bought a ticket out on one of the morning flights. Then I would know for sure if he got away."

"Yes."

Nina called the captain. He was grumpy because it was so late, but Nina expected it, he'd been grumpy a lot lately. She told him what she wanted to know and ten minutes later he called back and told her that Mick had managed to get a ticket on a charter plane full of Germans bound for Tobago and that the plane had left two hours ago.

"He must be going to his boat in Trinidad," Nina said.

She called the airport only to find the morning flight to Port of Spain was full. She called Captain da Silva back and he assured her there would be a place for her on the flight if her passport was in order.

That taken care of, Nina counted out five thousand

dollars from the stack of money, then said to Joana, "I'll take this with me, just in case. You keep the rest safe till I get back."

"I can't believe you're going. We haven't been apart in ten years."

"I have to go, I love him. And even if I didn't, it's what's best for the baby."

"I know." Joana opened her arms and Nina fell into the hug. "I'll hold down the fort till you get back."

"What fort?" Nina said.

"It's an expression, it means, I'll keep everything all right till you come home."

"I hate it that your English is better than mine," Nina said.

"You should read more comic books."

"I will, I promise." Nina broke the hug. The Port of Spain flight left at five-thirty, they only had a couple hours to get back over to Mick's room, finish packing up his stuff, get her things packed and get to the airport.

Nina lugged her suitcase through the airport lobby toward the ticket counter, Joana alongside, was dragging Mick's duffel bag. Nina had never flown, never been more than twenty miles outside of Fortaleza, never had to pack for a trip. Captain da Silva, a man who had traveled the world, brought her a suitcase along with his advice during the small hours of the morning.

Nina told him everything, lying only about the amount of money they'd found in the camera bag, saying it was three instead of thirty-thousand. Captain da Silva was a good and kind friend, but he was the port captain and had been stealing from the government, ship captains and yacht skippers for over thirty years. If he knew the true amount, he'd want a share, he wouldn't be able to help himself and Nina and Joana were not about to part with any of their new found gain.

At the ticket counter, Nina bought a round trip ticket and asked for a window seat. She was as excited as she'd ever been.

"I wish I was going with you," Joana said as she hefted the duffel bag onto the scale.

"I'll be all right." Nina hugged her friend for about the tenth time since they'd been in the airport lobby, then she paid for her ticket.

"I'm going to miss you," Joana said when they were at Passport Control.

"I'll miss you, too," Nina said and they hugged still again, then kissed cheeks.

"You be careful and e-mail me as soon as you get there."

"Yes, Mother," Nina said and they laughed, then they hugged one last time.

"Merry Christmas," Joana said as Nina was walking away.

"And a happy New Year," Nina called back.

On the plane Nina took her seat by the window. She was anxious, but tried not to show it. She was leaving Brazil on serious business, but the thrill of her first airplane ride made her feel like a little girl. Her heart thumped when the plane was towed away from the gate and she felt like it was beating in her throat when it taxied down the runway under its own power.

"First time on a plane?" the man next to her said.

"Yes, how could you tell?" Nina pulled her eyes away from the window and the dark morning outside.

"The way you're gripping the arm rests." He had soft blue eyes, the color of a shallow sea.

"Are you a yachtie?" She relaxed her grip, felt the blood flow back to her fingers.

"Kind of," he laughed. "Name's Norm Evans. How could you tell?"

"Shorts, floppy hat, Hawaiian shirt, nice beard. It wasn't too hard." She liked the way he looked at her, like a human being, not a woman he wanted to go to bed with. It was one of the things she liked about the Americans. "My name's Nina Brava."

"I guess it is almost like a uniform," he said, "the shorts and hat." He smiled at her. It made his eyes twinkle. He looked like he was in his early sixties.

"How come you're flying and not taking your boat?"

"My boat's been stuck forever at the Yacht Club in Trinidad. I'm a surveyor. I flew down to price a boat for a Trinidadian."

"Is he going to buy it?"

"I think he might have if I hadn't looked her over, but now I don't think he will. The engine needs a complete overhaul, the rigging has to be changed, the refrigeration is on its last legs, one of the battery banks is dead and the other one is just about to go."

"You're talking about *Friendship Three*. Jan's been trying to sell that boat for over a year now. How much is he asking?"

"Ninety-three thousand dollars. He says it's firm."

"It's not, he'll take seventy."

"Really, how do you know?"

"That's how far he came down for the last buyer, but it was still too much, the guy wanted it for fifty-five."

"Thanks for the info. I'll pass it on to the guy that hired me." Then, "How come you're going to Trinidad?"

"I married an American who lives on a boat. Mick Sapphire on *Satisfaction*, do you know him?"

"No, but I know the boat. It's docked at the Carib Inn Marina. A friend of mine worked on the sails a few weeks ago. You'll like her, nice boat."

All of a sudden the plane seemed to shake. An earthquake, Nina thought. "Oh boy." She gripped the arm rests again.

"It's nothing. We're about to start the takeoff roll."

"Oh my!" Nina said as the plane started down the runway. "I don't think I like this." She felt herself being pushed back in her seat as the big jets screamed and the plane shuddered. This was worse than an earthquake. Nothing could survive this.

"Look out the window," Norm said.

She did and gasped. The outside was rushing by so fast. Everything was a blur. "Hold on!" she said as the nose left the ground. She couldn't believe it. She saw headlights below, cars that looked like toys. The plane was in a climbing turn and Nina felt butterflies in her stomach. It was wonderful.

She reached under the seat in front of herself and took out the camera bag as soon as the fasten seatbelt sign went off.

"What do you have there?" Norm said when she

opened it.

"A camera, but I don't know how to work it."

"Let me see." He took the camera. "Olympus digital camera, newer and more expensive than mine. This baby costs about five hundred dollars."

"So much for a camera?"

"You can spend up to four or five thousand dollars for a camera if you want."

"Who would do such a thing?"

"Everything's relative, it depends on how much money you have." He fidgeted with the camera, looked through the view finder. "Okay, you take a flashcard," he pulled one of the tiny cards out of the case, "and stick it in here." He put the card into the camera. "Then you just point and shoot." He took her picture and Nina blinked when the flash went off.

"Now look." He turned the camera around.

"Look at me!" she squealed. "There I am on the back of the camera." She smiled, took the camera from him and examined the picture of herself on the tiny LED screen on the camera back.

"These are forty megabyte cards, so each one holds an awful lot of pictures, but if you do manage to fill one up, all you have to do is push this button to erase it." He started to push the button.

"No, stop. I want to save it."

"Okay." He handed the camera back to her. "You can probably stop in any camera store and get an instruction book that'll teach you all the advanced features, but for now you've got the basics. Stick the card in, point and shoot."

"I love it." She pointed the camera at Norm. "Smile." She took his picture then laughed. "Rich is so much better than poor."

"Lord, you ain't telling no lie," Norm said.

CHAPTER SEVEN

PAUL SNELLING DIDN'T KNOW what to think. Clayton wouldn't meet his eyes, but that didn't necessarily mean he was lying. Clayton had a habit of darting his eyes around, looking everywhere but at the person he was talking to. That made him hard to read, because he looked like he was lying even when he wasn't.

"Sapphire made you in a restaurant?"

"God's truth," Clayton said.

"And waited for you outside, then got the drop on you?"

"They jumped me. I'd a took 'em, but they got me from behind. Fact is, I was winning when his woman did this to me." He touched the scabs on his cheek. "I hesitated because she's a girl and Sapphire clobbered me. It's my fault, I know, and I'm sorry. I won't let it happen again."

Snelling shook his head. This wasn't the way it was supposed to work, These were just kids they were dealing with, it should all be over by now. He went to the open window, looked down at her boat. The air outside was hot and humid. The sun was straight up. There was no wind, not a hint of breeze. A bug landed on his neck. Snelling slapped it.

"We'll stay here till we see what develops," he said. "You can wait in the room next door and keep watch. I was up all night, so I'm gonna get forty winks. Wake me if she leaves the boat."

"First we need to do a little renegotiating," Clayton said.

"You're kidding, right?" Snelling almost enjoyed Clayton's attempt to stand up to him. It had been a long time coming. He'd come close before, but he'd always been paid too well to risk losing Snelling's business.

"I'm not kidding. Mick Sapphire had thirty thousand dollars in his camera case," Clayton said. "I saw it when I searched his room."

"I don't recall telling you to do that."

"I was taking a little initiative."

"So what are you saying?" Snelling said.

"You always told me what was what," Clayton said. "This time you're not doing that and it doesn't seem to me you're doing the government's work. I think you're out on your own."

"What kind of plane have you been flying around?" Snelling said.

"Air Force Citation jet."

"Did you have any trouble clearing in when you got to Brazil? Did anybody look at your passport?"

"No."

"How about here? Any trouble?"

"No."

"What does that tell you?"

"Look, I know you got connections. You got IOUs lined up longer than your arm. There's probably a half dozen generals that would give you a plane and military hardware without a blink. But I still think there's money here, and a lot of it."

"Or you'd have taken Sapphire's thirty thousand?"

"I wouldn't a done that. I do my job, you've always been able to count on me."

For a second he thought about killing him, but he'd used Clayton and his bombs so many times over the years that he was starting to like him. Besides, he needed him to fly the jet and the helicopter. He may be getting greedy in his old age, but the son of a bitch could fly anything. In the air he was a god.

"All right, a hundred thousand dollars. But not till it's over. You obey orders without question. You do your job. And if you try to renegotiate again, you don't get a cent. Am I clear?"

"Perfectly," Clayton said.

"Now I'm going to get some sleep." Snelling went to

the door, opened it. "You got the room next door. Keep watch." He held out a key to Clayton.

Alone he went to the bed, stretched out. He'd been up all night unable to sleep. That had never been a problem before, but then he'd never hit a woman before. It had been bad luck that she'd been awake. He'd searched hundreds of places in his lifetime without waking the occupants, but there was always a first time for everything.

He rubbed the base of his neck where she'd bitten him. Thankfully the wound was hidden under his collar, so he was spared the embarrassment of having to explain it to Clayton. He shook his head, Joey Sapphire was a fighter, cornered, she turned feral. If he hadn't have winded her, she might've chomped into his carotid. She was something. He was lucky he'd managed to plant the bug before the confrontation.

He closed his eyes, slipped the headphone in his ear. If anything happened aboard *Satisfaction*, he'd hear and wake up. But having Clayton on watch couldn't hurt. Besides, he wanted him to earn all that extra money.

* * *

"Hello, *Satisfaction*." It was a woman's voice calling from the dock. Someone Joey didn't know. She climbed out of her berth, glanced at the clock. Twelve-thirty and hot. She'd slept late, but then she'd lain awake all night, emotions running between fear and worry.

"I'll be right up," she shouted. She went to the head, splashed water on her face, then stared at herself in the mirror above the basin. "Jesus, Joey, you look horrible."

She had puffy bags under her eyes, her hair was tangled, she felt lousy. "What a way to greet company." She put a washcloth under a cold spray, ran it under her eyes, then ran a quick brush through her hair.

"Coming." She stuck her head through the companionway, saw a young woman on the dock with a suitcase, Mick's duffel bag and his leather camera bag over her shoulder. Joey knew her, but she couldn't remember from where.

"What are you doing here?" the woman said and recognition came with her accent. It was the girl from that e-mail place in Brazil that Mick couldn't keep his eyes away from. Why was she here? The answer couldn't be good.

"I think I should be the one asking that question." Joey eyed the duffel bag.

"It's hot out here." The girl's shoulders slumped as if a barrel of sad had rolled over her and stolen her spirit away.

"Yeah, I see that. What do you want?" Bad things had been happening to her in the last couple of days and Joey had a sinking feeling that the girl on the dock was one more.

"My husband," the girl said.

"Your what?" Joey tried to push away the dread that shot through her body, couldn't.

"Mick Sapphire. We were married yesterday."

"That's nuts! Mick wouldn't do that. You're mistaken!" She'd been sick with worry most of the night, thinking things couldn't get much worse. But she'd been wrong. Things were worse. The girl on the dock was proof of that. This day wasn't Christmas, it was just the opposite, whatever that was.

"It seems maybe we've both been mistaken about Mick." The girl had those pouty lips that the models on the cover of Vogue all seemed to have and a cute, perky little nose. She had the beauty found only in youth. Skin that radiated, not a wrinkle under her hazel eyes. She was just a wisp of a thing, and beautiful to a fault. It wasn't only Mick's eyes that had been captivated by her when they were in Fortaleza, all the men were afflicted with the disease of her. Her and her broody roommate. Devil women, the kind men die for.

"Hand me your bags." Joey couldn't turn her away, because in addition to her beauty there was something else there. The girl was hurting, even more than Joey. It was all over her face. She remembered how efficient she was in Brazil, how she handled everyone's paper work, how she was always around to help out. There she was strong, here she was a waif, out of her environment and helpless.

"I don't feel too good," the girl said. Joey didn't remember her name.

"Come on, give me the bags, then come aboard." Joey took them as the girl hefted them over the lifelines. "What do you have in here, everything you own?"

"Pretty much. I've never traveled before and didn't know what to bring." She sounded like she was about to cry. What had Mick gone and done?

"Let's get this stuff below."

"You're not divorced are you?" the girl said as she handed one of the bags down the companionway to Joey.

"No." Joey set the baggage on the floor in the middle of the salon as the girl came down.

"I'm going to be sick."

Joey showed her to the head, where the girl dropped to her knees and vomited into the bowl. It seemed to go on forever. The girl really was sick.

Joey's stomach cramped. She felt bile in her own throat. She was going to be sick, too. Not. She fought to hold it down, choked it down, kept it down. Thank God.

The girl finished, rolled some paper off the roll, wiped her mouth, then flushed the toilet. She was familiar with boat heads. Did Mick teach her that on *Satisfaction* back in Fortaleza during one of Joey's many shopping trips with the other yachtie girls? Probably. They had to have spent time together, otherwise he wouldn't have gone back to Brazil and married her.

Married.

It couldn't be true.

It had to be true. The girl was shivering in the heat, arms wrapped around herself, eyes wide in disbelief.

"My name's Nina, and I'm really sorry about this." She moved away from the head, went to the salon, sat on the settee. Her hands were in her lap now, fingers laced, knuckles white. She was still shaking. Was she going to cry?

"I'm sure it's not your fault." Joey sat next to her. Something about the girl begged to be mothered. Joey had always been a sucker for someone in trouble.

"I never would have come if it wasn't for the baby."

"The what? Oh, shit. It just keeps getting better." Joey felt like she was under a giant hammer and it was coming down.

"I don't understand, what does this mean, *getting better*, the way you said it?"

"It's an expression, it means the opposite of what it sounds."

"Oh, my friend Joana is always doing that, teaching me expressions."

"Why?"

"So I can speak English like an American. I want my baby to have all the advantages." She put her hands on her stomach, seemed to press against it, almost as if she were checking to see if the baby was really there.

"Swell."

"It is swell." Nina hadn't caught the sarcasm.

"Nina, we're going to put this stuff in the side cabin, then we're gonna make some tea and you're gonna tell me everything that's going on." Joey picked up Mick's duffel, she needed time to think. Nina got her suitcase and in less than a minute the baggage was stowed and Joey was making tea as Nina sat back down and fidgeted on the settee.

"He said you were divorced." The girl sounded scared now, and again Joey thought she was going to cry. Well, she could certainly understand that, she was scared herself, wanted to cry herself.

"Listen, Nina. Under ordinary circumstances I'd be out of my tree, you coming here and telling me this, but the circumstances are far from ordinary." Joey took the first cup of tea out of the microwave. Added cream.

"What does it mean, *Out of your tree?*"

"It mean's, I'd be madder than hell." She put the next

cup in the microwave, set the timer.

"That's what I thought."

"I'm in big trouble and from the looks of you, I'd say you are too. I don't have anyone I trust enough to tell what's happened to me and I'm afraid to go to the police, so I'm going to trust you." She laughed. The microwave beeped. "Stupid, I know, but I have to tell someone." She took the second cup out of the oven, added cream, took the cups to the settee.

"If you trust me, I'll trust you," Nina said.

"Okay, I'll go first." Joey told her everything, starting from when she woke up next to David Atwood, the American Ambassador's dead son, and continuing right through to last night when the guy in the ski mask broke into the boat. "I shot him in the face with hairspray and bit into his neck like a wild animal or something. It scared him so much, he smacked into the bulkhead and took off."

"*Bulkhead*?" Nina had a question mark in her voice. She was a woman in all the right places, but she seemed like a kid, too.

"A bulkhead is a wall on a boat."

"Why not just say wall?" Nina said, making Joey smile. The girl was pregnant by a two-timing, who-knew-what, and it hadn't dampened her spirit. Joey couldn't help it, she found herself liking the girl.

"Everything on a boat has a different name, you know, like a kitchen is a galley and a bathroom is a head."

"The same word as this?" Nina touched her head.

"Same word." Then, "We're getting sidetracked." Joey laughed. She couldn't help it.

"*Sidetracked?*"

"It means we're getting off the subject."

"I understand." Nina took a sip of her tea. "How come you told me all this? You know, the whole story. How come you just didn't send me away? I would have sent you away if the table was turned around."

"If *the tables were turned*," Joey said. "And no you wouldn't. I've only known you a few minutes, but I know you well enough to know you'd take me in. We have to stick together, you and me."

"*Tables were turned*, I'll remember that. Why do we have to stick together?"

"Because I think Mick must be behind it all, but more than that, we're women in trouble who don't have anywhere else to turn."

"I think you are right." She was quiet for a second, took another sip of tea, then said, "I should tell you about a camera bag, thirty thousand dollars and a man with a red beard that tried to kill Mick yesterday."

Nina told her story.

"Jesus!" Joey said when she'd finished.

"You shouldn't say his name like that," Nina said. "Especially on Christmas day."

"Sorry." Then after a pause. "He ran away and left you?" Joey said. "And went to Tobago?"

"Yes. But he wasn't running away from me. That Red Beard scared him off. Mick must be in some kind of trouble."

"Didn't you listen to a word I just told you? Of course he's in trouble and the trouble he's in is spilling over onto us."

"So, what are we going to do?"

"I'm going to Tobago and find out what he's done."

"But he won't be there. He'll come here straightaway, won't he?"

"No, he's got someone he can stay with there." And that thought really made her blood boil, because Katie Ortega had a seaside villa in Tobago and if Mick was on that island, that's where he'd be.

CHAPTER EIGHT

SNELLING PULLED THE HEADPHONES from his ear, picked up the phone, dialed the room next door. "Get over here," he said when Clayton answered. He hadn't even gotten an hour's sleep.

"Sapphire's in Tobago," Snelling said to Clayton when he came into his room. "How come you didn't know that? How come you don't know what hotel?"

"He'd a used the VISA card," Clayton said, "and we'd a got a hit. He must've paid cash."

"Not only that, the new wife is here," Snelling said.

"I know, I saw her go aboard."

"And you didn't call me?" Snelling felt the blood going to his head, tried to control it.

"Relax, you said you wanted some sleep. I'd a come over if they looked like they were gonna leave." Clayton went to the chair, sat. "Sort of an interesting development, don't you think?" Clayton eyed the receiver and the headphones on the nightstand. "I was watching and you were listening the whole time?"

"You could've seen something I couldn't hear," Snelling said.

"So we're going to Tobago?" Clayton still had his eyes on the listening gear.

"We are."

"Think the wife, the real one, knows where he's at?"

"Maybe."

"We taking the jet?"

"No, I've got a chopper at the heliport, we can be in Tobago quicker than we can get to the airport by car."

"Hot damn, I like flying choppers. We leaving right away?"

"Pretty quick. But first I'm going to buy a half pound of sugar."

"Gonna bribe some cops?" Clayton said.

Snelling nodded. They'd planted sugar and used crooked cops before. It always worked. Tell someone they were going to jail for forever because they were caught smuggling cocaine and after the denials and a couple hours alone in a bare room, they always talked, usually telling more than you ever wanted to know.

"While I'm watching wife number one squirm, do you

think you can keep tabs on number two?"

"She don't have a clue," Clayton said.

"Your point?" Snelling said.

"We're wasting our time with little Latin Loop de Lou."

"What if Sapphire finds *her*?" Snelling said.

"Okay, okay, I'll watch her while you have all the fun."

* * *

Again Joey was at the public phone at the end of the pier. She'd just finished talking with the airport. There were flights to Tobago every hour, retuning on the half, but because it was Christmas they were all full, save for the 6:00 pm flight and the only return available for the next week was at 9:30 am the next day, Boxing day, the day after Christmas holiday celebrated in Trinidad, a hold over from British rule. It didn't give them much time to find Katie Ortega's villa and find Mick, but it would have to do.

"I agree," Nina said as soon as Joey hung up the phone. "I think we need to talk to Mick and straighten everything out, but what do we do if he isn't in Tobago?"

"I think he is."

"But what if he isn't?"

"Then I don't know. I'd go to the States, to his parents, but I don't have a visa," Joey said. Then, "Actually, going to his parents would be good if we could do that, not just to find Mick. His father is a famous lawyer. If anybody can get to the bottom of all this, he can." Joey was thinking about the ambassador's son, dead at the bottom of the ocean. If anybody found out about it, she'd want a good attorney and Mick's father was the best.

"You think we should go to America?" Nina said.

"Yes, but we can forget that, they're not going to give us visas, a Brazilian and a South African. Not without money in the bank and some serious family ties, neither of which I have, how about you?"

"No, but I know someone who can help us get into America. Can we call Brazil on this phone?"

Joey said yes and listened while Nina spoke in Portuguese to someone named Captain da Silva. Having grown up with a best friend from Mozambique, which is next door to South Africa, she understood most of what Nina said when she told him of their problems and how they needed to go to America after they returned from Tobago.

"He said to call back in an hour," Nina said after the call was finished, so they had a quiet lunch at the marina restaurant, then she called back. Joey tried to listen, but the conversation was mostly one way, da Silva talking, Nina listening.

"Do you know where Corbeau Yacht Services are?" Nina asked after she hung up.

"Yes."

"We have to be there tomorrow at noon, two hours after our flight comes back from Tobago. Can we do that?"

"Yes, but why?" Joey said.

"Somebody there is going to fix it so we can go to America."

"Who?" Joey said.

"I don't know, but I guess we will find out," Nina said.

About seven hours later, Joey was sitting next to Nina as they neared the end of the twenty minute flight from Trinidad's Piarco airport south of Port of Spain to the airport in Tobago at Crown Point.

"It's going to be okay." Joey squeezed Nina's hand. She couldn't help comforting the girl. Nina was in the window seat, looking out at the black night. Clouds covered the sky. Lightning flashed in the distance. Joey felt a shudder ripple through Nina's hand to hers. She squeezed tighter. The plane shook as it rocked through turbulence.

"It's not the weather." Nina took her hand back, brushed her flowing hair out of her eyes. Beautiful the way it flowed around her face when she moved. Any man would find it so. "I was thinking about Mick," she said. "And what he'll do when he sees us together."

The plane hit another patch of turbulence and she grabbed onto Joey's arm.

"Ouch!

"Sorry." The plane shook again, more lightning flashed outside the window. "I take it back, I am afraid of the weather," she said.

The plane hit turbulence again. It rattled and shook. Then they were through it and on a long final approach. Nina bit into her lip and tightened her hold on Joey's arm.

"Relax, they do this kind of stuff all the time." Joey hoped she sounded more reassuring than she felt.

KEN DOUGLAS

"Sorry about the shaking." The captain's calm voice
came from speakers throughout the plane. "It's just a little
turbulence, nothing to worry about. We'll be on the
ground in about five minutes."

"See, you heard him, nothing to worry about," Joey
said, but Nina clung to her arm till the plane was taxiing
off the runway.

"It's still raining out," Nina said.

Joey had her hand back now. Nina was pulling her
long hair into a ponytail. She tied it back with a squeezy
she dug out of Mick's camera bag, her purse now. Then
she pulled out a compact and checked her lipstick. A chill
ran through Joey as she watched. Nina was drop dead
gorgeous, just her smile must have set Mick's heart
pounding. She looked like a beauty queen.

Joey moved her eyes away from Nina's lips and looked
out the window. An airport vehicle was coming toward
the plane with four or five cars behind it, sort of like a
miniature train without tracks.

"Not just rain," Nina said, still looking out the
window, "it's pouring." Then, "Uh oh, police."

"What?"

"Police," Nina said again.

Joey looked back out the window. A car with flashing
blue lights was coming toward the plane, following the
path of the luggage carrier.

The flight attendants were leaving their seats. One
went to the front of the cabin and picked up a telephone,
drawing Joey's eyes from the police car outside. "Ladies
and gentlemen, we're ready to disembark. We'll be met by
an airport tram which will take you to the arrival hall

84

where you can pick up your luggage." People started getting up and retrieving their carry-on baggage. Joey stood, too. "You will find taxies right outside the airport," the stewardess continued. "Thank you for flying with us."

"Are you worried about the police?" Nina said as they were making their way down the crowded aisle.

"No," Joey said. "They can't be here for us." At the door she started down the steps to the tarmac below and the waiting trams.

"Look, more police." Nina was ahead of Joey and pointed to four policemen standing in front of two police cars.

"Probably just routine," Joey said as she stepped off the movable stairway. They looked grim. "I wouldn't want to be down a dark alley on the wrong side of them."

"Me neither." Nina stepped into the tram.

The tram whisked them to the arrival hall where they followed the herd of people to baggage claim. But they didn't have to wait for any luggage to come off the carousel as Joey had a change of clothes in her carry-on bag and Nina had stuffed something into Mick's fancy leather camera bag.

"Hold a minute." Joey stopped when she heard the ring of authority in the voice. "You can put your bag up here." The speaker was a short, squat black man, wearing the uniform of a policeman.

"I don't understand, it's not an international flight," Joey said.

"We check some at random, only takes a minute," the policeman said. Nina started to put the camera bag up to the counter. "No, that one." The man pointed to Joey's carry-on.

"Not a problem." Joey set the carry-on before the policeman.

"You want to open it," he said. It wasn't a question.

"Sure thing." Joey unzipped it and opened the flap. Then she turned it toward the officer.

He ran his hands over the top of the bag, patting down her clothes. "Everything looks okay," he said, then he ran his hands under the clothes. "What's this?" He pulled out a bag of white powder.

"Not mine," Joey said.

"Everybody says that," the officer said.

"Well, this time it's true." Joey stiffened as panic rippled through her. The police car she saw outside the airplane window flashed through her mind. "What are you guys trying to pull?" She was agitated now.

"Easy ma'am." The new voice had a touch of gravel in it and it accompanied a large black hand that clamped down on her shoulder. "What do you have here, Jackson?" The man with the big hands was speaking to the officer searching her bag. He was one of the policemen they'd seen as they got off the plane.

"Lots of white powder in a Zip-Lock bag." He turned a scowl toward Joey. "What is it girl? Cocaine or Heroin?"

"I told you it's not mine!" Joey said. How could that have gotten in there? "There has to be some kind of mistake. I've never seen that stuff before and if I had, do you think I'd be stupid enough to stick it in my bag like that?" She couldn't believe what was happening. The hand on her shoulder was a vice, every bit as strong as the fear gripping her heart. First the dead man, then the break-in, now this. Somebody was out to get her.

"So you admit it's yours," the policeman holding onto her shoulder said.

"She did not. How can you be so stupid?" Nina said.

"Easy, Miss," the big man said. "You want to stay out this or you could be in trouble, too." And, with that said, the man squeezed Joey's shoulder as he turned her around and started to escort her away.

"Where are you taking her?" Nina grabbed onto the big man's arm.

"You should be careful, Miss," the big policeman said. "I could accidentally hurt you. We wouldn't want that."

"Nina, I'll get this straightened out," Joey said, but she didn't know how she'd do that. "Go back to Trinidad. Wait for me on the boat."

"Come along," the big man said. It wasn't right. This kind of thing didn't happen.

"I'm coming, you don't have to hold on so tight." And to Joey's surprise the man let go. The two officers led her to a small room with four folding chairs and a wooden table. They looked like they'd been in place for several years.

"Wait here. We'll be back." The big man closed the door, leaving her alone in the room to sit and contemplate a naked overhead light and a clock on the wall. A roach scurried across the floor. Grayish-white, dirty paint was peeling from the walls. Several names had been carved into the table. The door wasn't locked.

She looked at the clock. Five minutes after seven. She was still looking at it an hour later as she struggled to keep the panic from overwhelming her. Was this what it was like for those poor black kids her father used to torment? Shivers rippled through her, because she knew the answer. She'd been grabbed by the police on trumped up charges, stuck in a bare room with nothing but a light bulb and a ticking clock. Did they expect her to panic, run out the door like a crazy person?

But she wouldn't. She was her father's daughter. She knew how he and his police pals had dangled escape in front of a man, only to shoot him down when he grabbed at the false hope. She wouldn't do that, not in a million years. She looked over at the door. No way was she going to open it. She was in enough trouble already. They'd told her to wait and that's what she was going to do.

She got up, started to pace. That made it worse. She sat back down as a thin black man entered. He was angular, tall and wiry, like he could fight. He had close cropped hair, ears that looked like they were pasted on, thin lips and fierce eyes. He was pushing a bucket with a mop, like a janitor, but he studied her like a cop.

"What are you doing here?" the man asked.

"Waiting," Joey said.

"For what?"

"The police told me to wait. That's all I know."

"I'm supposed to clean the room." The man leaned on his mop, looking down at her, like he was waiting for her to get up and leave so he could mop the floor.

"Sorry, I'm staying."

"How am I gonna work?"

"They didn't lock the door," Joey said.

"What?"

"Didn't lock it," she repeated. "I'm not stupid, I think you people want me to try and leave."

"You're talking crazy. I'm just here to clean the floor, like I do every week."

"I don't think I'll get very far."

"I don't know what you're talking about."

"You people found a bag of white powder in my bag. It's not mine. Someone put it there. I don't know who. I don't know why. Then you put me in this room. Why no lock on the door? Why no handcuffs? Why no police guard? Why no questions? Now you want me to leave. Why? Who are you?"

"I'm just the man that cleans the floors."

"I'm not anybody special. You made a mistake. You got the wrong girl."

"That why you don't try to run away?"

"Yeah, because I didn't do anything wrong." Then all of a sudden it hit her, the only time her carry-on was remotely out of her sight was when they went through security in Trinidad. The police there must have put the drugs in her bag, then called ahead. She was really in trouble.

Just then two huge policemen burst through the door. "Up," one of them said. He was the one that had been holding onto her shoulder earlier. She stood and they propelled her through the door, across the airport lobby, toward a waiting police car. There was another officer behind the wheel and the engine was running. One of the giants climbed into the front seat, the other pushed her into the back, then folded himself in after her. Joey shivered as the car pulled away from the curb.

"Where are we going?" she asked.

"Scarborough Police Station," the man in the shotgun seat said. "You're going to be in jail for a mighty long time."

CHAPTER
NINE

NINA LOOKED ON IN HORROR as the officers escorted Joey away. It was a mistake. It had to be. She wanted to scream, but that would only get her arrested, too. She could deal with this. Trinidad and Tobago had to be like Brazil. Find the right official, give him some money and the problem was suddenly solved.

She looked up at the policeman that had asked to see Joey's bag. He looked away, refusing to meet her eyes. Why had he picked on Joey? How did that stuff get in her bag? It had to have been deliberate, but how could anyone have known they were coming to Tobago? They hadn't told a soul.

"Excuse me."

"You speaking to me?" the policeman looked up, surprised. He was a big man, as were the policemen that had taken Joey away. They all looked like they spent hours in the gym making muscles.

"Yes, can you tell me where I can change some money?" She smiled and moved in close to him. She knew how to make a man uncomfortable and in her experience the more muscles the man had on his body, the less brains he had in his head.

"Just outside that door." He pointed.

"Thank you." She made like she was going to go. Stopped, looked up into the big man's eyes. "Do you know what it was all about?" She gave him that look that she knew sent men wild. Was it her fault they were so stupid?

"Ma'am?" the policeman said, clearly uncomfortable now.

"That drug stuff in my friend's suitcase. Do you know why?"

"It wasn't my fault. I only do what they tell me. I've got a wife and kids. I didn't have any choice." He was looking at the ground, avoiding her eyes again.

"What are you saying?"

"I'm sorry about your friend."

"What do you mean exactly?" A chill began to cool the back of her neck.

"Nothing, just that I don't like to be responsible for someone's sorrow, but I have a job to do and that's just how it is."

"I understand," she said. "And I don't blame you." She could still see Joey in her mind's eye, being led away, her fright evident. She hoped she was all right.

"You go out that door and turn to your right. You can't miss the money changers," the policeman said, dismissing her.

Nina pushed through the double doors and found herself outside, but inside. The airport lobby was covered against the rain, but open to the night. Taxies were lined up at the curb, people were shoving their luggage into their trunks. There was a bank of ticket counters to her right, past them she saw the change sign.

Whatever happened she was going to need money. She went to the change window.

"Can I have a thousand dollars US in your currency?" She took ten hundred dollar bills out of the camera bag.

"A lot of money," the woman behind the glass said. "You have a passport?"

Nina handed it over along with the money, watching while the smiling woman checked her photo. Nina judged her to be about thirty, but black people had always looked younger than they were to her. She could be as old as fifty.

"Do you have any children?" Nina said, surprising herself.

"Why, yes," the woman said. "Why do you ask?"

"I'm pregnant," Nina said. "I never thought about kids before, now it's almost all I think about."

"I have two boys, three girls and two grandchildren."

"Really? You don't look that old."

"Must be the clean and healthy living," the woman

said.

"Are you ever sorry, about the kids, I mean?"

"Lord yes. Everyday I'm sorry, but everyday I'm happy, too. They are so much bother, so much trouble, and so much love. I wouldn't have traded them for all the money in the world."

"Thank you, I needed to hear that."

"Are you in trouble, girl?"

"I'm in a lot of trouble. My friend was arrested for drug smuggling and I don't know what to do."

"So that's what all the fuss was about earlier."

"I guess so," Nina said.

"Listen up, child. There's nothing you can do tonight. Just go across the way and get a hotel room. You can walk right out those doors, it's only a few steps. They're open all night. You get a good night's sleep and tomorrow you call Clarence Sparger, he's the best lawyer in Tobago. If anybody can help you, Clarence can."

"But what about Joey, my friend? I have to do something."

"You can't do anything tonight, so get a room and some sleep. Do it for the baby. Clarence will do you right in the morning. You tell him 'Lisbeth said to call. He knows me."

"Do I need your last name?"

"No, honey, you don't, Clarence is my brother-in-law."

"Thank you." Nina held out her hand as the woman counted out the money. It seemed like a lot to her. "What's the exchange rate?"

"About six to one. That's a lot of money, you best be

careful. People here are real friendly, but that's a mighty big temptation. Don't tell anyone you have that much, you hear?"

"Yes, ma'am, I hear," Nina said.

"Go straight, about a block and you'll find the hotel."

"Okay, thank you again," Nina said, but a taxi pulled up as she neared the curb and she held her hand up.

"Where to?" the driver asked.

"Can you take me to the police station?"

"Lord, that's in Scarborough, best you go to your hotel first."

"I want to go to the police station."

"Then that's where we'll go."

She waved to Elizabeth at the change window as she got in the cab and frowned when Elizabeth shook her head. Maybe she should have listened to her and gone to the hotel, but Joey was in trouble. If there was anything she could do to help, she was going to do it. She had money now, maybe she could bail her out, so she at least wouldn't have to spend the night in jail.

"You ever been to Tobago before?" the driver asked as he pulled away from the curb. He was short, bald and dark, with a pencil thin mustache that reminded her of a Jimmy Buffet song the yachties in Fortaleza were always listening to.

"No."

"It's the most unspoiled island in the Caribbean. The most friendly people, the safest roads, no crime to speak of, everybody knows everybody else, almost like a big island family."

"Do you know Clarence Sparger?"

"Certainly, my cousin. He's a good man and a fine lawyer. How do you know him?"

"My friend's in jail. I was told Mr. Sparger could help."

"You were told right, Clarence will be your man."

"Does your cousin mind being called in the middle of the night?"

"He hates it. Nothing you can do anyway. Once they put a body in that jail and lock the doors, the Lord himself couldn't get them open till eight in the morning."

Nina leaned back and closed her eyes as he started humming along with a soft rock song on the radio. She hadn't slept on either of the flights. She was too excited and jittery and now she was too upset and too frightened.

"How long before we're there?" She opened her eyes back up. She might as well not even try.

"Ten or fifteen minutes." He continued his humming. It was soothing and helped to calm her nerves as she watched the view slide by. The ocean, black and forbidding, was on her left for a while. Then they turned away from the beach and onto a wide road. He picked up the speed as she watched trees blur by. She heard the sound of the surf again. This time the ocean was on her right. They had crossed over to the other side of the island. He made a turn and in a few minutes they were in a small town. He made another turn and parked.

"We're here." He shut off the engine in front of the Scarborough Police Station. She paid him and he left. She started up the steps, went inside.

"Can I help you?" a lanky man in a gray police uniform with dark blue sergeant's stripes and skin black as the night asked her.

"My friend was arrested at the airport," she said. "I was wondering if I could see her?" She looked about the room. There were a few yellowed newspaper clippings tacked to the wall behind the sergeant and she imagined that they were stories about local police heroes. The wall to the sergeant's right had black and white photos of men in uniform, probably one of every officer on staff.

"Don't know anything about anyone arrested out at the airport tonight."

"I saw the police take her away."

"They didn't bring her here. Don't know why. Should have, if she was arrested."

"Where else would they have taken her?"

"Nowhere else, unless they took her straight to Trinidad. Might have if she was a big time criminal, like a murderer, but I think we woulda heard about it."

"What should I do?"

"The only thing you can do is wait till morning."

"Okay." Nina looked around the police station for a place to wait. She started toward a bench

"I didn't mean here."

"All right," she said, shoulders slumped.

"You know of a hotel around here?" he asked.

"No."

"Just out the door, maybe three blocks up the street. Not far. They'll have a room for you."

"Thank you." She wanted to shout her head off, but she knew it wouldn't do any good. The man was just trying to help. It wasn't his fault Joey wasn't here. She decided to get the hotel room and try to get some sleep.

She'd be better able to help Joey in the morning if she was refreshed. Besides, a young girl, lost and out of her depth, would get a lot more information out of these people than a tired and demanding foreigner.

She took another look around the police station before starting for the door. Twin overhead fans did little to kill the oppressive heat. The windows open to the outside might have been a help if there was a breeze, but there wasn't. She smiled at the policeman, wanting to give him a good impression, in case he was still on duty when she returned.

"Will you be here when I get back in the morning?"

"Yes, ma'am."

"I'll see you then." She tossed him a last smile, then went back out the door, down the steps and headed up a hill. Scarborough seemed to be built on a hillside overlooking the sea. The street looked clean, the businesses prosperous, but now they were closed and dark. It was a quiet night, the only sound, the gentle lapping of the waves as they rolled into the shore off in the distance. The town was closed up tight. She was on the street alone.

She thought she heard something. Footsteps. She stopped, looked behind. There was nobody there. She started up again, taking quiet steps, straining her ears against the dark. She heard it again. Footsteps echoing through the night. They stopped. She wanted to turn around and go back to the police station, but the footsteps sounded like they were coming from that direction.

"Is there anybody there?"

No answer.

A chill ran through her. She was alone on a dark street in a foreign country. She listened, but heard nothing. She started back up the hill, the camera bag slung over her shoulder all of a sudden seemed heavy.

Light caught her and she jumped as a car came around the corner and sped up the street. The driver was going too fast. She was still standing in place, still stunned by the speeding car, when another came around the corner just as fast as the first and, like the first, it was quickly gone.

The night was quiet again. She started back up the hill.

"Hey, lady." The voice came from behind. Harsh. Unfriendly. She turned. There was nobody there. She picked up her pace.

"I won't hurt you lady." This time she didn't stop. She didn't look back. She started walking even faster.

"Hey, lady, lady fly away home, don't belong where you don't belong," the voice said in a grating sing song. She started to run. "Come on, lady, I won't hurt you none."

She ran harder. There were some houses with doors that edged right up to the sidewalk, sandwiched between small retail shops and boutiques, and for a second she thought about stopping, banging on one of them and asking for help, but the footsteps behind seemed to be gaining.

Then she saw someone on top of the hill, about to cross the street. Thank God. She was safe. She was saved.

"Help," she tried to call out, but it rasped out of her

panicked throat, more a harsh whisper than a scream. She heard the footsteps clamping up the hill behind. She picked up her pace. "Help," she rasped again, panting, heaving, struggling to make a sound loud enough to be heard by the man up ahead.

The footsteps were louder, getting closer. She imagined a large black hand coming out of the night, reaching for her, grabbing at her. "Help me," she croaked.

The man stopped, looked down the hill. She couldn't make him out in the dim light, but it appeared he saw her. She pumped her arms in a vain attempt to get her legs to match their rhythm. She was running up hill, her feet were moving, but it seemed she was standing still.

The man started toward her. Thank God. She was breathing fast, wanted to shout out, tried. "Help me." But it came out a frog-like croak, not much louder than a whisper.

Would she never get there?

Her breath was coming in and out in ragged gasps now and something seemed to be pounding in her head. She was so tired, but she couldn't stop.

She wasn't a quitter. Not a quitter, she thought, again and again, not a quitter, not a quitter. She kept running, the footsteps behind fading.

She was getting away. She was going to be okay, but she didn't slow down, instead she put on a burst of speed. She didn't want to take any chances. She wanted to be well away from whoever was back there.

The man she'd seen at the top of the hill was coming closer, walking fast now.

"Can you help me?" she said, fighting to control her

rapid breathing.

"Yes," he said, and she saw the red beard as his balled fist slammed into her stomach. The pain was intense. Then she felt herself falling.

CHAPTER TEN

JOEY RAN HER TONGUE around her dry mouth and looked out the back window of the small police car as they passed a beach side hotel. The airport was behind them now, the police station somewhere ahead. Joey felt like she was going to wet herself, she was so scared. Did they know about the American Ambassador's son? Is that why they planted the drugs, so they'd have an excuse to hold her till they got more proof? Were they going to charge her with murder? Were they going to hang her?

She had to do something. She had to get away. Now,

before they got to the jail, because once they locked her up she'd be history. They'd find out what she'd done to David Atwood, they'd say she'd killed him, they'd hang her. She really had to pee now. She started to tremble. She fought to control it. Maybe they wanted her to try and escape, maybe not, but she didn't have any choice, she was going to go for it.

They stopped at a light next to a lighted park between the beach and the road. Some boys were playing cricket under the lights, they couldn't be more then ten or twelve.

"Kinda late for kids to be out," she said, making conversation, hoping to put the policeman sitting next to her at ease for a few seconds.

"It's only a little after eight. Besides, it's Christmas," the driver said. "Anyway, their parents don't worry. We don't have crime in Tobago." Joey knew that wasn't true. She'd been in Trinidad for over a month and she read the papers every day. They had crime.

She looked out at the black ocean and the three anchor lights on top of the tall masts of the boats anchored in Store Bay. A welcome sight. A sailboat, the sea, home.

"The airport police in Trinidad must have planted that stuff in my bag?" she said as she turned her attention to the traffic light. She was going to have to time it just right.

"You accusing the police? Us? That's a new one. Most people blame someone else, a friend or their wife."

"But we know better, don't we?" Joey said. "I saw you guys out the window of the plane. You were waiting for me? What are you after?"

"It's not very smart, blaming the police," the man next to her said. She felt the hostility oozing off him, filling the car with its odor.

"Oftentimes the truth isn't smart," Joey said. That had to be the longest traffic light in the world. Why wouldn't it change?

It did.

Now or never.

"That man's got a gun," she screamed, pointing to the right, as she jerked open the door and jumped out of the left side of the car. She hit the ground running for all she was worth to the hotel they'd just passed.

"Hey, stop!" One of the policemen shouted. He sounded close. She wanted to turn and look, but instead pumped her legs harder, sprinting toward the hotel. She'd hoped they'd think she was headed back toward the airport, but they weren't going to be fooled, not with that man right behind her.

"Stop!" the policeman's voice rang out again. He sounded closer, was closer. Joey was an athlete, she was in shape, but he was gaining. He was in shape too. A muscle bound policeman that could run.

She had to do something. What?

She veered right, toward the cricket game, charging for the batter like he was holding the tape at the finish line. Swimming wasn't the only sport she was good at. She'd run track in college, she knew how to run for a tape. She passed the bowler, a gangly kid who jumped out of the way to let her pass. Nothing between her and the batter now.

The kid with the bat couldn't have been more than ten. Joey caught his wide eyes as she raced toward him. She knew instinctively that it wasn't her that had him so frightened. It was the policeman behind.

"What?" the kid shouted as Joey snatched the bat out of his hand. The kid jumped back, not wanting to be a part of whatever was about to happen, while Joey whirled around, swinging the bat like a professional batsman, catching the policeman on the knee.

A popping sound, not unlike a good hit, rang through the field as the cop went down. He grabbed for his holstered gun, jerked it free and was about to bring it on target when Joey smacked him in the hand with the bat and the gun went flying as the policeman's scream woke up the night.

"Cool," the kid said.

"Gotta go," Joey tossed him the bat and charged across the field for the hotel with new energy. She saw the police car up on the road, two policeman standing by it, mouths open. One of them was pointing. Would they come for her or aid their wounded companion? She half expected them to pull their guns, but they didn't.

She'd closed half the distance to the hotel without taking her eyes off the cops on the road. Something decided them, because they took off as one, coming for her, running flat out. But she had a good start and they weren't nearly as fast as their downed comrade. If they didn't shoot her, she'd win the race.

The hotel was one of those beach resort places she'd seen so many of while cruising with Mick. Two wings of two story beach front rooms, each snaking along the ocean, with the lobby in the center. She burst through double glass doors and into a group of tourists on their way out.

"Out of the way!" she yelled as she plowed into them, pushing through. Then she was past them, running through the lobby. Long couches covered in tropical fabric with European looking people, chatting, drinking, looking at her as if she were some kind of freak bashing through, spoiling their party.

"Stop her!" someone shouted. The police she thought as she burst through another set of double doors and found herself dashing along a large, kidney shaped swimming pool. Chaise lounges surrounded the pool, empty because of the hour. In seconds she was past the pool, banging her way through an outdoor restaurant decorated with Christmas lights, the ocean so close.

"Hey you!" A black man dressed in black tie blocked her way. The maître'd, Joey supposed as she lowered her shoulder like an American football player blocking for the quarterback. She hit him mid-chest and sent him sprawling across a table of four, rolling in beef Stroganoff, lobster and filet mignon. Joey caught it all in the blink of an eye, a fraction of a second.

"Get her!" The policeman again.

"Out of the way!" she screamed as a big Germanic looking woman stood to block her path.

"Maggie!" her male companion shouted. "Mind your own business!" And the woman stepped aside. Not German, English. Thank God she wasn't German, Joey thought, as she lunged for the wall, otherwise she might not have gotten out of the way.

At the wall Joey grabbed hold, vaulted over and landed in the cool ocean. Her feet hit bottom, with her head above the water.

Her first impulse was to swim out to sea, but she checked it and stood still in the calm water for a fraction of a second that seemed an eon. In front of her was the dark space underneath the seaside restaurant. Thick pylons supported the floor about two feet above the water. She turned toward the bay. She was a strong swimmer, was about to head out that way when her world was lit up. They'd turned on the restaurant's overhead lights.

No time to think, she moved under the floor, stepping into the dark, moving her arms back and forth in the shoulder high water to keep from stumbling. At first she only went a few feet under and stood next to a pylon.

"I see her, out that way." It was the English woman, Maggie. Joey imagined her up there pointing. Thank God for her bad eyesight. Or maybe she did see something. A dolphin perhaps, who knew?

"You can't see anything, Maggie." It was the man who'd told the woman to mind her own business. Why couldn't he mind his?

"I know what I saw. She's over there, swimming toward that other hotel." Maggie sounded adamant.

"You're wrong," her man said. "Nobody could have gotten that far, that fast."

"Yes, sir." The new voice was out of breath. One of the policemen? "She's an Olympic swimmer." Definitely one of the policeman. How'd he know that?

"There, I saw her again," Maggie said.

"Where?" One of the cops. He was right on top of her, Joey caught glimpses of him in his policeman's uniform through the cracks between the planks that made up the floor. For a second she thought if she could see him up there, then he'd be able to see her down below, but she dismissed the thought when she realized she was looking up into the light. He couldn't see through the small space between the planks. She was surrounded by the dark.

"Don't see nothing," the other policeman said. Joey could see him, too.

Something moved by her shoulder. She almost shouted out, almost jumped, but she remained quiet as she turned her head.

Crab.

Big one, clinging to the pylon. Inching around it, bathed in the light coming down through the cracks from above, a star on a hidden stage, nobody to see but her. She shook involuntarily in the water as another crab crept around the pylon and she stayed still as wet tingles rippled along her skin.

All of a sudden it went quiet, totally quiet. She hadn't noticed it before, but there'd been music in the background. Pan music, the national instrument of Trinidad and Tobago. You heard it wherever tourists congregated. Hotels, restaurants, it was even piped through speakers at the airport. Pan muzak.

Without it, the place where Joey was seemed more alien than ever. A third crab joined its mates on the pylon. Apparently when she invaded their domain they'd been scared and scampered away. How come they weren't afraid now?

"Have to be pretty dumb to swim out in the bay after dark," policeman number one said. "I don't care how good she can swim in a pool, that's the ocean out there. The sea don't allow for fools."

"No telling how foolish people are," policeman number two said. Then, "You think she's gone?"

"She could be down there," policeman number one said. Between the cracks Joey saw him pointing right at her.

"She's not down there," policeman number two said. The lady said she saw her out there." Now Joey could see him pointing out to sea.

"Someone's gotta go down and look," policeman number two said.

"Not me."

"I'm senior, it's your job."

Oh, Lord, Joey thought, if he climbed over that wall, he'd see her for sure. She took a deep breath and backed up under the floor a bit. Maybe he wouldn't come down here. After all, that Maggie lady said she'd seen her swimming toward one of the other hotels.

She bumped something sharp. Stopped, clamped her mouth shut against a scream. She backed into another pylon. This one was covered with barnacles and thousands of those bugs the locals called sea cockroaches were running every which way. The hotel must clean the barnacles off the pylons in front to keep the outside of the restaurant looking clean and wholesome for the tourist that might pass by on one of those peddle boats or a windsurfer. But they didn't clean the pylons underneath.

No reason, the place was off limits to tourists.

She turned to face back into the dark and resolved not
to go any farther unless she absolutely had to. It was more
than dark back there. It was the kind of place every horror
writer writes about. A place of bats and spiders. Snakes
and rats. She didn't want to go back there.

She shook in the dark water. With the absence of the
music above, the quiet noise down below sent shivers
shimmying from the back of her neck to all the parts of
her body. The snapping sound of shrimp on the bottom,
the gentle waves slapping the pylons, the creaking of the
overhead planks as the people above moved about, the
shrieking of a chair being pulled from a table, all of it
unnerved her.

And, of course, the background buzz of talking as the
patrons had to be wondering about the crazy woman that
had come bursting through the restaurant only to leap
over the wall into the night sea. They all seemed white,
therefore American or European, so they wouldn't be
afraid of the police. They were on vacation from places
where the police helped and assisted, protected and
served, they wouldn't understand that the men in uniform
among them should be feared.

And as if to prove her thoughts, she heard one of them
say, "Clear out the restaurant!"

"But, sir," Joey assumed it was the maître'd speaking,
"these people are having dinner. They haven't paid yet."

"Clear them out!" And in seconds the restaurant above
was empty, save for the two policemen.

"Okay, it's time for you to go look," policeman
number two said.

"I'm going!"

And so was Joey. Using her arms to help her move through the water, she went further under the restaurant. Her way was dimly lit by the little light that filtered through the cracks between the planks and she didn't like what she saw.

Barnacles covered the pylons, thick and black, about a foot above the water. She gasped, that meant the water was going to rise. She looked up, at absolute high tide there was maybe a foot between the floor and the sea. Was the tide coming in? She didn't know, but what she did know was that if it was, she wouldn't be able to touch. The thought of treading water under there with only inches of space between the water and the floor sent even more shivers rippling through her.

There was grassy slime growing among the barnacles, too, but she had no choice and continued on, moving toward a dark corner, probably under the kitchen, she thought, because no light came down from above. She heard a chirping kind of sound and now she was really scared, because the last time she'd heard that sound she was fourteen years old, staying overnight at her best friend's, back in Scotland. They were scaring themselves silly with a video of the movie *Ben*. A horror story about rats. More chirping jerked her mind back to the here and now. These weren't movie rats down here. They were the real thing.

She heard a splash. The policeman was in the water. She turned, saw his torch go on. She slipped under the surface as the light played over where she had been. Something moved by her in the water. Some kind of big fish. It took all her will power to keep herself under. She could hold her breath a long time, and she did, till her lungs were screaming for oxygen. She surfaced. The torch was out.

"She ain't down here," policeman number one said.

"Okay, come on up."

"What's going on?" A new voice from above, American.

"She got away," policeman number two said.

"I told you to keep her in that room." The American sounded angry.

"She had drugs, it was our job to move her to the police station," the policeman said.

"It was sugar, or did you forget?"

"She belongs at the police station." He was as stubborn as Joey had come to learn the officials in Trinidad and Tobago often were.

"Christ!" the American said. He sounded disgusted. Then he said, "What's going on down there?"

"Officer Brumbeau's checking to see if she's hiding."

"I thought you said she got away?"

"A woman said she saw her swimming that way." Joey imagined him pointing.

"Where's this woman?"

"We sent all the people in the restaurant away."

"You sent away the witnesses?" The American was talking loud now. Then, "You down there, Brumbeau, you see anything?"

"No, sir," Brumbeau shouted.

"Get up here."

"Coming, coming." Brumbeau sounded glad to be

away from this place. Joey certainly understood that.

"I paid you to baby sit the girl at the airport, then as soon as I turn my back you go and screw it all up," the American said as Joey moved slowly toward the ocean. Halfway she looked up through the floor and got a good look at him. He was blond, she couldn't tell from below, but he seemed tall. He was good looking, with a baby face and, even from where she was, she could see the fire in his deep blue eyes.

"Sorry," the policeman said.

"Let's get the fuck out of here," the handsome American said.

Joey wanted to hear more, but all she heard was the American's footsteps as he thundered out of the restaurant. The policeman followed. Now all she had to do was wait a few minutes, till the coast was clear, then swim out to one of those boats.

CHAPTER ELEVEN

"I THINK SHE'S COMING OUT OF IT." Nina heard the voice as if it were filtered through a tunnel. She couldn't feel anything. She was floating. Lost in a cool blue sea. Then the dark came again, stealing the light. She tried to fight the thief. She was going under, gasping for air.

"She's not breathing. I need help here." The voice was strong, but not reassuring.

Something covered her face. Heavy hands slammed into her chest, pushing and pushing. She was blind. She railed against the dark. People were shouting. She couldn't make out what they were saying. She was sinking.

Later she woke again. This time she was covered in darkness of a different nature. The lights were out, but enough light sneaked in from the corridor for her to make out that she was in a hospital. She stared at the ceiling. She could see the cracking paint. The hum of an air-conditioner blew cold air from the wall at the foot of the bed. She shivered. She felt like she was at the dock at the Bay View Hotel on a cold Brazilian evening right after the rain.

She started to reach down to pull up the blanket. She felt a pain in her left hand. She eased it back. She balled her hand into a fist. It hurt. She relaxed the hand and looked up at an IV. There was a unit of blood hanging from a chrome stand. The chrome was reflecting light from the corridor. It looked spooky. Her eyes followed the red blood as it slid down the clear plastic tube connected to the back of her hand.

Blood, they were giving her blood. Why? She looked away from the plastic tube. She closed her eyes and flexed the fingers on her other hand. Her palm hurt. It felt raw. She remembered falling, throwing her hands out in front of herself. The pain sharp as she skinned her palms on the pavement. She relaxed her hand. It was too cold to sleep. She tried to sit up, almost making it before she fell back down. She was weak, that must be why there were giving her blood.

She was so tired, but she was cold, too. She edged her right hand down toward the covers she felt on her legs, snaking her fingers as far as she could, but the blanket was still out of reach. She closed her eyes, ready to drift back to the safety offered by sleep. But not yet. That would be like quitting. She wasn't a quitter.

She was going to get that cover. She wasn't going to quit. She balled her right hand into a loose fist. Then she pushed her fist into the mattress and pushed herself up into a sitting position. She was surprised at the amount of energy it took. She grabbed the blanket. Joana would have been proud.

Then she crashed back down and closed her eyes. When she opened them again the light was on. She squinted her eyes against it. The air-conditioner was still chugging away, still keeping her room hovering just below igloo temperature. And again the blanket was at her feet. She didn't remember dreaming, but she must have had a fitful nightmare.

"How do you feel?" The voice was warm and caring, like Joana's. The young black woman was dressed in white with a nurses cap standing out like a beckon among her sea of dark curls. Her smile was wide, her teeth as white as the uniform and cap.

"Who are you?" Nina asked.

"My name's Angel."

"Where am I?"

"Hospital."

"I know, but where?"

"Scarborough."

"In Tobago?"

"Yeah, in Tobago. You got hurt."

"How long?"

"A few hours. They gave you something to help you

sleep, but you had a bad reaction to it. It scared them."

"They?"

"The doctors."

"Oh." She closed her eyes and tried to remember. Then it all came flooding back. The flight. The thunder and lightning. Holding Joey's hand during the landing. The policemen. Them taking Joey away. The man with the red beard. He'd hit her in the stomach. "Oh my God. My baby."

"I better call the doctor."

"Tell me." Nina grabbed Angel's hand.

"I'm sorry. I'm truly sorry." Her eyes were misting up. She was crying. She was feeling Nina's pain. Nina melted into the girl's brown eyes, sharing her tears.

"Do you know what happened to my friend?" Nina asked Angel.

"I'm not supposed to speak about that."

"Please, I have to know." She heard the pleading in her own voice. She hoped Joey was all right. She didn't exactly know why, maybe it was because Joey was all she had right now.

Angel looked over her shoulder as if she expected someone to come in any second. "You won't tell I told?"

"No," Nina said. "I won't."

"They don't want anyone to know, but in Trinidad and Tobago everybody knows everything. The prime minister, the police, the bank robbers, not my own mother can keep a secret. Especially in Tobago. Lord, Tobago's small and no one has any privacy. Because of that, I know what I'm not supposed to know."

"What? What do you know?"

She bent lower, face centimeters from Nina's. "She got away from the police. But they say they're gonna catch her right back."

"She really got away?" Nina sighed, heart relieved. "How do you know this?"

"I told you, everybody knows everything, but it helps that one of my boyfriends is with the police. They're gonna catch her because she's a white woman without any money on this small island. They're saying she's a big drug dealer."

"She's not a drug dealer."

"They're sayin' she is."

"It's not true," Nina said. "They set her up."

"What do you mean?"

"When we got off the plane from Trinidad, they found drugs in her bag, but it wasn't hers. She didn't put it there."

"How do you know?"

"Because I was there when she packed it."

Angel was about to say something, but they were interrupted.

"How's my patient? Better I hope." The voice was male, harsh.

"I'm feeling better. Did I lose the baby?" She hated asking when she knew the answer, but if she didn't, the doctor would suspect that Angel had told.

"I'm Doctor Ramsaran, and yes, you did. It's a shame, but sometimes accidents happen."

"Accident?"

"The man that brought you in said you slipped stepping off a curb and landed on your stomach."

"I don't remember anything," Nina said, but she did. It was no accident. That man deliberately hit her in the stomach. But she didn't want to say anything about it. If she'd learned anything in her young life, it was to remain silent until you had all the facts, and even then it was usually better to keep your mouth shut. "When can I get out of here?"

"Not for a couple of days. We want to run some tests." The doctor was short, obviously Indian, maybe part Chinese. Dark skinned, beady eyes, sinister smile. His face was a sneer without trying. She didn't believe a word he was saying.

"What kind of tests?"

"Oh, you know, routine. That's all," he said through thin lips.

"What kind of routine tests?"

"Just routine. Nothing to worry about." He looked at his watch. "I have to go now, other patients. Glad you're feeling better."

"He's not a nice man. He didn't even say he was sorry about the baby," Nina said.

"And he lied," Angel said. "He doesn't have any other patients to see right now, they're all asleep. He wouldn't even be seeing you, except you're a special patient."

"How special?" Nina asked, fearing the answer.

"There's been a policeman asking about you."

"What do you mean?"

"You best be careful, that's what I mean. Watch what you say and who you say it to."

"Thank you, Angel. Thank you for telling me."

"What are you gonna do?"

"I don't know."

"You had a lot of money in your leather bag when they brought you in. So I took it when no one was looking. I didn't want anyone else to get it. It's happened before. Some of the people who work here don't have much. They see that much money and they can't help themselves. You know what I mean?"

"I know."

"I have it downstairs in the nurse's lounge. It's safe, but you're going to need clothes. They took yours and I don't know where they put 'em. Seems they got a mind to keep you here."

"What are you saying?" Nina asked. The whole situation was unreal. Why would anyone steal her clothes? Why would anyone want to keep her in the hospital if she was well enough to leave?

"If your friend doesn't get herself a lawyer, she's going away to prison for a long time when they catch her. You should get to Port of Spain and do what you can for her. That's what I would do." Nina stared hard into Angel's liquid eyes and saw only truth. "You might not be able to do anything at all," Angel continued, "but it's for certain that you can't do anything if you stay here."

"Do you think I'm well enough to get out of here?"

"I don't know, but even if you were, you're gonna have to sneak. I don't think they're gonna let you just walk out."

"Can you help me?"

"They said my brother was a big drug dealer. I've been to Trinidad to visit him in that jail. It's not a fit place to be, your friend wouldn't like it there. You rest.

Eat all you can. Try and get strong. I'll come by tonight with some clothes and we'll see about getting you to Port of Spain. Maybe one of those fancy lawyers that think they're better than everyone else can help you."

"You really think they will catch Joey?"

"Like I said, Tobago's a small place. Where can she hide?"

"Was your brother a drug dealer?" Nina asked.

"Yes, but not like they made out. He just sold a little smoke to help pay the bills. They made it sound like it was his fault everybody's smoking crack. He never did that. Marijuana's the only thing he ever messed with and he didn't do too much of that."

"What did they do to him, your brother?" Nina asked.

"They gave him fifteen years."

"Oh shit," Nina said.

"Exactly," Angel said. She looked over her shoulder again, nervous, not wanting to be overheard. "I'll be coming in less than an hour. You should be ready."

"I'll be ready," Nina said. She had to get to Trinidad, had to get a lawyer for Joey. She didn't want her in jail. In a very short time her allegiance had shifted from Mick to Joey. Mick was a rat. Joey was real.

She spent the time waiting on edge. She cried for her lost child. A nurse came in with a pill to help Nina sleep. She pretended to take it as the nurse was pouring the water. It wasn't hard. The nurse had no reason to suspect she wouldn't want to sleep.

"Are you awake, Miss?" a male voice. Nina didn't answer.

"She's asleep." Now the voice was talking to someone else. She recognized the American accent. For a second the thought about shouting out, but then she remembered Red Beard. It could be him. She remained silent and heard them whispering as they walked away. Now, more than ever, she wanted out of the hospital and out of Tobago. She pressed her eyes shut, bit into her lips and tried to understand what was happening.

"I'm here." Nina recognized Angel's whisper. She'd been laying in a fetal position, facing the wall. It seemed like she'd been staring at the cracked paint forever. She turned over.

"There's men here, watching me," Nina whispered back.

"Don't I know it. Don't move, this might hurt some." She ripped off the bandage that was holding the IV needle into the back of her hand. "I'm supposed to be adjusting the IV, but I'm taking it out instead." She pulled out the needle. "Okay, we're set," Angel said.

"So we're going now?" Nina asked.

"They paid one of the nurses to watch this room. She's out at the nurse's station right now, staring at this door like it's Jesus Christ himself come back to earth."

"What are we going to do?"

"I'm gonna make a diversion, like in the movies."

"How?"

"I'm gonna start a fire down the hall."

"You can't," Nina whispered. "This is a hospital, people will get hurt."

"Not a real fire. I'm gonna burn some papers in a

wastebasket, when everyone comes running, you get up and get out of here. You cross by the nurse's station, go through the door on the right. It's a stairway going down. We're on the second floor. When you come out the door on the bottom, you turn right and go in the first door. That's the nurse's lounge. I'll meet your there."

"How do you know the nurse watching my room will go?"

"She's a Tobago lady, she'll go. She'll be too curious not to. Besides, she won't wanna miss the fire. It'll be a good story to sit around and talk about over a glass of rum. She'll be going. You can count on it."

Nina nodded.

"Okay, I'm gone."

Nina sat up on the bed. For the first time she considered her state of dress, or rather undress. She was wearing a worn hospital gown, open at the back. She felt she might as well be naked. She clenched her hands, wondering how she'd know when Angel would be ready. She didn't have to wonder for long.

"Fire!" Angel's voice rang through the ward. "Fire!" she shouted again.

Nina heard someone yell, "Where?" Then the sound of a scuffling chair—footsteps running, fading—running away from her room, toward the fire. She stepped off the high hospital bed. She had a pain in her abdomen. She felt a dampness between her legs. She was sore. She padded to the door. It hurt to walk. She peeked out. There was no one there. Quickly, quietly she moved across the corridor, past the nurse's station and through the door. Safe, she thought, as she eased the door closed behind herself.

Her stomach burned. She felt the wet between her legs. She felt nauseous. She took a deep breath, grabbed the hand rail and started going down, each step a private agony. Halfway down, she thought her stomach was going to explode. Sweat glistened on the back of her hands, she felt it under her arms, wet and slippery.

She grit her teeth and forced herself to go on. A siren went off, blasting its warning throughout the hospital. The blaring noise gave her the courage to continue. She took two more steps. Stumbled and fell down the stairs. She screamed, but the siren drowned out her cry. The stairs mauled her as she tumbled down. She felt each one, like a blow from a determined tormenter. Then she was on the bottom. She was breathing fast. In and out. She tried to slow it down. Fought to catch her breath, finally regaining control. In and out, slowly now.

She flexed her fists. Then her arms. Then her legs. She curled her toes. Then wiggled her feet. Nothing seemed broken, though she hurt all over. She struggled up, grabbed onto the handrail and pulled herself to her feet. She had to go on, she wouldn't quit.

The siren was still wailing when she peeked her head out the door. She gasped. Had it not been for the siren, he would have heard her. The man with the red beard was standing in the center of the ground floor lobby, eyes roving around the room. Sniffing the air. Smelling for trouble.

He turned away from her, looking down the corridor toward the patient's rooms. She held her breath, stepped out though the door and scooted along the wall. She opened the door to the nurse's lounge, thankful for the siren. She slipped inside and closed it just as the siren went silent.

She looked around the room. Antiseptic white walls, paint cracking, like in her hospital room, but clean like her hospital room, too. Old building, worn down, worn out, out dated. The world had passed it by. She wondered about the medical equipment in the hospital and the doctors. There were two rows of gray lockers in the center of the room, gray benches in front of them. She shuffled over and sat. Where was Angel?

She looked between her legs. Blood. She was spotting. She needed a doctor. She needed to be in a hospital. She should just go back to her room and let them take care of her. Then she remembered the man with the red beard. She remembered his face under that street light just before he hit her. Narrow eyes, bushy brows, pink cheeks, A florid face on a fat neck. And the beard. A devil with a smile. She had to get out of here. Where was Angel?

CHAPTER TWELVE

THE OVERHEAD LIGHTS WENT OFF a few minutes after the policemen left. Joey shivered under the restaurant. Who was the American? Why had they planted sugar in her bag? Why had they said it was drugs? Not because of the dead man she'd dropped overboard, they would've said, so it had to be because of Mick. What had he done?

Katie Ortega had a house in Tobago. Mick and her were close, but not lovers, at least that's what he'd said. Could she believe anything he'd said now? Was he with her, lounging his night away with a rum and coke in hand while she shivered and shook in this awful place?

She'd planned on going straight to Katie's with the pregnant Nina in tow and confronting him. She couldn't do that now. She'd be lucky if she got out of Tobago in one piece. All of a sudden she realized the water had risen. If she didn't do something, she wasn't going to get out of Tobago at all.

She started to make her way out, skirting around the barnacle encrusted pylons. When she passed the last one, she dropped to her belly and swam underwater away from the restaurant, toward the yachts at anchor.

She was several strokes away from the shore when she surfaced and heard the sirens. She stopped, treading water, turned to look. Flashing blue lights sped by on the ocean road. Were they still looking for her? Probably.

She grabbed a few breaths, calming her nerves, then started out for those bobbing anchor lights. She hoped to find a boat with nobody aboard. After she judged she was a safe distance from shore, she stopped again, shucked out of her running shoes. For a second she thought about pulling off her jeans, then decided against it, they'd slow her down, but she didn't have that far to go. She shivered, but it wasn't from the cold.

Someone had set her up.

Why?

She grabbed another breath and struck out for the closest yacht. It was a ketch, about forty-five feet, flying a German flag. She'd get no help there. They'd be calling the Coast Guard on the VHF before she managed to get on board. She swam past, striking out toward a Taiwanese built schooner off in the distance. She heard the dog barking before she got close, so she turned away and headed toward a sloop anchored to its right. It was lit up, there were people home. When she got closer she saw the American flag. Americans in the Caribbean had the reputation of shooting first and asking questions later.

She saw another boat farther out. Dark, no anchor light. She struck out for it. It turned out to be a small sloop that had seen better days. She grabbed on to a rope boarding ladder, held on for a few minutes, dangling in the water to catch her breath, then she pulled herself out of the sea and climbed onto the deck. Once up, she stretched out on her back and looked up at the cloud covered sky. Usually she shied away from bad weather, but a storm tonight would be a blessing. After a few minutes she got up and made her way to the cockpit.

The boat was locked and any noise she made breaking in would echo across the bay. But that was okay, she didn't need to get in to move the boat. Mick had taught her how to sail on and off the hook, she didn't need the engine.

She went to the bow and studied the automatic windless. If the batteries were switched on, all she'd have to do was push the deck button and the windless would bring up the anchor. But the sound of it coming up would ricochet throughout the bay. She could bring it up manually, but that, too, would be loud on this still night. She checked the anchor rode.

Rope.

She calculated that the boat was anchored in about thirty feet of water. She guessed that the skipper probably used seventy-five to a hundred feet of chain spliced or tied to rope as anchor rode. In thirty feet of water he would have another fifty to seventy-five feet of rope out. If the rope was tied to the chain with a bowline or a fisherman's bend she could haul it up and simply untie it. If it was spliced to the chain, she'd have to let it back out and think of something else, because even if she brought it up by hand the chain would make noise as it clanged over the bow roller. She grasped the rope and started hauling it in. Silently the boat moved forward.

A dog started barking. Joey froze and squinted through the dark. She couldn't see it, but she could imagine it, angry eyes, fangs bared, drooling. It was the dog on the schooner. Joey let out the rope and the boat gently drifted back to its original position.

"Quiet Hannibal." Joey heard a woman's voice drift over the water. She sounded hard. She wondered what kind of person named a dog Hannibal. One who had a dog that meant business. The dog kept barking, louder than before. "All right, all right, we'll check it out." Then Joey heard. "Rudy, Hannibal's staring out at *Mariah* barking to beat the band."

"Think someone's out there?" A man's voice, as hard sounding as the woman's. Joey didn't want them to come out and investigate.

"He doesn't bark without a reason."

"I'll get the light," the man said.

Joey slipped over the side as the boat was bathed in white. The man was using one of those million candle power lights, lighting up the small boat as sure as a searchlight stalking a prisoner during a prison break.

"See anything?" The woman's voice.

"No. Let's go over and have a look."

Joey heard the sound of a small outboard starting up. Probably a four horse. Not very fast, but faster than she could swim. She lay in the water with a hand on the boarding ladder as the sound of the outboard came closer. The dog was quiet now. That was the worst kind. Now that his master had been notified of the danger, he was all business. The dog had sounded big. Most boat dogs were small and wiry, but some had the big ones. Some were trained as guard dogs. Joey was afraid.

The dog barked once as the dinghy approached. "Easy, boy," the man said. He had a deep voice. He sounded big, too.

"Think there's someone here, Rudy?" The woman didn't sound afraid.

"Don't know," the man said. "Sometimes he barks at dolphins."

"You have the gun?"

"Yeah."

Joey had no doubt about what the man would do with the gun if he caught her. Boat owner's were clannish and protective. They looked out for one another, because many of the third world governments looked upon the cruisers as a source of revenue and nothing more, often looking the other way when a local robbed a boat. Joey had heard more than one story about how a boat owner had taken the law into his own hands, firing at or shooting an intruder. You didn't board a boat without being invited. It wasn't done.

The boat was between her and them, but any second they were going to come around the stern and they'd see her hanging on the ladder. She felt like she was one with the sea and the night. She waited till she saw the dog's great head hunched forward over the dinghy's bow, eyes reflecting the moonlight, then she grabbed a breath and let go of the ladder.

She sank into the sea and with a couple of powerful strokes was under the boat. She swam with eyes open in a dark watery world. The saltwater stung. Chills crawled up her spine, sending electric tingles to the back of her neck. She shivered with cold and fear. She was in no danger from the sea, but a primitive part of her wanted out.

She maneuvered herself between the rudder and the keel, felt the bottom of the boat, slippery with sea moss. She kept a hand on it as she came up on the other side, quiet and slick, eel-like.

The dog barked again and she shuddered, picturing those eyes. It was a Doberman, ears cropped, fangs bared, snarling, vicious. The dog knew she was there, but would he be able to convince his masters? How many times would they circle the boat? How many times would she be able to swim under without being detected? She had nothing to hold onto on the starboard side, but she didn't care. She could tread water all night if she had to. The dog barked once more, then was quiet.

But they couldn't quiet the motor. This time they were coming around the sloop's bow and once again Joey sucked air and slipped under the boat, coming up on the other side. She reached out of the water, grabbed onto the ladder and held on.

"There's no one here," the woman said.

"Yeah, let's go."

"As long as we're out, let's go to shore and eat," the woman said.

Joey held onto the ladder, remaining still as the couple in the dinghy talked. She let out a long sigh as she heard the man add power and head for shore. She didn't move till the sound of the motor was only a buzz in the distance.

Satisfied that they weren't coming back, she pulled herself out of the sea, climbed the ladder and was once again on deck. This time she decided to search the boat before attempting to bring up the anchor. She scooted back to the cockpit, staying as low as possible. She didn't want to present a silhouette to anybody that might be looking from one of the other anchored boats.

The ignition key was in the ignition. That wasn't unusual, in safe anchorages many cruisers left it that way. Without a key, another boater couldn't board, start the motor and safely re-anchor the boat if she started dragging in high winds.

Joey lifted up the cockpit cushions and looked in the storage area underneath. Like on most small boats, there was a hodgepodge stored there. She rummaged through dive fins, scuba masks, snorkels, fishing line and then she found something she could use. A rusty scaling knife. It hadn't been used in a long time and wasn't very sharp, but it was sharp enough.

Eager, breathing fast, she put everything back, replaced the cover and cushion, then crawled up to the bow. Now she didn't have to worry about the chain rattling when she brought the anchor up, because she didn't have to bring it up.

She raised her head to the wind. It was blowing from out of the east. Perfect for sailing downwind to Venezuela. She had no money. No passport. She'd have to ditch the boat and go ashore somewhere and find a sympathetic villager with a phone, so she could call Mick's parents for help. It didn't sound like an impossible task. She was beginning to have hope.

She checked the tide. The current was going out. She reached forward and cut through the anchor rode. The rope cut easily and in seconds the small sloop was drifting out of Tobago's Store Bay, heading north with the tide. She glanced at the heavens, the clouds aloft were on a gentle march eastward, the moon winking through them gave the night a ghostly feel and it chilled her.

She had no charts, but she'd be able to find Venezuela. All she had to do was sail west. South America was hard to miss.

She waited, satisfied with the direction she was heading, until she could no longer see the boats anchored in the bay. She wondered how long the couple with the gun and the Doberman would stay ashore. They'd miss the small sloop as soon as they returned and sound the alarm.

In a hurry now, she went to the mast, took the main halyard off a cleat and started hauling it up. She didn't have the luxury of turning into the wind, but the wind was still slight, the sail small. She kept hauling, till it was all the way up, then she cleated off the halyard and headed back to the cockpit. She grabbed the tiller and pointed the boat westward, letting the wind fill the sail as she worked the main sheet.

The small boat had no instruments, so she had no idea how fast she was going, but she figured that she'd be past Trinidad and in Venezuelan waters by sunup if she was lucky. She lashed the tiller and scooted up to the bow. The boat had no roller furling. The jib was bagged and tied to the forestay.

She untied the drawstring, pulled the sail out of the bag, hanked it onto the forestay, went back to the mast, found the jib halyard and hauled it up. It started filling even as she was cleating off the halyard. Now there was nothing else she could do, except go back to the cockpit, work the tiller and try to get as much speed out of the little boat as possible.

The breeze on the back of her neck told her that she was sailing directly down wind. The lights of Tobago were fading in the distance. She'd done it. Escaped from the police. It only happened in the movies, but then you were only set up like that in the movies, too. Someone was really messing with her life, and damned if she could figure out who, unless it was Mick, and that didn't make any sense.

A slight rain tingled her arms, bringing her out of her reverie. She looked up. The clouds ahead were blacking out the stars. No time to be tired now, she was sailing into a squall. Then she remembered the weather she'd seen from the window on the plane. Maybe it wasn't a squall. Maybe it was a storm.

The wind picked up. She turned her face toward it and guessed it to be about twenty-five knots. She counted six seconds between the swells. Could be a storm. She didn't want to take any chances. She couldn't face a storm on an unfamiliar boat with everything out. It was too dangerous. Once again she counted the seconds between the swells. Maybe a little less than six now. Not the kind of night to be taking chances.

She turned into the wind, put the boat in irons, then, with sails flapping, she crawled out of the cockpit and scurried up to the mast where she released the jib halyard and dropped the headsail. It billowed and flapped as it came down. She threw her body on it as the boat rocked with the swells. Lightning cracked the sky. Thunder boomed. A wave crashed over the bow, drenching her as she struggled the sail into the bag. She didn't have time to be neat about it and she left it hanked to the forestay.

Another wave crashed over the bow, surprising her. She wasn't holding on to anything and she slid against the lifelines, grabbing them at the last possible instant to keep from sliding under and into the sea.

The deck was slippery as she crawled her way to the mast. The wind had picked up. The boat was being slammed by the swells, and floundering. Still on all fours she pulled herself to her feet, using the main halyard for support. She released it from the mast cleat, lowered the main to the second reefing point and tied it down.

Standing and holding onto the mast, she looked ahead into the black and tried to picture a map of the southern Caribbean in her mind. Trinidad would be off her port side. She saw stars out in that direction. Maybe she could skirt between the island and the storm. It looked like a good possibility.

She dropped back to her hands and knees with her hopes buoyed. She was about to start her slippery crawl back to the cockpit when she saw it. Green and red running lights, bobbing off her stern. A long way back. They couldn't see her as she was running without lights, but she imagined that she was lit up on their radar.

Chapter Thirteen

THE DOOR OPENED PART WAY. Angel squeezed through. She was panting, like she'd been running. Sweat ringed her dark curls. There were sweat spots under her arms. Like her, Angel was running scared.

"I found your camera bag." She started to hand it over, gasped. "Lord, you're bleeding."

"I know."

"Let's get this gown off." Angel helped her take it off, then she dumped it into a laundry basket. She went to a sink, rinsed out a washcloth and gingerly dabbed it between Nina's legs. "You're gonna need a Kotex." She went to a locker, opened it and pulled out a blue box and handed it to Nina.

"What about clothes?"

"I brought you blue jeans and a T-shirt. Also got a pair of tennis shoes. Good that you're my size."

Nina put on the Kotex. "Do you have panties?"

"Here." Angel handed over a pair.

"Thank you." Nina put them on, pulled up the faded jeans, then slipped the plain white T-shirt over her head. She turned to Angel, surprised to see her dressed identically, White T-shirt, faded jeans. She laced up the white high top tennis shoes, same as the ones Angel was wearing.

"Come on." Angel handed Nina the camera bag. "We've got to hurry, before they see you're gone."

"Okay."

Angel looked out the door. "The coast is clear. We're going out the back. Follow me." And she was out the door with Nina in her wake. The lobby was deserted. "They're all upstairs where they think the action is," Angel whispered. "They're so dumb, 'cause we're the real action, you and me."

Yeah, Nina thought, you and me.

"Emergency room, we're going right through," Angel said.

Nina followed her. No paint peeling here. Lights bright. Stainless steel gleaming. A black man with a bandaged head on a gurney. Another with a broken arm, sitting on sofa, looking bored. No doctors, two nurses.

"Hey, Angel," one of the nurses said.

"Hey, yourself," Angel answered.

Then they pushed through the double exit doors and out into the night. It was sprinkling lightly, a fine mist mingled with the tropical heat, sticking to the skin, mating with the sweat. Angel crossed the street. There were no cars out, no people walking the streets. The town was shut up tight. The night was dark, the town like a graveyard.

"There." Angel pointed to a new Toyota pickup down the road.

They crossed the street, slipped between two cars and stepped up onto the sidewalk. They'd made it. They were out of the hospital. She was on her way to save Joey. Then Nina felt hands digging into her shoulders, pushing her. She landed on her skinned palms. Pain shot up her arms. She didn't scream.

Angel dropped on top of her. Nina clenched her fingers into her skinned palms to keep from crying out.

"Sorry," Angel whispered. "You okay?"

"Yes," Nina whispered back. "What's wrong?"

"That man with the red beard." Angel rolled off Nina and scooted to the front of the car and peeked across the street. "He's just standing there. That's not good."

"What?"

"The other one. He's a policeman in plain clothes. They know you escaped."

"What are we going to do?"

"I have a plan," Angel said. "You scoot up between those two houses and hide in the bushes. They don't know I'm helping you, so I'll just get up and get in the car. I'll drive around the block and stop right here. Then you run out and jump in and we're outta here."

Nina looked at the two houses. They weren't really houses anymore. One had been converted into an auto supply store, the other was now a restaurant. There was a dark space between them. Bushes shielded the space from the street. Nina wondered what was in there. She didn't want to find out.

"Can't I just stay here?"

"Not good, what if they come this way. I'm gonna distract them, then you crawl up there. It's a long block, I might be a few minutes, but don't worry. I'll come back for you." She took a deep breath. She seemed scared. "Give me your bag."

Nina handed it over.

"Okay, wish me luck."

"Luck," Joey said.

Angel waited a few seconds, till the men weren't looking in her direction, then she rolled over to the sidewalk and stood. Nina watched her walk away, feeling more alone with every step she took. Angel stopped at the Toyota and fished her keys out of her pocket. Then she dropped them along with Nina's bag and screamed. She grabbed at her T-shirt, pulled it over her head. Her breasts bobbed in the half light of the partial moon.

"Get away," she screamed, making motions with her hands like she was pushing something off her breasts. "Go, go, go," she yelled and Nina realized that she was yelling at her, not the imaginary thing she was trying to brush away.

Nina took a deep breath, then crawled on her hands and knees toward the dark space between the auto parts store and the restaurant. Even though the grass was soft and mushy, she still felt searing pain each time her raw palms touched it. But she kept on. She wasn't going to quit.

"Lookee those tittys," the plain clothes policeman said. His laughter carried across the street. Sailing through the night, chilling her blood.

"It was one of those big flying roaches," Angel said. She faced the men, naked from the waist up, hands covering her breasts. "You boys look the other way so I can get my shirt on."

"No, you took it off, you can't 'spect us to look away," the policeman said.

"Leave your shirt off, we don't care." Nina heard the voice as she scooted between the bushes. American, deep. It must be the man with the red beard. The one that had hit her. He'd killed her baby, but she'd gotten a good look at him.

She scooted around and lay on her stomach, facing out, hugging the damp ground. She heard a scraping sound. Then a rustling behind her. She fought the urge to run out into the night and she stuck her thumb into her mouth to keep from screaming out.

"Okay, boys, you wanna look, look." Nina heard Angel's voice and watched as she dropped her hands and shook her breasts. The men laughed as she bent over, picked up her T-shirt, the camera bag and the keys. She put the shirt on, unlocked the car, then turned back to the men before she got in. "Bye, boys." She slid into the car, started it and pulled away from the curb.

Something growled, or groaned. Nina held her

breath. She heard it move. There was something in there with her. She wanted to turn around and look, but she was afraid. From where she was, hugging the ground, she could see the emergency room exit between two parked cars. The man with the red beard was there, standing under the light, the black policeman was gone.

"Is she up there?" Red Beard was calling to someone up the hill. Nina remembered that Scarborough was a hill town. She'd been running up a hill when he'd slammed his fist into her stomach. She wished she had a gun.

"Someone's turning the corner." It was the voice that had been taunting Angel only a few seconds ago. Nina wondered who he'd seen, probably just a woman out for a walk. She let out a sigh of thanks when Red Beard went trotting up the hill.

The thing behind her moved. It felt big. She wondered what could live back here. Maybe it was a dog. Were homeless dogs violent? She didn't think so. She'd seen the thin dogs wandering the streets back home. They seemed harmless. It was only hiding from the evils in the night, just like she was.

It groaned. Not a dog groan.

She saw lights coming up the bottom of the hill. Please, God, let it be Angel.

It groaned. Not a groan, a yawn. Shit. She turned.

"Hey, woman, my spot." Enough light filtered in from the partial moon for her to see his bloodshot eyes. His stubble covered, black face. Sunken cheeks. Scraggly, dirt matted hair. Fat nose and a fat chin on a skinny skull. Hideous.

Nina screamed.

She tried to scoot away, but she wasn't fast enough. The scarecrow lashed out and grabbed her ankle with a bony hand and flipped her over.

She screamed again, kicking out at him with her free foot, but he held fast.

"Mine. Woman for me." He climbed on top of her.

"No," she screamed. She punch his fat nose.

"Hurt me!" the man said.

She hit him again, landing a blow on his mouth. She felt one of his few remaining teeth slice into her knuckles as she knocked it out. But she failed to stop him. He was on top of her now, mounting her, feeling between her legs. She snarled, like a crazed dog and bit into his shoulder. Hard, just like Joey had said she'd done to the man that boarded *Satisfaction* in the middle of the night.

"Fuck!" The apparition jumped back. Nina drew her knees to her breasts, kicked out toward his head.

He was fast, dodging the blow, but her foot connected with his shoulder blade, snapping it like a twig under a lion's claw. He roared as he flew back into the dark space.

Nina pushed herself through the bushes.

"There she is." It was the policeman, a monster of a man, and he was running toward her. Hogging the middle of the road. He didn't see the headlights coming up from behind, didn't hear the horn, didn't feel his back breaking as the pickup truck plowed into him, thumping over him, crushing his life away.

The tires chirped as Angel stomped on the brakes. "Hurry!" Nina saw Red Beard framed in Angel's headlights. She jumped in the car and Angel stepped on the gas.

"You killed him!"

"He killed himself, wouldn't get out of the way. Not my fault." Red Beard was ahead, blocking the road. Angel pushed the horn, keeping a hand on it as the Toyota gobbled up the distance between them and Red Beard. The horn, a siren now, blasted its deadly warning.

"Hold on," Angel yelled. She pulled her hand from the horn, but Nina barely noticed, because someone was screaming, the sound wailing into the night as sure as the horn. Angel clutched the wheel with both hands, gave Nina a quick look, then turned back to the man in the road. Nina clamped her mouth closed and the screaming stopped. Milliseconds ticked by. Everything out of focus, so slow.

She saw Red Beard. The demon that had killed her baby. His face etched forever in her memory. Fat eyes. Round head. Acres of curly red hair that matched his lumberjack-like beard. A drinker's nose. A jolly, roly poly demon. A belly laughing man that had stolen her baby's life away.

"Kill him!" Nina screamed as they ran into him, striking a glancing blow as he tried to jump out of the way.

Nina looked out the back window. "He's getting up," she said as Angel wheeled the truck around the corner, leaving Red Beard out of sight. She cinched her seatbelt as Angel turned the car onto the highway.

* * *

Fuck, it hurt. Clayton tried to fist the hand that hung on

the end of his throbbing right arm. Couldn't. Bitch had run into him sure as if he'd been a rabid dog. He wanted to shout at her to come back as she sped the truck around the corner, but he knew it was no use.

He faced down the hill, saw the policeman's body dead in the street. Least he looked dead. Clayton started down, stopped when he realized it wouldn't do for a foreigner to be associated with a dead cop. That could be bad. He turned away, started back up the hill to where they'd parked the rental.

In the car he slid down. The arm was broken. It hurt like hell, but he'd have to wait till they cleared the dead body from the street and the gathering crowd had all gone home. Then he'd walk into the emergency and get it set.

A little over an hour later he left the hospital, got back into the car. He took off the sling. The cast covered only his right forearm, it wouldn't even be a hindrance. He knocked on it. No pain now. What the fuck did he need a sling for anyway? He tossed it in the back seat.

Now to get the car to the airport. It couldn't be that hard, he'd been to England, seen thousands of people driving on the wrong side of the road. Africa too, just like here. If all them could do it, he could too. But he immediately put the car on the wrong side of the street and barely avoided a head on with a van full of people. They honked at him as they swerved to avoid him, then passed in a sea of smiles. Was everything a joke here?

At the airport he unfolded the Yagi antenna, saw that the Brazilian babe was near. He'd been on his way to the chopper, to wait for Snelling, when he decided to check the receiver. She was in the parking lot somewhere. He could have her if he wanted, decided he did. There was just a chance she knew about the money. He folded the antenna into his grip when he saw Snelling's rental heading to the chopper. Snelling got out.

The little girl was gonna have to wait. Bummer. Clayton got out of the car, started toward the chopper.

* * *

Angel and Nina were sitting in the airport parking lot, parked next to a police car, because Angel thought the best place to hide was in plain sight. They'd been there for the last two hours, because the flight to Port of Spain didn't leave till 9:30 in the morning, check in wasn't till 8:00.

They couldn't sleep, so they spent the time talking away.

"I lost a baby once," Angel said. "I wasn't married to the father, he didn't want it, but I sure did. He didn't hit me or anything, he just kept after me and kept after me, till I got an abortion. It was horrible, they're not legal here, so I had to go to this creepy doctor in this filthy hotel room. I got sick afterwards, but it could have been worse. I can still have kids. I guess I was lucky. It's why I became a nurse, so I could help people in trouble. And honey, I think you're in about as much trouble as a human can get herself into."

"I think the bleeding's stopped," Nina said.

"It wasn't much, I didn't think you were in any danger. But I'd be careful if I was you, even though the doctor said you were going to be okay, you never know about these things."

"What's that?" Nina said.

"Helicopter." Angel pointed out her open window. "The Coast Guard's got a helicopter that comes in here sometimes, but that's not it," Angel said. "It's different, smaller."

"It's him up there, Red Beard," Nina said.

"How can you know that?"

"I don't know." Nina shivered. "But I do."

CHAPTER
FOURTEEN

SNELLING WAS SITTING next to Clayton as the big man piloted the helicopter through the dark. He wondered about the cast, but decided not to say anything, Clayton would tell him in his own way.

"Put your headset on!" Clayton shouted.

"Right." Snelling could understand why Clayton wanted to talk to him through the headset rather than shout. "What?" he said as soon as the headphones covered his ears and the mike was in place in front of his mouth.

"Where we going?" Clayton said.

"Over the ocean. Someone just reported a stolen boat. She's a sailor, she must be on it."

"What are you talking about?"

"Joey Sapphire, she's on the lose."

"You let her get away?" Clayton chuckled, then went quiet.

"What?" Snelling said.

"The other one got away from me, too. Did this." He held up the cast.

"Tell me later." Snelling wanted to berate the man, but couldn't. He'd been just as incompetent himself. "Two professionals," he said. "What a pair of fuckups we are."

"Least it's not just me this time." Clayton laughed.

Snelling couldn't help himself, he laughed, too.

* * *

The boat behind must be the schooner with the Doberman, Joey thought. It was the only explanation. The other boats were settled in for the night and the only reason for any of them to be out from the safe anchorage would be to chase after the pirate who had stolen a boat. She wondered if they'd called the Coast Guard. But of course they would have.

She shivered in the cold and with the thought that they would probably catch her. The schooner was bigger, faster and they'd be fully crewed, probably sailing with all the canvas out, despite the weather.

Giving up wasn't in the cards. She turned her face into the wind, no longer coming from behind, but off her starboard side. She'd need to get that headsail back up if she was going to make a run for it. And there was too much wind for her to do it on the run, she'd have to turn into it, lash the tiller, get it up as quickly as possible, then get back on course.

She'd lose a lot of her lead by the time she'd done that, but she didn't have any choice. She was about to shove the tiller to turn the boat when she heard a helicopter.

She looked up. Oh, Lord, she'd never get away now. Why in the world were they after her like this? If it wasn't because of the dead man back in Trinidad or anything she had done, then Mick must have done something really bad, really awful.

* * *

Clayton moved the stick a little to the left and the helicopter went into a slight bank.

The weather didn't look good, not from where he sat, but Snelling wasn't worried, nobody flew better than Clayton. He tightened his seatbelt.

"I'm gonna hit her with the light." Clayton dropped lower, till they were about a hundred feet above her mast, then trained a spotlight on her, lighting up the boat below.

"I see her!" Snelling looked down at the woman behind the tiller. She was something. He didn't admire many people, but he was starting to admire Joey Sapphire. She took everything he threw at her and shrugged it off. She was one tough woman.

"Look at that, she gave me the finger." Clayton had anger in his voice as he shoved the stick forward.

* * *

Joey flashed the finger up into the blazing light, then screamed as the helicopter seemed to fall out of the sky. They were dive bombing her. Were they crazy? For a second she thought the pilot was intent on impaling the metal monster on her mast, but he swerved aside at the last minute, light still shining on her as he descended almost to sea level, flying only a boat length away.

She fisted her hand, took back the finger and shoved the tiller to port, as she was afraid of hitting the chopper. The helicopter changed it's course to match hers. She couldn't see through the light. Were they planning on using that to herd her where they wanted her to go as if she were a runaway lamb?

"No!" she screamed into the light. She reached for the ignition key, turned it and felt, rather than heard, the small diesel rumble to life. She prayed it would make up the speed lost by whatever wind might be killed by the helicopter's rotors. She gave them the finger again, then pulled the tiller back to starboard.

The small boat caught the wind and jumped to obey. Joey had her bow pointed right into the light now. A wave caught the boat, giving her speed as she closed in on the flying machine.

* * *

"Oh, shit!" Clayton yelled as he jerked on the stick in a frantic effort to get the chopper up. They were only a few feet above the water, the blades were whipping up spray from the ocean so close. The sailboat was pointed toward them, the bow as deadly as that of a destroyer right now. The machine roared as Clayton added power into the maneuver, pulling the aircraft away from the boat, missing the mast by inches.

Snelling had his eyes locked onto Joey Sapphire through the whole exercise. She was terrified, but she was fighting back, a doe against a lion. Snelling had been to Africa—Kenya, Tanzania, Uganda—had seen what happened when an antelope or springbok turned on a giant cat to protect its young. The lion always won.

He forced himself to take his eyes off her and was surprised to find everything outside the field of light was pitch dark. The light had killed his night vision. Probably Clayton's too. Joey Sapphire's for sure.

Clayton stopped his climb at two hundred feet and hovered above the sailboat, the spot still on Joey Sapphire. The man was a remarkable pilot, working both the plane and the light as if he'd been born to it. Snelling started to feel more at ease, felt his nerves calming.

"She could have killed us," Clayton said. Snelling still had the headphones on, could hear him above the noise of the overhead blades as sure as if he'd been playing Billy Holiday at full volume on his CD Walkman.

"She probably thought that's what we were trying to do to her and if I wasn't so damned scared, I'd be laughing," Snelling said. What a girl, she'd fingered them again, then swung that little boat around as if to ram them.

"Nothing funny about what she almost did. When I get my hands on her—"

"You'll do nothing."

"Whatever you say, you're the boss," Clayton said, then he was working the stick as the helicopter dropped again.

* * *

Joey stared into the light as the chopper seemed to drop from the sky. Not again. Her nerves were on edge. She was being pushed beyond reason. She was half tempted to throw her hands in the air and give up, let them drop a line and haul her away, let them do what they would with her. But she trashed the thought as quickly as it had come.

She'd keep fighting, trying to get away, as long as she could draw breath. There was a squall ahead, she could feel the wind off it, though she couldn't see it, couldn't see where the clouds blanked out the stars, couldn't see anything, save for what was bathed in that brilliant light.

The chopper dropped right down in front of the boat, halfway between the top of the mast and the sea, with that light forever in her eyes, blinding. This time she wouldn't be able to surprise them with a quick turn, they were going backwards, matching her speed, blinding her with that light, always blinding her with the light.

She couldn't see, couldn't think. All she could do was continue on with dogged determination. A few drops of rain splashed against her face, a wave washed over the side. She couldn't be making much headway. She turned aft, strained her eyes into the night. She couldn't see the boat behind, but at the rate she was going now, they'd be on her soon. Was that the chopper's plan, to slow her down until they caught up? That made sense to her and it seemed as if that's what they were doing, flying backwards in front of her, forcing her to go slow.

Though the main was reefed, the cracking noise it made as it flapped and whip snapped in the night wind was audible even above the sound of the screaming blades atop the chopper. All her life Joey had hated the sound of snapping sails, preferring always the sound of the wind caressing them as a boat moved through the sea, but now, right now, she loved that sound, anything to take away the incessant whirring of those blades, even if only for a few seconds.

* * *

"What's she doing?" Clayton shouted. Raising his voice wasn't necessary as Snelling still heard him in both ears, as if he'd been shouting inside of his head. Was flying close over the choppy seas getting to him? Was the girl getting the better of him? Snelling hoped not, because his life was in Clayton's hands and there wasn't a thing he could do about it, short of jumping into the murky water below.

"She's not doing anything."

"I don't get it," Clayton said.

"Maybe she's tired." Snelling could well imagine her tired as he watched her steer the tiny boat, almost close enough to touch. He saw her muscles ripple through the wet T-Shirt. She wasn't wearing a bra and her breasts jiggled as she frantically moved the tiller back and forth. He'd seen her nude the night he'd killed the Atwood kid and hadn't been aroused as he was now. It wasn't the sight of a pretty young woman that excited him. He'd seen more naked women than the Emir of Kuwait, been with more than a feudal king. With Snelling, character counted, and Joey Sapphire had character to spare.

If he had it to do over, he'd've done it another way. Probably should've. Probably should've waited for Mick Sapphire to show up in Trinidad and confronted him and David Atwood together, got the photos and dispatched them. But he didn't. He'd been so sure he'd flush out her husband when Joey was charged with murder. So sure the husband would be terrified about what could happen, so terrified that he'd fork over the photos post haste.

In over thirty years of clandestine work for his country, never had he misjudged a situation so completely. Never had he had to involve locals to the extent he had in this case. Of course the circumstances were special, but he should've been able to handle it alone, shouldn't've even brought in Clayton. Should've been patient.

Now he was paying the price in more ways than one.

He continued watching in admiration as the little boat jumped around in the bumpy seas, giving her a rough ride, but she wasn't giving up. Any normal person knows when it's over, when to throw in the towel. Extraordinary people keep working the controls right up till the plane plows into the ground, letting out only a final explicative just before impact. Joey Sapphire's plane was going down, but she was bound and determined to pilot on, fighting the odds till the last.

Then he saw white off in the distance.

"Shit, lightning."

"Too far away to worry us," Clayton said.

"Seemed close to me." Snelling started mentally

counting off the seconds. Ten to the loud boom of thunder. "Two miles."

"Not even close," Clayton said.

"Oh yeah, that's close."

"You worry too much."

* * *

Joey saw lightning flash. Normally, she'd turn and hightail it away from a storm if she could, but now it offered protection. If it was thick enough, and she hoped it was, she'd be like a stealth bomber to the boat behind, concealed from its radar by the heavy rain and dense clouds. And as for the chopper, could they fly in a thunderstorm? She didn't think so. She hoped not. Maybe they'd crash and die. Serve them right the way they were hassling her. It wasn't right.

And it wasn't right that she was so cold. She shook, chilled to the bone, colder now than she'd ever been in her whole life. Too cold to imagine it away as she did on long ocean crossings. But during those she had foul weather gear on, and shoes. The cold that was shooting through her now started at her bare feet, shot up through her body, needling her at the back of the neck.

Cold mixed with fear and she had to pee so bad, she felt like she was going to burst. That she could do something about. She let go, feeling the warmth worm down her legs as she held onto the tiller. Her hands were so cold, her fingers screamed, she couldn't feel her toes.

Another wave washed over the side, drenching her again, but she was already wet and shivering, she hardly noticed and as the next one came up, she turned into it, easing off, letting the boat ride it down. A couple more and she was in the groove. It seemed a tough little boat, maybe misused and abused by it's present owner, but whoever built her knew what he was doing. The boat took the swells as if she'd been made to sail in heavy weather.

Lightning flashed again. Five seconds to the thunder, heard well above the rotors of the chopper now flying alongside. Again she turned into the light and for a third time she flashed them the finger. She didn't know who they were, villains or police, but whoever they were, they had no business messing with her the way they were.

Lightning again, this time brighter than the spotlight. For an electric instant the chopper was lit up from behind and Joey got a look at the men tormenting her. The red beard stood out straightaway, the man that had attacked Nina and Mick in Brazil. The other man was the American from the restaurant. Two devils whose faces she'd never forget.

Lightning again, this time a ragged bolt across the overhead sky, showing off dark clouds. Thunder boomed and a wave washed over the deck, burying the boat in dark water. Joey held on to the tiller for all she was worth as the wind rose. She had no windspeed indicator, but she guessed over forty knots. However there was no rain and that chopper and it's damn light were still flying right in front of her.

Another wave, more dark water. Any sensible person would turn around, put the wind at her stern and run from the storm. But then she'd be sailing right into their hands. So she scrunched down in the cockpit, steeled her grip on the tiller and held on.

* * *

"I think we should turn back," Snelling said.

"We're fine," Clayton said, but Snelling didn't think so. The wind was buffeting the chopper around as if it were suspended by a rope being jerked by a giant's hand. Clayton was still controlling the aircraft, still keeping the woman covered by the light, but the cockpit was thick with tension. If they didn't get out of the weather, they could be in trouble.

Lightning again. The sky was awash with white as the thunder rolled through the night. Clayton was covering Joey Sapphire in light, God was covering them and Snelling didn't like it a bit. He was no coward, but he wasn't stupid either. He wanted out.

"Let's get out of here!"

"Scared?" Clayton taunted.

"Damn right." Snelling clenched his fists as lightning struck again, instantaneous with the thunder, blasting before their eyes, blinding them as they'd been trying to blind Joey Sapphire. "That was too close! At least get a little altitude. And kill that light. Fly the plane!"

"Maybe you're right." Clayton flicked off the spot and brought the chopper up to two hundred and fifty feet, still flying over the boat below. "Feel better?"

"Immensely."

Again a lightning blast accompanied by thunder. And for an instant it appeared as if the top of the mast on Joey Sapphire's little boat below was blazing as the glow of St. Elmo's fire flashed bright. Joey too, for an instant, seemed on fire.

"Jesus, she's been hit."

* * *

Joey screamed, but the sound was killed by the thunder. She squeezed the tiller still tighter as the boat shook with the blast. Her fingers were aglow, she imagined her hair sparking. She saw the illusion of fire atop the mast.

A lightning strike. She shivered. Was the boat bonded so that the blast would be carried harmlessly through it to the sea, or not? Had the lightning sought ground, coming down the mast, only to blow a hole through the bottom of the boat? Please God, no.

* * *

Clayton, panicked by the blast, screamed as he jerked forward, almost like he was trying to jump up, but he was repelled back into the seat by the shoulder harness, the back of his head smacking into the headrest as the helicopter shook with the booming thunder, then careened out of control. Snelling was helpless as Clayton slumped forward, now held in place by the shoulder harness.

"Are you all right?" Snelling shouted into the mike.

Nothing.

"Clayton!" Snelling grabbed the man's shoulder, shook him as the plane started an uncontrolled climb. At least they were going up. "Are you okay?"

"What happened?" Clayton mumbled. Snelling heard him through the headset. Thank God they still had their electronics.

"Can you get control of the plane?" Their climb had peaked, now they were on their side, going down. "Clayton! Snap out of it!"

The rotors were roaring, the sea was closing fast. Time was in suspension. Snelling's heart skipped a beat, then raced out of control. He was alive like he'd never been alive and in a fraction of a second he was going to be dead if Clayton didn't do something.

"Get a grip, man!" Snelling squeezed Clayton's shoulder, hard. He couldn't think of anything else.

"Okay!" Clayton screamed. He grabbed the stick, righted the chopper, but they were still falling.

"Oh, Lord!" Snelling said as they shot over the sailboat's mast, missing it by inches. Then they were closing fast on the hungry sea when all of a sudden the descent stopped and they were roaring along at sixty miles-per-hour scant feet above the waves.

Then thunder boomed without lightning and it started to rain.

"Let's get the fuck out of here!" Snelling said.

"We're gone," Clayton said.

* * *

It was a few seconds after the lighting strike before Joey realized that the megawatt light the chopper had been covering her with was out. Now her world was black, no moon, no stars, no landfall. Just the black beyond and black water crashing into the boat.

She was squinting into the dark, trying to get her night vision back, when she heard the roar of the helicopter coming down. She looked up as it rotated past the masthead, shooting for the frothy ocean, but at the last minute the pilot regained control and they whooshed away, flying over the sea barely above wave level till they were out of sight, leaving Joey alone with the raging sea.

A roaring thunderclap sounded without warning and the heavens opened up, pelting her with tropical rain. She had to run with the sea now or risk rolling the boat. That would dismast her and probably throw her overboard.

She shoved the tiller to port, then turned off the engine, keeping the boat in the turn till the wind and waves were coming from the aft. She had to try and keep it like that and ride out the storm. Where she would wind up when it was all over was anybody's guess.

After three hours she was worn out. Then the wind settled down to about twenty to twenty-five knots and the swells calmed, the period between them, about seven seconds. She allowed herself some hope as the waves rode under the boat, helping the wind and the current to move it along.

Occasionally lightning cracked the sky, followed a few seconds later by deafening thunder. But she was no longer taking water over the side. The storm was letting up.

An hour later, the storm was over. She saw Trinidad off the bow. That was the last place she wanted to be, but it was the place she had to be if she was going to get to the bottom of whatever was going on.

The Coast Guard of the twin island republic would be on the lookout for her, and the police in Trinidad were the same as the police in Tobago, so she wasn't going to get the tourist treatment if she were caught, that was for sure. But she had to get to the airport and meet Nina, otherwise she'd never get a visa for America, wouldn't get to Mick's father and would probably wind up the rest of her life in jail for a murder she didn't commit.

Soon she was past Maracas Beach where she'd spent several wonderful weekends with Mick. Mick, he hadn't been in her thoughts for hours, but he was there now and there he stayed as she moved west along the peninsula at the northwestern end of Trinidad that separated the Caribbean Sea from the Gulf of Paria.

Whatever it was that he'd done, it was bad, so bad she couldn't imagine. And she couldn't see how he could have done such a thing even if he'd wanted. He was just a rich kid with a sailboat. He wasn't a drug smuggler, spy or murderer. So how come he was in so much trouble? What had he done?

She encountered a current rushing out of the Boca and she sailed into it, through confused and boiling seas. Then she was past it and passing the small Monos island on the right where Trinidad's wealthy and elite had their weekend homes.

Joey couldn't imagine having enough money to own a second home, though she imagined Mick's parents were that wealthy. They'd flown to South Africa for the wedding. But after she was married, it was boat life for her. True, *Satisfaction* was a million dollar boat, but other than that, she'd seen no evidence of his parent's money, however she'd always assumed it was there in the background in case Mick ever got in trouble. Well he was in trouble now.

She sailed past quiet and picturesque Scotland Bay, where she'd spent a few quiet days at anchor with Mick not so long ago. She shivered at the memory, then she shivered again when she went past the Coast Guard station. They only had three boats to patrol the northern and western coasts, but usually one or two were tied up to the dock. This morning all three boats were at sea. Looking for her probably. They'd never believe that she was sailing by right under their noses.

She sailed the small boat in to the great Chaguaramas Bay and dropped the sails. She motored close to the Carib Inn Marina and picked up one of the fisherman's moorings, as she had no anchor or dinghy. It only took a few minutes to flag down someone headed for shore. She didn't want to risk going back to *Satisfaction*, but she had no shoes and looked a mess, besides she needed her passport, money and credit card.

She sighed, for once Mick's paranoia about her carrying that stuff around had paid off. She kept her documents and most of her money hidden on board, traveling with only a copy of the front page of her passport and enough cash to get by.

Back on *Satisfaction* she took a quick look around. Whatever happened, this was probably the last time she'd be here. She was through with Mick, that meant she was through with the boat, and that was sad.

It was on *Satisfaction* that she'd learned to love the sea, learned to live her own life, her way. It was on *Satisfaction* that she'd learned that the sins of the father are not necessarily visited upon the daughter. And it was on *Satisfaction* that she was going to sail around the world, now that wouldn't happen. It was hard for her to come to grips with, but she was going to miss the boat more than the man.

She checked the time. It was 9:00, just barely enough time to shower, change and get a taxi to the airport before Nina's flight arrived.

CHAPTER

FIFTEEN

NINA MOVED THROUGH that long tube that connected the
airport to the plane. She felt like an ant in a tunnel,
people behind, people in front, holiday ants back from
vacation, ready to work. Not her, she was descending
from the plane into an uncertain future and she was
depressed, down like she'd never been before.

Back in Tobago Angel had been her lifeline, talking to
her the night through, staying with her right up till she
boarded the flight to Trinidad. It had been a tear filled,
hard goodbye. Angel was a special person, who was going

to be her friend for the rest of her life, like Joey. Joey, Nina thought, she didn't know why, couldn't understand it, but she felt as close to Joey, this woman she didn't used to like, as she did to Joana. Women had to stick together.

"Nina!" someone shouted.

Nina turned, it was Joey, running through the concourse. She looked out of breath.

"Am I glad to see you," Nina said. "I was so worried."

"I'm glad to see you, too. I almost didn't make it." Joey was panting, looked like she hadn't slept in a long time. She held her arms open and Nina fell into the hug.

"I lost my baby," Nina whispered into Joey's ear.

"Oh, Nina, I'm so sorry." Joey broke the hug, looked into Nina's eyes and Nina saw the hurt there. She really was sorry for her. She wasn't just saying it.

"We can cry later," Nina said. "Right now we have to meet someone and get our visas, remember?"

"Yeah." Joey led Nina to the curbside, raised her hand for a taxi.

A rusty Toyota pulled up to the curb. The car was old, but the tires were new.

"You want a taxi?" The driver's rich baritone and ebony skin conspired to hide his age, but the gray hair and wrinkled hands gave it away.

"We're going to Chaguaramas," Joey said. "Corbeau Yacht Services. Do you know it?"

"I know every place and street in this country." The driver opened his door, started to step out of the car.

Nina held a hand up. "That's okay, we don't have any baggage."

"Makes it easy on these old bones." The driver pulled

his door closed.

Nina went around the car, reached a hand inside the open passenger window, started to drop her camera bag in the front seat, but changed her mind and got in the back, after Joey, clutching the bag in her lap.

"Dependable Ted, at your service." The driver handed Nina a card. "You need a taxi, anytime, day or night, you call me, hear? I'm dependable, like my name, the name on the card, Dependable Ted."

"I'll be sure to do that." Nina put the card in her back pocket.

"Now relax and enjoy the ride. I might not be the fastest taxi in Trinidad, but I'm the most dependable."

Nina sat back as the taxi started winding its way along the airport access road.

"We'll be on the highway in ten minutes. Port of Spain's just up the road."

Joey laughed.

"What?" The driver said.

"Port of Spain is at least a half hour from here."

"Like I said, just up the road." He kept to the slow lane. Cars and trucks of all ages and sizes flew by the cab. Junkyard fugitives racing along with cars fresh off the showroom floor. Speed tempered by chaos seemed to be the order of the day. Everybody was in a hurry to get somewhere. Everybody wanted to pass the car in front, but nobody wanted to be passed.

"Do they always drive like this?" Nina said.

"Mostly, except me and a few others that have lived long enough to develop common sense. And of course the car that's been following us since the airport."

Nina turned and looked through the back window. "The BMW? How can you be sure?"

"I'm sure. Besides, even if I wasn't, you can see how people drive here. That's a new car and he's not passing. He's following us or my name isn't Ted and I'm not dependable."

"How could they have found us so fast?" Nina said.

"It's my fault," Joey said. "I stopped at the boat before I came here. They must have been waiting."

"You ladies in trouble?" Ted asked.

"I think so," Joey said.

"Can you get away from them?" Nina said.

"You running from the police?" Ted said.

"No, sir." Nina leaned forward, put a hand on his shoulder. "Those are bad men. They hurt me. They made me lose my baby,"

"That why you look so weak." Ted eyed her through the rearview mirror.

"Yes, sir, it is."

"Shit, ladies, I can lose the tail. Didn't you hear me say I know all the roads in this country? I was driving them before you were born. Just say the word and it'll get done."

"We'd like you to lose them," Joey said.

"That's all I needed to here. Sit back, ladies and stop your worrying. I'll be losing them when we get to the city."

Nina did as he said and looked out the window, the conversation killed by the car following. The scenery flashing by was covered in green and dotted with billboards bearing familiar names—KFC, Pizza Hut,

McDonald's—and although the billboards were in English, the houses on the side of the road reminded Nina of the poor section of Fortaleza. Like Brazil, there was poverty here.

She saw a short bridge up ahead where the road changed from four to two lanes. Cars were putting on the gas. Everybody wanted to pass the slow moving taxi before the bridge. Nina turned and looked out the back window. Not everybody was trying to pass. The BMW was three cars back, still following. She continued watching as a battered, left-hand-drive American Ford flew past the car immediately behind them and kept on coming.

"I think he's going to try and pass us, too." Nina was more than a little surprised that the car wouldn't slow down.

"He can't make it!" Ted said, but the car kept coming.

"He's not passing! He's coming in on the left!" Nina shouted as the car plowed into the left quarter of the taxi, then slammed on its brakes as Ted lost control.

Joey threw an arm in front of Nina, keeping her pinned to her seat as the taxi spun onto the other side of the road. A pickup, coming in the opposite direction, clipped the cab's rear bumper, tearing it off.

Then they were off the road and spinning through a park toward a football game. Children screamed and fled the oncoming taxi and for an instant, Nina thought they were going to roll, but Ted let out a whoop and spun the wheel into the slide, managing to turn the car away from the fleeing children, pumping the brakes all the while, trying to slow the car as they scraped along a huge tree.

Ted screamed again as the car slid by the tree with a soul wrenching sound that shrilled through the morning. The tree slowed the car, but didn't stop it, and Dependable Ted never stopped working the wheel.

"Hold on," he yelled from the front seat. Nina looked up and saw what he saw. Another tree, this one thicker than the last, and it seemed to be charging straight for them as it loomed larger and larger in the front window, a giant green Jaguar with raking claws on the end of its branches. Claws and jaws, reaching for her, reaching to tear her apart, but at the last instant the roaring rear wheels found purchase in the wet grass. The old Toyota shot forward like a race horse. Ted yelled again, because even though he was heading for the tree, he was back in control.

He spun the wheel to the right, missing the tree, but the branches scraped the side of the car as it headed into a huge mass of green, the very edge of the rain forest. Ted jerked the wheel one last time and stomped on the brakes. The engine died, but the car continued its slide through the green vegetation, twice missing trees that would have brought it to a crashing stop, coming softly to rest in an almost anticlimactic absence of sound.

"Sheeit," Dependable Ted said under his breath, but Nina heard.

"Is anybody hurt?" Joey said.

"Don't think so," Ted said.

"I'm okay." Nina looked out of the car. Seconds ago she'd been on a highway, with cars, houses, stores and people. Now she was surrounded by green—leaves, grass, weeds, bushes and trees. There were places like this in Brazil, but she'd never been to them. She was in an ancient world, a primitive place, and something deep in her heart told her that she wasn't welcome.

"That car hit us on purpose." Ted turned toward them. His smile was gone. There was a glazed look in his dark brown eyes.

"Looked like it," Joey said and, even as she said it, the glaze faded from Dependable Ted's eyes, and as they cleared Nina saw anger.

"It's good that I got insurance," Ted said.

Nina put her hand on Ted's shoulder again. "I'm sorry about your car."

"Don't you worry about that. I said I got insurance. They never paid for nothing in all the years I had it, it's about time I got some back from them." He turned and offered his hand.

Nina took it.

"You get out of here. I'll stall them as long as I can."

"Thank you." Nina said.

"You best get going," Ted said. Then, "Go straight into the green till you get to the river, it's not far, then turn right and follow it back to the road. Bridge goes under, you come out on the opposite side. It's easy. I used to do all the time when I was a boy."

"Thank you again." Nina grabbed the camera bag, got out of the car. Then she saw where Ted wanted her to go. "I don't think I can go in there."

"Sure you can." Joey took her by the hand, pulling her. Nina offered no resistance. Joey led her around a large teak tree and pulled her further into the tall grass

KEN DOUGLAS

and dense growth. Nina heard the running water and in seconds they were confronted with a small river that wound from the mountains down to the sea. Still holding Joey's hand she started to step down the bank.

"Wait," Joey said.

Nina stopped.

"Listen," Joey said.

"They went in there," Nina heard a voice say, gravelly and menacing, not friendly.

"I bet it's Red Beard," Joey said. "Let's go."

Nina felt Joey tighten her grip as she turned back toward the river and started down the bank. The ground was wet, muddy and it smelled. People up in the mountains had been using the river as a dump for too long. The water that should have been fresh and sweet was polluted with litter—plastic bottles, Styrofoam cups, Coke cans and other odd bits of trash. The river was taking it all toward the sea.

At the bottom Joey sloshed through it, still pulling Nina along behind. The water was only inches deep, but the mud was tugging at her shoes, threatening to pull them off. The growth was dense and oppressive. Nina was grateful that Joey was breaking trail for her. Chills ran up her spine, sliding under the sweat running down her back. She squeezed Joey's hand tighter as she led her toward the unknown.

"Shit, I think they're headed back toward the road," the gravel voice from behind said, and Nina answered Joey's squeeze by gripping her hand even tighter as Joey picked up the pace through the shallow river, pushing low overhanging branches aside with her other hand.

"Bridge up ahead," Joey said. "We have to go under."

But when Nina looked ahead she didn't see a bridge at all, just the highway above the trees and a place where the river vanished into the undergrowth beneath it and Joey was pulling her steadily toward it.

"No!" She jerked on Joey's hand, forced her to stop. "Let's climb up this side."

"That's what they'll expect," Joey said. "They might have somebody up there waiting."

"Who?" Nina said.

"Don't know and we don't have time to discuss it." Joey released her hand and turned toward the spot where the river disappeared under the road. "I hope there's no snakes under there," she said. "I hate snakes."

"Me too." Nina slung the camera bag over her back as Joey dropped to a crouch, making her way toward the dense growth.

"Gonna have to crawl." Joey went to her hands and knees into the water. Nina watched as she forced herself through the wet and slimy foliage that guarded the area under the bridge. Then she couldn't see her anymore and she was alone. She heard the slight murmuring of people overhead, the sound of a siren off in the distance, but there were no traffic sounds on the highway, no cars whizzing by above. Traffic was stopped. She didn't want to go in there. Maybe she could climb up on this side. There were people there, she'd be safe.

"Hurry up." It was the gravel voice behind her. "Not much farther," it said and it made her mind up. She dropped to a crawl and scooted through the slimy muck, pushing as much of it away from her face as she could.

Her heart was racing, sweat chilled her skin. Insects crawled on the back of her neck. She wanted to scream each time her fingers curled into the mud, but she fought it back and pushed forward.

She was closed in by the dark, like a dead man in a coffin, and she was waiting for somebody to nail her in. Then she felt something else under her hands. The mud had a bottom to it and it was solid. A chill rippled through her as she pulled a hand out of the river. She reached out to her left and struck something hard. A wall. She thrust her hand above her head and whimpered when it touched the concrete top.

She was in a drain pipe.

Every ounce and fiber of herself screamed, *Go back*, but she closed her eyes and plunged on ahead. Then she felt sunlight on her eyelids. When she opened them she saw Joey. She pushed herself out of the pipe as a great wave of relief flooded through her. But as quickly as it came, it went.

They'd only gone halfway. They were under the highway, between the lanes. There was another drain pipe on the other side. She was going to have to do it all again.

She couldn't.

She just couldn't.

Joey leaned toward her and put her lips to Nina's ear. "You're doing fine." Joey's whisper soothed her. She closed her eyes for a second, took a deep breath. "That's the way," Joey said. "It's going to be all right."

Nina shivered, but not as much as before. She opened her eyes, looked around. She was in a place where trolls lived. Under the bridge, under the feet of people and the wheels of cars. A mythical, fairy tale, dangerous place. There were things here she didn't want to know about. Creepy crawlies and slithering slimies. She wanted out and the only way was to slide through that other drain pipe.

Joey took her hand again and gave it a squeeze. Then she went back down on all fours. Nina followed and again she was in the dark and again she felt the chills shoot through her, but this time she wasn't alone, because she grabbed onto one of Joey's feet as she crawled ahead and not God nor the Devil himself could have made her let go.

Then they were through it and on the other side. She let go of Joey's foot and they started up the embankment onto the far side of the highway. Up on the street she saw why she'd heard no traffic sounds. The car that hit them had itself been rear ended and the result was an accident on the bridge, causing traffic to be backed up in both directions. People were out of their cars, some were helping the victims on the bridge, others were watching, talking, laughing, having a good time. Most of the drivers were apparently viewing the accident more as entertainment than aggravation.

The BMW was sitting four cars back from the bridge. It was unoccupied.

"Come on." Joey led Nina over to the car. Joey peeked in the open window. "Keys are in it. Let's go, before they come back." Joey opened the door, got in. Nina hurried around to the passenger side. Joey had the engine started before she had the door closed.

Joey threw the car in reverse, backed up till she tapped the car behind, then she shifted into drive, cranking the wheel all the way to the right, moving forward till she bumped the car in front. The accident on the bridge had traffic blocked and the cars were packed in tight.

The driver behind saw what Joey was trying to do and backed up a few inches, giving her that much more room to maneuver. Joey stuck a hand out the window and flashed him the thumbs up sign. The driver responded with a short honk.

"Friendly people," Joey said.

"Seems so," Nina answered.

"Stop them!" a voice rang out.

"You better hurry!" Nina said.

Joey backed up till she tapped the bumper again, cranked the wheel and moved forward, but she still didn't have enough room to get out of the squeeze.

"It's Red Beard and he's running!" Nina said.

Joey must have heard the urgency in Nina's voice because she jammed the BMW back into reverse, this time tapping the car harder and this time the honk wasn't as short, didn't sound as friendly.

"He's getting closer!" Nina said.

Joey again cranked the wheel and banged the car in front, pushing it a few inches forward. Back into reverse, she hit the car in the rear. Hard. The driver honked— loud, long—not friendly at all anymore.

"He's got a gun!" Nina said.

Joey cranked the wheel and stepped on the gas. She hit the front car's bumper with a hard glancing blow as she squeezed out. She turned onto the right shoulder.

"He's getting ready to shoot!" Nina said.

Joey put her foot to the floor and the BMW

responded like the thoroughbred it was, tires spinning, sending dirt and grass flying from behind as they flew along the stalled cars going in the opposite direction.

"Cross there," Nina said.

Joey followed her pointed finger, spinning the wheel to the left. They charged across the wide center strip. Then they had the two lanes all to themselves as they sped back toward the airport and away from the danger behind.

"Look out!" Nina screamed.

Joey stomped on the brakes, swerved to avoid an old Toyota Land Cruiser that turned onto the highway going the wrong direction. They started to slide toward the car and all Nina could see was the flashing blue light on top of the Toyota.

The policeman's reaction was faster than Joey's and the Land Cruiser swerved and jerked out of the way as Joey clung to the wheel. They slid sideways, past the police cruiser and Joey screamed, jerking Nina's eyes off the Toyota and back onto the road.

"Look out!" she shouted.

"Yeah, yeah!" Joey pulled the wheel into the direction of the slide as she pulled her foot off the brakes, attempting to bring the car back under control.

But the car resisted.

Nina screamed as Joey panicked and jammed her foot back on the brakes, sending the car into a three hundred and sixty degree spin. The outside circled by and Nina saw lightning glimpses of houses, highway and hills as her screams mingled with the sounds of the racing engine and the squealing tires.

Most cars would have rolled, but the stable BMW

came to a jerky stop in the center of the road and Joey quickly shifted into neutral.

"You sure know how to scare someone," Nina said.

Joey leaned back and started laughing.

"What's so funny?"

"You should see yourself," Joey said.

Nina's T-shirt and jeans were torn and covered with the drying mud and muck from the river. The stuff was already turning hard on her skin. Her shoes looked like she'd been walking through a cow pasture. She raised a hand to her face, her hair, then she laughed, too.

"You look the same," she said. "We're a mess."

Nina looked behind them. Saw that the police car, far away now, had turned around. "He's coming back."

"I think it's time to make ourselves scarce." Joey put her foot to the floor and Nina felt herself pushed back into the seat as the car accelerated, tires spinning. Then the tires dug into the pavement. Nina turned back, grabbed a glance behind. The police cruiser was turning into a speck in the distance.

"Another one," Joey said, her voice calm, like a pilot's, but tense like the plane was going down.

"I see it," Nina said. The second cruiser was coming head on, driving on the wrong side of the street as the two lanes coming from the airport were backed up because of the accident.

"What are you going to do?" Nina said.

"See who's chicken."

Nina stole a look at the speedometer. They were flying and the other police Land Cruiser was looming larger in the windscreen with each heart beat.

"He's not going to turn," Joey said, still calm, but Nina heard stiffness in her voice as she stiffened her hands on the wheel. Any sane person would pull aside, pull over and pull out her license, but the memory of Red Beard back at the bridge was still sending shivers up Nina's spine that turned into sparks at the base of her neck.

"Run him off the road!" she said.

"Hang on!" The edge was gone from Joey's voice and Nina admired her for not screaming.

At the last possible instant, Joey pulled the wheel a few inches to the right and the police car flew by, close enough to touch.

"Boy, you got my blood jumping," Nina said.

"Pumping." Joey laughed. "We say you really got my blood pumping."

"Pumping, I'll remember," Nina said. Then, "I think we should get off the highway. How about that turn there?"

"Good idea." Joey stomped on the brakes, sending the car into a slide, laying rubber all over the road as they flew through a long circular exit behind a football stadium. She worked the brakes through the turn and was down to a reasonable speed as they shot out of the exit and into the evening traffic.

CHAPTER
SIXTEEN

JOEY STOPPED AT THE SECURITY GATE at Corbeau Yacht Services. Smiled at the West Indian guard. He gave their disheveled appearance a quick once over, frowned back.

"We heard we can get a ride here out to the Five Islands for the Boxing Day Barbecue," Joey said.

"Been partying a little early?" the guard said.

"Mud wrestling," Joey lied. "You should've been there."

"Americans." The guard raised the gate.

"What's a Boxing Day Barbecue?" Nina said.

"Boxing Day is the day after Christmas. It's a hold over from British rule. On Boxing Day the lord and lady of the house would box up a present for the servants. In Trinidad it's just an excuse to extend the Christmas holiday."

"And the barbecue?"

"There's a yachtie who's been here forever. A guy named Frank that lives on a boat called *Shogun*. Every year he has a Barbecue out at the Five Islands, they're tiny little things about a mile or so out in the gulf. I figured if we told the guard that, he'd let us in, because from what I've heard the yachties get pretty drunk and rowdy at those things. He thought we were going from one drunken affair to another. Not an unusual thing in Trinidad."

"That was fast thinking," Nina said.

"Thanks," Joey said. Then. "How will we know how to find your friend?"

"He's found us." Nina pointed to an Hispanic looking man dressed in jeans and a white shirt open at the collar. The man had a long handlebar mustache, was short and squat and though he appeared to be in his middle sixties, Joey didn't see any fat on his stocky frame and, even from where she was in the car, she saw the steel hard look in his dark eyes. He was a man you didn't want to mess with. A man who could make your life very uncomfortable if you did. This, Joey saw in an instant. Next to him stood a pretty girl in a yellow summer dress. She looked enough like Nina to be her sister.

"Who is he?"

"Captain da Silva from back home. When I called

him, I never thought he'd come himself."

"Who's the girl next to him?"

"Joana do Campo, my best friend in all the world."

The captain motioned for them to drive over to the dinghy dock and Joey did. He pointed to a dinghy and Joey climbed in, followed by Nina, Joana and lastly the captain, who pulled the starter cord and motored them out to a Venezuelan flagged fishing boat named *Buenas Noticias*.

"What's the name mean?" Joey said as the captain pulled along side.

"*Good News.*" His voice had a hard edge to it, but somehow it didn't seem menacing. "Let's hope the *News* is good for us and we get out of this country undetected." He had no trace of a Brazilian accent. He sounded American. He cut the motor as Joana stood and secured the painter to a deck cleat.

Aboard, da Silva started up the engines, then pointed the boat out to sea as Nina and Joana kissed cheeks, hugged, then started babbling in Portuguese like little kids.

"Only a few days apart and they forget their rule," da Silva said.

"What rule?" Joey said.

"They only speak English among themselves," da Silva said. "So when they get to America they'll fit in." He sighed and Joey saw the hard look fade from his eyes as he took in the two girls. It was obvious he loved them.

"Can you take the wheel?" da Silva said to Joana after a few minutes. He was still speaking English, Joey guessed for her benefit. "I need a word with Nina and her friend below."

"Sure." Joana scooted behind the wheel.

"Let's go inside and talk," da Silva said.

Joey and Nina followed him into a large cabin forward of the pilot house. A galley, cooker and sink ran along the forward bulkhead of the cabin, bunks, three high, ran along both side bulkheads. The boat slept six, a head was on the aft bulkhead and a table was bolted to the floor in the center of the cabin with picnic like benches on both sides of it, also bolted to the floor.

Da Silva sat at the table, Joey and Nina sat opposite him.

"Tell me all about it," he said.

They did.

"And you think this Mick's father can make it so everything is safe for Nina?" da Silva said to Joey. "Because if he can't, I'm going to hunt the boy down and kill him." Joey didn't need the proof of his presence or the fishing boat to believe him, just the way he said it told her he could do it.

"Yes," Joey said. "Mick's father is a powerful and famous man. Somehow Nina and I are caught up in something very bad, but if anybody can make it right, he can."

"Reuben," Nina said to the captain, "How did you do all of this?"

"Nina, my brave one, my reach is longer than you could have ever imagined." Then to Joey, "I understand my Nina has lost her child, when this is all over, you will tell me who is responsible, so I can have my vengeance."

"Yes, sir," Joey said, meaning it.

"Good." He put a hand up to his mustache, twisted it. "I'm sorry about the circuitous method of travel, but I didn't think it wise to fly my jet into Port of Spain. Too many questions here, so I flew to Margarita and Joana and I borrowed this old boat."

"How'd you do that, Reuben, get this boat so fast?" Nina asked.

"Many people owe me many things, and those that don't do me favors, so that I'll owe them. It's a hazy world I live in."

"But how, Reuben?" Nina said.

"I'm a thief." Da Silva fairly twinkled.

"I knew that," Nina said.

"A very big thief." He thumped his hard stomach, laughed.

"And how come I never knew you spoke English? And so good."

"So well," he corrected. "I went to Harvard. I'm an educated man."

"I never knew."

"So now you do." He looked at Nina like a father and Joey wondered about their relationship. He was so rough looking and Nina seemed so innocent. Obviously she wasn't rich, but she wasn't poor either. She worked in that internet cafe, she was educated. Joey envied her, she probably had a happy childhood. But da Silva bugged her, she had to know about him.

"How do you two know each other?" Joey blurted out.

"Family friend," da Silva said.

"Yes, family friends," Nina said.

"It's good to have friends," da Silva said. "And it's good to remember who they are." He looked right at her, bore into her eyes.

"I remember my friends." Joey met his gaze, nodded.

"And is Nina your friend." Da Silva's eyes were brown and deep, but there was a softness there that seemed to smooth over his rough edges.

"Yes she is."

"Good." He turned to Nina. "Do you want to do as this woman wishes, go to America?"

"Yes, Reuben."

"Then you shall."

"How?" Joey said.

"It's been arranged. Shortly after we anchor we'll be met by a launch. Then a quick cab ride to the airport where we'll board my jet. While we're flying through the night to Bogota, Colombian passports will be being made up for the both of you. There will be multiple entries logged in and out of the United States. You'll enter as crew of the Avianca, Bogota-Miami flight. It's a twenty-four hour turn around, so the crew routinely clears in and overnights in the city.

"Once you're through Customs and Immigration, you'll board an American flight to Los Angeles. It's the best I could do on such short notice. All the Miami-Dallas flights were full. Besides the Los Angeles flight takes off within an hour of your flight's landing. Under the circumstances, it's probably best you're out of Miami as quickly as possible and lost to your pursuers somewhere in the great American West.

Joey couldn't talk. She was stunned.

"How about the photos?" Nina said.

"They'll be taken on board the aircraft. Don't worry, little one, we've done this before. However, always before our people have made the return flight to Bogota, thus not arousing any suspicions in America. You, on the other hand, will not be taking the flight back and we haven't anybody to return in your place. So, the government's going to know two woman from Colombia have jumped ship, so to speak."

So, Joey thought, Nina's friend Captain da Silva was more than a thief. He was a drug smuggler, and from the sound of it, a big one.

Captain da Silva was behind the wheel as they motored into the large bay off Porlamar, a bustling city on Venezuela's duty free island of Margarita. It was a little before midnight, and the tall buildings at the water's edge lit up the shoreline, making landfall as pretty as Joey had ever seen it after dark.

Two days later, Nina sitting in the window seat, reached over, took Joey by the hand and squeezed. Joey squeezed back. She thought of the tearful farewell between Nina and Joana. They weren't sisters, something more. Joey didn't know what, wondered if she'd ever find out, wondered if she'd ever be as close to someone as Nina was to Joana.

Then they were on final approach and soon Captain da Silva's passports were going to be put to the test. They'd spent the flight in first class, in jeans and T-shirts, going to the forward bathroom to change into the flight crew uniforms only as they neared the east coast of the

United States.

During the flight Joey had been surprised at the crew, treating them as if they were guests and not someone they were forced to smuggle into America for some drug lord. Eventually Joey came to the conclusion that Captain da Silva must reward the crew very well for their cooperation and she wondered how the world could ever stop the flow of drugs if people like him had so much money to throw around.

Joey felt Nina tense up as the plane's wheels squeaked on landing and she stiffened even more when the plane taxied up to the gate. Inside they followed the crew to the Immigration desks.

"What if they question us in Spanish?" Nina said.

"Why would they do that?"

"I learned on the internet that Spanish is almost the first language of Miami now," Nina said. "Because of all the Cubans."

"No matter what he says, answer in English. Like you're showing off your ability," Joey said.

"What if he won't speak English back?"

"This is America. They have to speak English," Joey said. But she wondered if it was true and she wished Nina hadn't brought it up, because now she was more worried than ever.

A few minutes later Joey saw that Nina's fears were bearing fruit, as the Immigration man crooked his finger at the girls and said. "*La proxima, por favor.*"

* * *

Joey started toward the Immigration officer, but Nina put

a hand on her shoulder, held her back, and walked up to the desk herself. The man was thin, wiry and would have looked official even if he wasn't wearing the uniform. He eyed Nina with a toothy smile that looked false. She wondered if he got up early every morning and practiced in front of the mirror.

The man said something in Spanish. Nina didn't have a clue.

"English please." She handed over the Colombian passport.

He said something else in Spanish.

"Look," she turned her own megawatt smile on him. "I spent five years with those damn Berlitz tapes, so when I come to America I want to use the English, please."

"Yes, ma'am," the officer said in English. He took Nina's passport, stamped it.

"My friend back there," Nina nodded toward Joey. "Isn't so good at English. Don't let her get by you. Make her talk." Nina smiled again at the officer as the blood rushed to Joey's face. She looked embarrassed and that was good.

"Yes ma'am." The officer handed back the passport.

"Thanks." Nina took it, then held her right hand out as if to shake.

"Welcome to the United States." The officer took the offered hand, shook it. Then he turned toward Joey and said, "Next."

"Damn, I was scared to death," Joey said once they were outside the Customs area.

"We have to change clothes and get ourselves over to American Airlines," Nina said. "We don't have much time." She looked at up at a screen that showed arrival and departure information. "We only have twenty minutes, we have to hurry."

They didn't make it, but when they got to the gate they saw that the plane had been delayed. There were two women at the boarding desk and they stepped up behind them to wait their turn. Nina was in awe of the giant airport. It seemed they did everything bigger and faster in America.

"I want to thank you for all you've done, holding the plane and all," one of the women in front of them said as she received her boarding pass.

"It was nothing, Mrs. Shannon. We all knew Frank. All of us here at American liked him," the airline representative behind the counter said.

"Well, you made it so much easier," Mrs. Shannon said.

"There's a lot of forms when you bring in a body. I'm just glad we were able to smooth things over for you."

Nina closed her eyes. They were bringing back a body. One of the women turned, as if she could feel Nina's eyes on the back of her head. She was crying.

"I'm so sorry," Nina said.

"My father," a raven haired woman said. Then, "My name's Noelle."

"I'm Nina, I know how you feel, I just lost my baby." Nina couldn't help it, she opened her arms and the woman fell into the hug. Nina didn't even try to hold back the tears. She just cried.

"I'll get the boarding passes," Joey said and Noelle led Nina away from the counter.

"It's supposed to get easier as time goes by." Noelle wiped her eyes with a finger. "Thanks, Nina. I really needed a hug."

"I think I did, too," Nina said.

"I'm sorry about your baby," Noelle said.

"And I'm sorry about your father."

"Come on, Noelle, we have to board now," the woman named Mrs. Shannon said.

"It was nice meeting you," Noelle said, then she was through the gate, boarding with the first class passengers.

"Her father died. His body's on the plane," Nina said to Joey.

"I heard," Joey said.

"That's so sad."

"Yeah," Joey said. "Everybody's got problems I guess. Some just worse than others."

"Hers were pretty bad," Nina said.

"Ours are pretty bad, too," Joey said. "Come on, it's our turn to board."

On the plane, Nina practiced with the digital camera. It was so stupid of her not to have used it earlier. She would have liked to have Angel's photo, and Reuben's, and Noelle's, the lady she just met, and Joey's, of course. Plus, she could have photographed the airplanes she'd flown on. By the time they landed in Los Angeles, she'd taken dozens of pictures on the plane, marveled at how they came out in the view finder and she took several more shots as the plane made an early morning landing at LAX, Los Angeles' International Airport.

In the terminal, Nina saw two men approach and recognized them right off as police, even though one was an albino and wore his hair down to his shoulders. She'd spent too much of her short life living on the edge of the law, no policeman could ever fool her, no matter how long his hair was or how he dressed.

"Police," she whispered to Joey.

"Where?"

"The albino and the guy with the shaved head."

"How could they have found out?"

"Look," Nina said. The policemen stopped Noelle and Mrs. Shannon. "They're not here for us."

"Okay, but it's a good lesson. We have to be careful till we get to Mick's parents. We don't take any chances."

"Right," Nina said. "We don't take any chances."

"I've got to call and tell them we're here."

"Okay." Nina followed Joey to a telephone, watched while she read the instructions, then inserted her credit card and made the call. After about a minute she hung up. "Answer machine. They're on vacation in Hawaii. They were supposed to be back by now, but they've extended their vacation till January Seventh."

"So what are we going to do?"

"America's a big place. They live in San Antonio, in Texas. Fifteen hundred miles away. How'd you like to drive it?"

"Really?" The thought of renting a car put goosebumps on her arms. She'd wanted to come to America her whole life. Now she was here. Now she was going to see it all. "Stay right there." Nina backed away from Joey, took her picture. "I want to remember this moment forever." Then she caught a glimpse of Noelle out of the corner of her eye, talking to the two policemen, and felt guilty. Noelle still looked sad, she should be too. She'd just lost her baby, it wasn't right to feel this good this soon. Then what Joey had said hit her. "January Seventh, that's ten days."

"Yeah." Joey put her credit card away. "Let's get out of here."

"Can we stay in Los Angeles for awhile, maybe go see Hollywood or Disneyland?" Nina said.

"No, I don't think that's a good idea. We should get on the road as soon as possible. We'll have plenty of time to play the tourist after this is all over."

"Okay," Nina said and she wondered what Joey meant by that. It sounded like she planned on staying in America. "Together?" Nina said. "We're going to play the tourist together after this is all over?"

"Sure," Joey said. "You don't think I'd dump you after all we've been through, do you? I wouldn't do that."

"But I slept with your husband. I married him."

"Yeah, you did. But it wasn't your fault. He's the bastard of this show. Not you, not me. Now, come on, let's get the H out of here."

"What does that mean, *the H?*" Nina said.

"H is short for Hell, so I don't have to swear."

"So I could say, *What the F are you doing*, and that would be okay?"

"Yeah," Joey said, "that would be okay."

* * *

Outside, Joey saw the Hertz shuttle bus and jumped in with Nina right behind. At the rental desk she used her credit card and her South African license to rent a car.

The woman behind the counter, thin to the point of being frail with a blue tint in her hair, asked what kind of car they'd like.

"A convertible," Nina said, "so I can take pictures as we drive."

"You have one of those?" Joey said. "A convertible?"

"Of course." The woman picked up a phone with bony fingers, spoke into it and in no time at all a red Ford Mustang convertible was brought around from the lot. "Will that do?" she said.

"Oh, yes." Nina clapped her hands.

Joey laughed at seeing the girl so happy, then as if she felt guilty about it, Nina frowned.

"It's okay to enjoy yourself, Nina."

A few minutes later Joey got behind the wheel. Nina got in the passenger side, then said, "Well, let's go."

"Everything's on the wrong side." Joey drummed her fingers on the wheel.

"Is that a problem?" Nina said.

"Maybe you should drive. I've never driven on the right before."

"I've never driven before at all."

"Swell."

"You better do something. That lady's looking at us funny." Nina sounded nervous.

"Okay, here goes." Joey keyed the ignition and the car rumbled to life. She pulled the stick into drive and eased her way forward.

"Come on!" Nina said. "Let's hit the mean streets."

"Where'd you learn that?" Joey said as she coaxed the car into a right turn out of the parking lot.

"Television," Nina said. "We have television from the sky at the hotel where I live. Eighty channels." She fumbled with the map provided by the blue-haired Hertz lady. "I think you were supposed to go left if you want to get to the freeway. That's what the lady said." Then, "Ah, I see it here. Highway number 10, the San Bernardino Freeway. We have to get to that and it'll take us all the way to Texas."

"I think I'll just drive around the block a few times, till I get used to the car."

"Imagine that," Nina said, "one road that goes all the way across America." She took Joey's picture.

"Stop that!"

"It's fun." Nina took another shot.

"You're making me feel self conscious."

"You don't have to be. If they're not any good, I can erase them." Nina took several more photos before they got to the freeway.

"Well here goes nothing," Joey said and she accelerated through the on ramp.

"What's that mean, *Here goes nothing*?" Nina said.

CHAPTER
SEVENTEEN

PAUL SNELLING ORDERED a second beer from the slowest bartender on earth, shook his head as the West Indian ambled away, supposedly to get it. The bar was above the mini market in the Carib Inn Marina, from where he sat he could see *Satisfaction* snug in her slip

He knew Clayton was right. Joey Sapphire wasn't coming back to the boat, but he couldn't think of what else to do, where else to go. So until he got a lead, he was going to sit tight and wait, dull as it was.

"Hey, chief," Clayton yelled out to the bartender as he

took the seat next to Snelling. "We'll have two cold ones here and make it snappy." All of the sudden the bartender started hustling like he was a calf running from the branding iron. "Had a little talk with the son of a bitch last night," Clayton said. "Told him if he ever kept me waiting on a brewski again, I'd cut off his balls and shove them down his throat."

"That's all it took?" Snelling said.

"I grabbed his rocks and squeezed a little. That might've helped." He laughed from the belly. "Then I smacked him up side the head with this." He held up the cast on his right forearm. "You know, every cloud really does have a silver lining. This baby," he knocked on the cast, "is like a built in weapon. Makes me feel like the Bionic Man or something."

The bartender set the beers down. Clayton took a long pull from the bottle, then said, "You wanna know what I found out about Mick Sapphire?"

"You're going to tell me, whether I want you to or not, so you might as well get it off your chest." Snelling didn't like admitting it, but Clayton, as obnoxious as he was, usually had good trade craft and he had good sources, sources he shouldn't have. But that was why he used him, because as crude as he was, he got the job done.

"Mick Sapphire is a little more than just Harry Sapphire's boy. Navy Seal, demolition. Fought behind the lines during the Iraqi war. Blew up so much shit, they nicknamed him D-Man, you know D for demolition."

"Like you, a bomb guy?" Snelling didn't like what he was hearing.

"Not exactly. I've used bombs, sure. And I've killed

people. But always in the line of duty. It was my job."

"Right," Snelling said. But he knew better. Clayton didn't directly work for the government, never had. He was a contract agent, a mercenary.

"This guy Sapphire, they say he wasn't just doing his duty, he enjoyed it, loved it. The more people he blew away, the happier he was, women, children, he didn't care. They say he's got no conscience, a true psychopath, thinks only of himself."

"That would explain why he married the girl in Brazil so readily." Snelling really hated getting information from Clayton. In the old days he wouldn't have allowed that to happen. "She was a means to an end. Free rent, a piece of ass. If he had to marry her to get it, no problem."

"Yeah," Clayton said.

"But it doesn't explain why he let you live."

"What do you mean?"

"You said you had a run in with him."

"Yeah, right. He must've thought I had back up, wanted to get away before they showed." Clayton's face turned redder than usual. He didn't like talking about fights he didn't win or jobs he fucked up.

Snelling was about to rub his nose in it a little more when Clayton's cell phone rang.

"Clayton," he said when he got the phone to his ear. He listened for a few seconds, then, "Thanks." He punched the end button and wore a grin that literally made his nose glow.

"What?" Snelling said

"A hit on Joey Sapphire's VISA card. Los Angeles, she rented a car."

"How the fuck did she get to Los Angeles?"

"Maybe we should get a move on and find out."

* * *

Once on Highway 10, Joey drove until they came to the California-Arizona border. For the first two hours of the trip they zoomed along with four lanes of east bound traffic, the only indication that one city ended and another started, the signs on the side of the road. Without the signs it would seem that Los Angeles went on forever. But finally the cities shrank in size, the distance between them increasing as they went ever eastward, until they were in the California high desert.

It was winter and it was cold. Joey wanted to raise the roof, but Nina stood firmly against it. The girl had to be freezing, but she soaked up the American air as if she had been too long in the desert and it was water.

Joey saw the sign for gas, piloted the car off the highway and drove up to a set of gas pumps in front of a restaurant.

"It's a truck stop, like in the movies," Nina said. "And a wooden American Indian. I've heard of those." She took a picture.

"They're called Cigar Store Indians," Joey said.

"Why?"

"Because in the Old West they put them in front of cigar stores. Some places still do, but I don't think it's politically correct."

"How do you know this?"

"Television, just like you," Joey said. After a few minutes Joey was beginning to think the famous American service she'd heard so much about was a myth. She'd been waited on faster back home, faster even in Trinidad, but then a station wagon full of people pulled up on the other side of the pumps, the driver got out and put in his own gas.

"You do it yourself?" Joey said.

"Yeah." The driver of the station wagon was watching the numbers roll by on the pump. "They don't do it that way in England?" He'd obviously mistaken her accent.

"No." Joey said. "They don't." She got out of the car and filled the tank as Nina went inside the restaurant. When she was finished, she went to the car to get her credit card.

"I took care of it," Nina said. "And I got us some pastries."

Then they were back on the road again, Joey shivering in the wind with the open top while Nina continued to take pictures. The sun was going down when they passed a sign telling them they were two miles from Phoenix. Joey saw a sign for a motel and took the next off ramp.

"We're stopping?" Nina said.

"I'm too tired to go on. We'll rest here."

At the reception, Joey handed over her VISA card and told the young man behind the counter they'd only be staying the night.

"Is there someplace close we can do some shopping?" Nina said.

"There's a mall five miles up the road."

"Nina, I need a break. I've been driving all day."

"Come on, Joey. We need warm American clothes." Then to the clerk, "What time does the mall close?"

"Most stores stay open till 9:00."

"Nina?"

"Please!"

"Then I'm putting the top up, it's freezing out there." Joey felt better once she was inside the giant mall. Nina's attitude was infectious. Every store delighted her, but save for a small English-Portuguese dictionary, she didn't buy anything. Then they got to the Eddie Bauer outback type clothing store and she started hopping around. The little kid was back.

"We need two of those, for sure." Nina pointed to a backpack that was displayed on the wall, too high to reach.

"That's a pretty serious pack," a young salesgirl said. She had dishwater blonde hair and a just washed looking moon face. She seemed like she was about sixteen.

"That's what we want, two of them."

"Why?" Joey said.

"For our clothes."

"We have the stewardess suitcases."

"These are way better than those. And don't even talk to me about our old clothes that we brought along. We're in America now. We're getting American clothes."

"But backpacks?" Joey said.

"We're on the road and we're traveling light," Nina said. "If it doesn't fit in the backpack then we don't buy it." All of a sudden Nina didn't seem like an excited little girl anymore. "With those, if we have to move fast, we won't lose our stuff. Besides, we won't need anymore than we can cram in them. The jeans will weigh the most. We'll need two pair, but we'll always have one pair on.

We'll each need a heavy sweater for the cold and a jacket. Some T-shirts and maybe a dress. That's all."

"Toothpaste, makeup?" Joey said.

"Toothpaste, yes, we'll share. No make up."

"Yes, boss," Joey said.

"And two of those." Nina pointed to a red Swiss Army knife.

"What for?" Joey said.

"Those are very useful. They have a scissors on them, a can opener, tweezers, all kinds of stuff."

"Aye, aye." Joey laughed and she let Nina take over outfitting them, because she had to admit what the girl said made sense. They left Eddie Bauer's store with their packs almost full.

"Okay, you can buy a couple more dresses than me and maybe some makeup."

"What do you mean?" Joey said.

"I've got to fit the camera bag in mine. I meant it. We wear everything, either on our bodies or our backs."

"Okay." Joey smiled. She was too tired to argue.

"Oh, look," Nina said as they passed a dress shop. "It's beautiful. I have to have it. Come on." She grabbed Joey's hand and led her into the store. She was the kid again.

But she was crestfallen when she found out the price.

"Two hundred and ten dollars. I've never paid that much for anything in my whole life."

"We just spent six hundred dollars at the Eddie Bauer store," Joey said.

"Yeah, but we got a lot of stuff. Stuff we need. The dress I can live without." Nina was an adult again. It amazed Joey how she could switch back and forth like that. It was almost as if she had two personalities fighting for control in her tiny body.

"Okay, let's get something to eat. I'm starved."

"We just had those pastries," Nina said.

"That was hours ago, and it's all we've had all day. Aren't you hungry?"

"I could be." Nina was quiet for a few seconds, as if in thought. "I guess I'm used to going a long time without food. I've kind of learned not to hear my stomach when it tells me to eat."

"Come on, I saw a Mexican restaurant by where we came in. Let's treat ourselves."

"I've never had Mexican food," Nina said.

"Neither have I," Joey said. "It'll be an adventure."

* * *

Snelling was asleep on the Citation with the seat back. He'd left Clayton orders not to be disturbed till they were on final at LAX. He hadn't had much sleep since Christmas and he wanted to be as fresh as possible when they caught up to Joey Sapphire. So he opened his eyes annoyed when Clayton shook him awake.

"Autopilot?" he said.

"Yeah," Clayton said. Then, "We just got another hit on Joey Sapphire's VISA card." He was backlit by the overhead lights and from Snelling's position, he looked like a red bearded Santa Claus with a halo.

"Christ, your nose is even glowing."

"What?"

"Nothing. Tell me about the hit."

"A motel just west of Phoenix, less than an hour ago. They must be driving."

"How far?" Snelling said.

"We're right on top of it. We'll be on the ground at Phoenix' Sky Harbor Airport in fifteen minutes. I've already made arrangements for a car."

* * *

Clayton closed the door to his room. He was seething. Snelling had dropped him off at the first no name motel they'd come across as they drove from the airport, with instructions to stay put and wait for further notice. It took a full ten minutes for him to get his anger in check, then he pulled the antenna out of his grip and hooked it up. It was a long shot. The Brazilian girl was probably still in Trinidad, but he got a reading on the signal strength meter. Nina Brava was hanging out with Joey Sapphire. Clayton wondered what kind of relations the two Mrs. Sapphires were having and decided it would be fun to watch. More fun to join in. Then he called the front desk and told them he wanted a rental car sometime before the kid that checked him in graduated from high school.

In ten minutes there was a car in front of his room. A Ford Pinto that had seen better days, but it was better than nothing. He signed the papers and in minutes he was off. Heading for the city, laughing all the way.

Glowing nose indeed.

Fucking Snelling and all his morals were probably checked into one of those rooms over at the hotel were Joey Sapphire had checked in. Maybe he was staking the place out in the car. No, too cold, not his style.

But the girls weren't there. They'd gone into the city. Leastwise whoever was carrying that camera bag had gone into the city. The signal got stronger as he approached the mall. They were shopping he reasoned, and he laughed again. Girls just had to have fun.

He parked the car, checked the time on his Rolex. It was just shy of 8:00. The mall probably closed at 9:00. That gave him over an hour to find them. He wanted to know what was worth a hundred thousand dollars to Paul Snelling and somehow, someway, they knew. After he got a hold of them and questioned them, the way only he could, then he'd know, too.

* * *

Nina looked at the menu as four guys dressed in white, wearing Mexican sombreros and serapes, sang in Spanish from a corner stage in the back of the dimly lit restaurant.

"Tacos, tostadas, burritos. I don't know what any of this is," Joey said. "But it all sounds good."

"I'm going to have the combination plate, a taco, two enchiladas, chili rellanos, rice and beans."

"That sounds like a lot of stuff," Joey said. "I'm going to have the bean tostadas."

"I want to try it all." Nina pointed the camera at Joey.

"Not in here."

"I have to learn how to use the flash." Nina took the picture.

Joey blinked because of the flash. "Are you erasing any of those pictures? Because you've taken more of me than I've had taken in my whole life."

"No, I have to find some way to get them on paper.

Maybe we could find a photo store."

"I think you probably need a computer store. It's a digital camera."

"Oh, yeah. We should find one of those. I only have a couple flashcards left."

"Nina!' You should go through those pictures and erase the one's you don't like."

"Can't. I like them all. They're like my diary, you know, a record of where I've been and who I've seen."

"You've only had the camera a few days."

"And I'm keeping it forever. So we have to find a computer store."

"First thing in the morning," Joey said.

"Really?"

"Yeah, let's order."

"You order for me. I'm going to go get that dress." She pushed her chair away from the table, got up.

"Good girl," Joey said.

"You don't think it's too expensive?"

"Heck yes, it's too expensive. Now go get it."

"I'll be quick." Nina started to pick up her new backpack.

"Leave the stuff. It'll be fine."

"Okay." Nina laughed to herself as she walked, almost skipped to the door. She did skip when she got out into the mall. This was a new feeling and she liked it. In her whole life she'd never gone out and bought something special, just for her. Sure she'd bought clothes, but not like that dress, she'd only been able to afford the cheapest jeans, the cheapest clothes. She felt good. She couldn't help it and she wasn't going to feel guilty about it.

In the changing room she marveled at the dress in mirrors that showed three different views of herself. Purple really was her color. She folded her jeans and T-shirt. She was going to wear the dress tonight, right now, while she had dinner in that Mexican restaurant. In fact, they had another one just like it, only two sizes larger, and it was the same blue as Joey's eyes. It'd be perfect for her. She'd take it, too. They were going to be some hot girls.

Back in the mall, she couldn't help but notice the stares. Men had always looked at her, the suggestive way she walked, the way she tilted her head, batted her eyes. But this was different. These were a different kind of men, these Americans. They wore wide smiles, had a bounce in their step and a sparkle in their eyes, not the hungry look she'd seen so often. She liked these stares, welcomed them.

* * *

Clayton caught sight of the girl in the purple summer dress and couldn't help staring. Dead of winter, colder than a witch's tit outside and you could see a girl dressed that way. Malls were beautiful. He watched her kind of sashay with that shorty dress as she swung a shopping bag. She moved through the mall as if it were a fashion runway and she was the top model. He loved to watch women walk, especially young ones, pretty ones. He traveled his eyes up to her face, caught the long hair and gasped.

It was her.

He stepped into a Foot Locker.

"Can I help you, sir?" A pimply faced girl wearing a black and white stripped shirt said.

"No." Clayton ignored the salesgirl, kept his eyes on Nina Brava.

"Excuse me," she said.

"I'm not here for shoes." Clayton turned to the girl. "I'm a police officer following a felon." He turned his eyes back onto the hot Brazilian girl.

"You don't look like a police officer."

"Go to the phone, dial 911. Tell them you're interfering with an officer in the line of duty. Do that before or after you talk to your boss, I don't care."

"I'm the manager."

"No kidding?" Clayton gave her a quick once over. She didn't look old enough to tie her own shoes. "Look, I'll be out of here in a couple minutes."

"Okay." The girl went to wait on a customer that just walked in the door as Clayton saw Nina Brava step into a See's Candy store. Perfect. The mall exit was two stores to the right of Mrs. See's place. His car was in the lot, not far outside. When she left with her candy, he'd grab her and walk her out, slicker than rat shit.

* * *

Joey had a clear view of the mall from where she sat inside the restaurant. The food had come. She didn't want to be rude and eat before Nina got back, but she was starving, so she dug in, keeping a guilty eye on the mall as she ate.

She saw Nina leave the dress shop, watched her stealing every male eye in the place as she glided along.

Joey sighed.

The woman was born to turn men's heads, to break their hearts. There was something about her innocent beauty that begged men to love her, women to mother her. If she'd been born in America or Europe she'd probably be an actress or married to somebody like Mick Jagger.

Joey watched Nina go into the candy store. The girl could probably eat a pound of chocolate a night and not gain weight.

Then she saw the big man with the red beard go into the Foot Locker.

CHAPTER

EIGHTEEN

NINA PUT THE WRAPPED BOX of assorted chocolates into her shopping bag with the clothes she'd worn into the dress shop and the dress she'd bought for Joey. She smiled. Would Joey ever be surprised, a new dress and American chocolates.

"Will that be all, Miss?" the blonde woman with the big Dolly Parton hair behind the counter said. Americans were so friendly.

"Maybe another box."

They weren't that expensive. Besides, they had a long

way to go. Chocolates on the American highway with Joey. She sighed and examined her feelings for Joey as the woman wrapped the second box. She hadn't like her in Brazil—of course Mick had been saying all those lies about her, saying he was going to get divorced, so she'd make love with him. Then Mick went away and left her pregnant, only to turn up three months later, saying the divorce had happened. What a liar. Then, when she saw Joey on the boat, she'd hated her instantly, but the hate went away fast. Now she thought of her like an older sister, someone she could trust. Someone she could be close to. Someone like Joana.

"Your second box, Miss." The lady handed over the box and Nina paid.

"Thank you," Nina said on her way out. Could she ever get used to how polite Americans were. They seemed to treat everybody with respect.

Outside of the candy store and back in the mall again, Nina started for the restaurant. All of a sudden she was so hungry she could eat snake and she hated snake.

"Don't scream." A giant hand pulled her into a bear of a man. She turned to see who, saw the red beard, the fat nose with the blue veins running through it. "I have a gun inside my coat. One peep out of you and you're toast."

She didn't know what a peep was, but she could imagine. She did know what toast was and didn't want to become it.

"That way." He pushed her toward the exit. She was about to shout out anyway, but he must have sensed it, because he said, "I mean it, raise your voice and I'll kill you." Now he grabbed her arm, wrapped an ape like hand around it as he moved her toward the glass doors and the outside, where he could do whatever he wanted.

"Rape!" The shrill voice rang out through the mall. "Rape!" Joey screamed again.

Red Beard turned and Joey clobbered him in the head with the camera bag.

"What?" Red Beard staggered, let go of Nina's arm. He was between them and the exit.

"The restaurant!" Joey shouted. "Run!"

Nina, free from Red Beard, charged into the restaurant. Saw a waiter in Mexican clothes blocking her way. He probably wanted them to pay for their meal. She dodged around him, grabbed the backpacks from the empty chair they'd set them on and ran toward an exit sign on a door next to the stage where the Mexican band was still playing.

She hit the bar on the door as if she were running from a fire. It was dark outside now and for a flash of a second Nina was disoriented, then she remembered the car was toward the back of the lot. The lot was full when they'd arrived. Now it was almost empty. She could see the convertible with it's white top, bright under a street light. She ran toward it.

"Stop police!" someone shouted. It had to be Red Beard. "I'll shoot!"

"Nina, Look out!" Joey screamed.

Nina looked up. There was a car bearing down on her without its lights on. Were they with Red Beard? They turned the lights on as Nina jumped aside, the car grazed her as it past, knocking her down. The door opened and a woman's voice shouted out. "Sherman kill!" And a beast charged out of the driver's door. Nina dropped to the pavement as it roared over her, howling loud enough for Joana back in Brazil to hear.

"Get away." It sounded like Red Beard. "Aarrgh." It was Red Beard. A gunshot rang out. Another.

Nina turned to the sound of the gunfire. Red Beard was on the ground. The biggest German Shepherd she had ever seen had him by the arm. The dog was shaking its great head back and forth, worrying the arm until the hand gave up the gun. Then the giant dog was on top of the giant man, fangs at his throat.

"Are you all right?" It was an old woman standing over Nina.

"Yeah." Nina pushed herself into a sitting position.

"There's probably someone else." Joey was panting. Fear, Nina saw, not exertion. "We gotta go."

"Hurry!" An old man was standing by the passenger door, holding it open.

"Come on!" Joey grabbed onto Nina's hand and pulled her the rest of the way up.

"Get in!" the old man again. The car was an old two door type. The old man was holding the seat forward so they could get in the back. Nina jumped in. Joey tossed in the backpacks and the camera bag, then piled in after.

"Sherman!" the old woman hollered and the dog jumped off the man, bounded toward the car and bullied his way into the back seat, worming his way between Joey and Nina.

"Hurry up, Dottie!" the old man said. "If he is police, there'll be more of them."

"Right, dear." Dottie got behind the wheel, had the

car in gear and her foot to the floor even as the old man was closing the passenger door.

"Police!" Red Beard shouted. He was pushing himself up as they drove by.

"Not!" Nina said as they drove away.

"Can you go any faster?" Joey said.

"I'm putting the pedal to the metal," Dottie said.

"What's it mean, *pedal to the metal*?" Nina said.

"I don't know," Joey said.

"She means she's going to floor it," the old man said. "But if they come after us, they'll catch us. This old girl's a wonderful car, but she's thirty-five years old. Not much good in a high speed chase."

"I don't understand, *floor it*," Nina said.

"This," Dottie said, and all of a sudden the car picked up speed as they squealed out of the parking lot.

"Now I get it."

Sherman licked Nina's cheek.

"Oooo, stop that." Nina giggled.

"My name's Malcolm," the old man said. "The lady driving is my wife Dottie. That's the General between you there."

"General Sherman," Dottie said as she drove at a respectable speed through the dark night.

Nina turned, looked out the back window.

"There's nobody following, dear," Dottie said. "I've been watching in the rearview mirror."

"Why are you helping us?" Joey said. "Most people would be afraid."

"My husband saw that man chasing you out of the mall and said 'Dottie, those girls are in trouble.' He's a regular Sir Walter Raleigh, my Malcolm is."

"What's a Sir Walter Raleigh?" Nina said.

"He was a man that honored women," Dottie said.

"I don't understand."

"Sir Walter Raleigh wouldn't let a man hurt a woman," Joey said.

"Now I get it."

"What if he was the police, weren't you afraid?" Joey said.

"Darlin'," Malcolm said. "I don't care who he was, no one has call to abuse a woman and no I wasn't afraid. I'm too damn old to be afraid of anything." He chuckled, then said, "Would I be far from the mark if I said you girls don't sound like you're from here?"

"South Africa," Joey said.

"Brazil," Nina said.

Sherman licked Nina's cheek again and she snaked her hand up and scratched his great head as Joey began to talk.

* * *

"Mother fuck," Clayton muttered as he got up from the pavement. Dog would have ripped right through his flesh if it wouldn't have been for the cast. As it was, his arm hurt like hell. At this rate the fucking bone was never gonna heal. "I really am too old for this shit." He dusted himself off. Looked around. A crowd was beginning to gather. Time to go. He picked up the gun. Several people saw him do it, but no one made any effort to stop him as he hustled himself to the piece of shit Pinto.

A couple security guys busted out of the mall as he

started the car. For a second it looked like one of them might try to block his exit, but the fucker jumped aside at the last minute, good thing, because Clayton had the toy car aimed right at his crotch, would've run the fucker down, the way that black bitch in Tobago had run him down.

On the street Clayton drove west. He had two choices. One, go back to the dump and wait for Snelling, a prospect that didn't excite him because by the time Snelling got back, he'd be in a mood. Or two, head out to where the man was staking out an empty motel room and tell him what had happened and that option stunk, too.

He'd gotten the license number on that old Ford. California tags, so they wouldn't get an address where they might be going in Arizona, but it was a lead. The only one now. No, he still had the receiver. He checked it. They seemed to be going the opposite direction. He thought about turning around, but his arm was screaming. He ran a hand along the cast, pulled it back when he felt something wet. Blood. That settled it. He'd get Snelling, then get himself to a hospital.

No, hospital first. He'd have them send a cop for Snelling.

* * *

"That's quite a story," Malcolm said when Joey finished. "But what I don't understand is why you two are together. I mean, he married both of you. Shouldn't you hate each other?"

"Oh, no," Nina said. "Joey's like my big sister."

"Really?" Joey said.

"Yeah, besides, Mick wasn't very nice."

"He's scum," Joey said, meaning it.

"Yet, you're headed for his parents," Dottie said.

"I've seen Harry Sapphire on television," Malcolm said. "It's hard for me to believe he could have a son like that."

"We don't always behave as if we're our father's children," Dottie said. "Your father was a minister and you haven't stepped into a church since I've known you."

"Point taken," Malcolm said. Then he turned around in his seat, faced Joey. "The American you saw from under that restaurant. You said he looked old, how old?"

"Not as old as you," Joey said.

"Thanks a lot."

"Maybe in his late fifties."

"And the guy with the red beard?"

"He looks even older," Nina said. "He's got a drinker's nose, you know, fat and blue veins. His cheeks are like that, too. And puffy."

"They don't sound like any policemen I've ever heard of," Malcolm said. "Sound more like criminals, if you ask me."

"They were with the police in Tobago," Joey said.

"That doesn't mean that's what they were. The cops are in the crook's pockets in a lot of third world countries."

"I know that," Joey said, thinking about Reuben da Silva and how he got them into America.

"I think the best thing for you girls to do is to lie low until Harry Sapphire gets back from his vacation," Dottie said.

"And you can't use your credit card, because even if the men after you aren't police, they have some pretty good connections," Malcolm said.

"What do you mean?" Joey didn't like the sound of what he was saying.

"He means they found us because we used your credit card to get the motel room," Nina said.

"I didn't think of that," Joey said and she wondered why she hadn't, because now it seemed obvious.

"And we can't go back for the car," Nina said. "They probably know all about that from the rental people."

"How do you know?" Joey said.

"We told them we were going to Texas, remember? You used your card to rent the car, they probably found out with only a phone call where we're going with it. They probably had people looking for it. Maybe someone spotted it in the mall and called them."

"This is spooky," Joey said.

"So, I guess that means you have to stay with us," Dottie said.

"You would do that for us?" Nina said.

"Of course. Sherman likes you. Consider yourself under the General's protection now. Just settle back and relax, we have a long ride ahead of us."

* * *

"Tell me why I shouldn't shoot you right here," Snelling said as he paced back and forth. They were alone in the emergency room of Phoenix' large Mariposa County Hospital. The doctor had just finished attending to Clayton who now sported a new cast.

"It wasn't my fault." Clayton was sitting on a gurney, meeting Snelling's eyes head on. The man wasn't a coward, didn't seem afraid. "I got bored and went to the mall."

"I told you to stay put."

"No, you said you wanted to go to that motel alone, and you did. You didn't say anything about me being under house arrest."

Snelling really did want to shoot the bastard. Would've, right here in the hospital, if he thought he could've gotten away with it. The man was probably lying, protecting himself, but from what? Maybe it was just a chance encounter, impossible as that was to believe.

"Okay, so if I buy your story, do you want to explain again how you let a hundred pound girl get away from you?"

"She had help, I told you. Some people with a big dog. Dog like to have killed me." He held up the new cast. "Bit right through the old one like it was paper. Never thought I'd be glad I had a broken arm, but without the cast, the damn dog woulda bit it right off."

"And they all drove away in a '56 Ford."

"Red, the Ford was red, and I got the license number."

Snelling went to the door, stuck his head out. "Nurse."

"Yes." The woman was tall, black and had an attitude.

"Shave his hair and beard off. Make him so his own mother won't know him."

"This is a hospital, not a barber shop."

"He'll give you a thousand dollars."

"What?" Clayton and the nurse said in unison.

"Give it to her," Snelling said. "I don't want that girl recognizing you and running for cover before we even know we're close."

"Right." Clayton pulled his wallet out, counted out ten hundreds and gave them to the nurse. Snelling shook his head. At least the man wasn't vain. Or cheap. He didn't whine about the money as most would have.

* * *

Nina scratched the dog between the ears as the car wound it's way through the mountains. She marveled at the sheer drops to who knew how far below. Certain death if you came around one of the hairpin turns too fast, lost control and smashed through the barrier, a short fence like thing that didn't look like it could stop a man on a bicycle, much less a car.

She'd read of Arizona on the internet, as she had most of the states, but nothing she'd read had prepared her for the two lane twisty road that seemed to wind ever higher, as if it were reaching for the stars. And there were so many of those. Somewhere she'd read that there were observatories, places where scientists studied the stars, in Arizona and she could see why.

But now she noticed the stars were twinkling out as if the darkness above was stealing them away. A light rain splashed against the windshield and Dottie turned on the wipers.

"Uh oh," Malcolm said. "Dark ahead."

"Is that bad?" Nina felt Sherman tense up.

"At sea, it means clouds," Joey said, "which could

mean a squall."

"Here it could mean snow," Malcolm said.

"The weatherman on TV said the road was clear." Dottie sounded apprehensive.

"Is snow a bad thing?" Nina said as she saw more stars disappear.

"We don't have snow tires, or chains," Malcolm said.

"That doesn't sound good," Nina said. Then, "Why not?"

"We're from California, we don't need 'em there," Malcolm said.

"But you're here now," Joey said.

"Yeah, we are," Malcolm said. Then, "Better pick it up, Dottie."

"Picking it up," Dottie said and Nina felt the increase in speed.

Now there was tension in the car as Dottie drove faster than she should on the mountain road. And all of a sudden the click clack sound of the wipers sent shivers up Nina's spine as tall Christmas-like trees whizzed by, looking to her every bit like ghosts swaying in the wind. It was spooky and she fisted her fingers in the thick hair on the back of the dog's neck.

"A couple more curves, then it's smooth sailing all the way into Prescott."

"Prescott?" Joey said.

"Where we're going," Dottie said. "Prescott, Arizona. Our new home, Malcolm's and mine. A small town nestled in the mountains, away from all the smog, pollution and crime you see so much of today."

"You sound like a commercial for the town," Malcolm

said.

"I am a commercial for the town," Dottie said.

For a second Nina thought they were starting an argument, but then they burst out laughing as a few snowflakes fluttered onto the windshield.

"Snow." Nina rolled down her window, stuck her hand out. "Like in the movies."

"Thank God it's going to be a light fall," Malcolm said.

"Thank God we're so close to town," Dottie said. Then to her husband, "A light fall, did you just make that up?"

"Yeah," he said. "But it sounded better than, 'Oh Lord, we're gonna get snowed in out here and freeze to death.'"

"How much farther?" Joey said.

"About ten miles."

"Then you better slow down," Joey said.

Immediately Dottie pulled her foot off the accelerator and the speed started to drop. "Why?"

"A light rain, now snow. We might get black ice."

"What?" Malcolm said.

"Oh my, God!" Dottie said as the car slid to the right.

"What's wrong?" Malcolm said.

"I'm not in control." Dottie spun the wheel, trying to get the car back on the road, but she only made it worse, sending the car into spin, then they were sliding sideways along the dark road, toward the barrier and a long drop down.

Joey reached forward, grabbed Dottie's shoulder. "Turn into the slide," she said as the rear end of the car

KEN DOUGLAS

hit the fence with a soul wrenching screech. "Now!" Joey raised her voice, but didn't shout.

"Doing it!" Dottie started spinning the wheel to the right. "I hope you know what I'm doing!" she shouted.

"Give it the gas!" Joey shouted back. The rear of the car was still sliding along the fence to the right. The drop on the other side, too deep to think about.

"It seems stupid!" Dottie said as she shoved her foot to floor, but the front of the car moved ahead of the slide. "I'm getting it back," Dottie whooped.

"Left, left, left!" Joey screamed and Dottie brought the car away from the dangerous side of the road. Then she put her foot on the brakes.

"Don't do that!" Joey screamed, but it was too late, the car was out of control again, sliding the other way now.

"Hang on!" Dottie shouted and they slammed into the shoulder, bounced off and again they were sliding down the road, but this time at least they were going straight.

"No brakes!" Joey said. She didn't have to shout now. She had Dottie's full attention.

"I gotcha!" Dottie said and somehow she managed to keep the car pointed straight, inching the wheel back and forth as she lost speed. Then as suddenly as they were on the slick spot, the wheels found traction and Dottie again had control of the car.

"What was that?" Malcolm said.

"Black ice," Joey said. "Very bad. It happens when you get a light rain then it drops below freezing real quick. The rain freezes on the road. You can't see it and it's very

222

slippery."

"How'd you know?" he said.

"The sudden snow right after the rain."

"Yeah, okay, but how'd *you* know?"

"Oh, you mean because I'm from Africa. My parents moved to Scotland when I was young. Lots of snow and ice there and I've spun out more times than I like to think about." Then, "We should pull over, there's probably more up ahead."

"Right." Dottie pulled over to the side of the road, parked next to the barrier. "I wouldn't want to go through that again."

Sherman barked.

"I think he wants out," Nina said.

"Yeah, me too." Malcolm opened his door, got out. "That was a little too close for comfort."

Then everybody was out of the car.

"Oh, Dottie, you shouldn't look." Malcolm was on the passenger side of the car surveying the damage.

Dottie walked around. "A good body shop can fix it. Besides, the important thing is, we're all right."

Sherman barked.

"So, how long do you think we should wait out here?" Dottie said to Joey.

"I don't know, till the ice melts, I suppose," Joey said.

"It's midnight, hours till sunup. We'll freeze," Malcolm said. Joey didn't sense fear, he was just stating the facts.

"He's right, we'll freeze." Nina was shivering in that summer dress, but shivering or not, Joey had to admit, she still looked wonderful in it.

"We could sit in the car and run the heater," Dottie said.

"No," Malcolm said. "We'd run out of gas. You could drive, Joey. We've only got about ten miles to go."

"Not me," Joey said. "We drive on the other side of the road in South Africa."

"Sure you could, Joey," Nina said. "You drove all the way from Los Angeles."

"There you go," Malcolm said.

"Driving on the wrong side is one thing," Joey said, "but in these conditions—"

"I've never driven on the ice," Malcolm said.

"Me neither," Dottie said.

"I've never even driven," Nina said.

The dog barked.

"All right, I'll drive."

"Wait, I want a group picture."

"Not now, Nina," Joey said.

"Just one, everybody stand by the car."

CHAPTER NINETEEN

IT HAD TAKEN AN HOUR and three phone calls from their motel room by the airport to find out that the '56 Ford was registered to Malcolm and Dorothy Morrison of Huntington Beach, California. It took another two hours and the dropping of several names to roust the Huntington Beach Police Department out of its lethargy, but once they believed the situation was urgent, they went right to work, and they didn't seem to mind waking up the Morrison's neighbors in the middle of the night.

At the address the car was registered to, they found a

young couple that had just bought the house. The new owners didn't know where the Morrisons had moved to, but after waking up almost the whole neighborhood, they found someone who knew that they had bought a place in Prescott, Arizona, a place with a couple of rentals so they could supplement their Social Security.

When he got off the phone with California, Snelling caught Clayton sitting on the end of one of the beds, admiring himself in the mirror above the bureau. Snelling groaned as Clayton ran a hand over his shaved head.

"What are you doing?"

"I like it."

"Maybe I went too far, you're just as conspicuous as you were before it was shaved off."

"No, it's cool. You were right about the hair and beard. Very unprofessional. I thought I was done with this kind of work, so I let it grow. I'd always wanted to do that, you know, be like a hippie. But because of the kind of life I've led, I missed all that."

"Not the dope, surely," Snelling said.

"Even that. I was always a straight arrow, bourbon and water kind of guy. So when I retired, I decided to find out what I'd missed. But I should've shaved it off when I hooked back up with you."

"Did you find it, what you missed?" Snelling hated himself for asking, but he had to know.

"No, but at least I didn't have to shave every morning."

"That's something," Snelling said.

"Shaving's a drag," Clayton said. Then his cell phone rang. He pulled it from his inside coat pocket, flipped it open. "Clayton," he said into it, then he listened for a couple minutes, hit the end button, flipped it closed and put it back in his pocket.

"What was that all about?" Snelling said.

"Joey Sapphire," Clayton said. "Ryder ain't her real maiden name. "It's Vanderveer."

"You're kidding?"

"No, I'm not. Harold Vanderveer was her old man."

"Christ." Snelling exhaled. "We were there."

"Yeah," Clayton said. "She must've changed her name so no one would know. Can't say as I blame her? The bastard burned up a bunch of kids. Burnt 'em alive."

"Yeah." Snelling thought back through the years. He and Clayton had been in Cape Town, tracking a diamond smuggler, when it came over the news. A cop up in Pretoria had been accused of setting fire to a black school. Eleven kids died. Someone, a white person, identified one of the arsonists as Harold Vanderveer. Eight cops testified they'd been playing poker with him when the school went up in flames. Vanderveer went free, but the whole world knew he was guilty. It must have been hell being his daughter. Snelling would've changed his name, too.

"Did you find out where they went?" Clayton asked, snapping Snelling back to the present.

"They're going to Prescott."

* * *

Joey drove the last ten miles into the outskirts of Prescott at fifteen miles per hour and encountered no more ice on the road, or cars. Malcolm found a news station on the radio and the weather forecast was grim. They were predicting a cold front and two days of snow.

"If the blizzard hits before we get to our cabin we could be in trouble." Dottie had traded places with Joey and was riding in the back now.

"They didn't say anything about a blizzard," Malcolm said.

"Two days of snow is a blizzard to this California girl."

"Don't worry, Dottie," Malcolm said. "We're going to be fine."

"It's like a fairy tale town. Like a Hansel and Gretel place," Nina said as they drove past a video store and a donut shop, covered in snow. The trees were tall pines, tops covered in snow, too. Snow lined the side of the road. It was falling in flurries now.

"We're going to be snowed in," Dottie said.

"Yes, we probably are," Malcolm said. Then to Joey, "Make the next right, just before Hungry Jack's. You'll find a road that twists through the trees for about a quarter mile. It dead ends at a group of cabins. That's our stop."

Joey saw the restaurant decorated in blinking Christmas lights and heard the country and western music drifting through the night as she made the right. The car slipped a bit, but Joey had the measure of the vehicle now and it didn't give her too much trouble.

"You live out in the woods?" Nina said.

"Yes, there." Malcolm pointed to a group of four log cabins.

"Like the Three Bears," Nina said. And once again Joey marveled how she shifted between girl and woman with such ease. Sometimes she seemed completely without guile, others it was as if she'd seen the weight of the world and wore it on her shoulders.

"Escrow doesn't clear till after the First, but they're ours."

"All of them?" Nina said.

"All of them," Dottie answered. "The one on the right is where we live."

"Not closing escrow. That means you don't own the cabins, not officially?" Nina said.

"That's right," Malcolm said. "Not till sometime next week."

"So, that means there's no record of you tied up to them, the cabins?"

"No," Malcolm said. "I guess not."

"So if Red Beard remembers your license number. He can't find us?"

"You think he did that?" Joey said. "Copied down the number?"

"He's not stupid. He got to Arizona almost as fast as we did and we didn't know where we were going." Nina was all adult now, thinking clearly. Joey was impressed.

"The license plate will take him to California," Dottie said. "We haven't had time to re-register the car yet."

"Then we should be safe here," Nina said. "Huh, Sherman?" Joey looked in the rearview mirror and saw her hug the dog, a child again.

"Hear that?" Dottie said.

"Airplane," Nina said.

"Who'd be crazy enough to fly on a night like this?" Malcolm said.

Joey shivered, because she thought she knew.

* * *

"You going to beat the storm?" Snelling said. Clayton thought he sounded worried. The snow hitting the windows was getting thicker by the second, but it wasn't a problem.

"Five minutes to touch down." Clayton said. Then, "What's it all about?" He knew the girls were close, could feel it. His pulse quickened as it always did near the end of a hunt. He couldn't say why, couldn't know for sure, but somehow he knew it would be over soon and he could retire again. This time for keeps and in grand style.

"You said you wouldn't ask. That was the deal."

"I know. But it's getting to me." All he needed was a few words out of the man, a clue. "We got an Air Force jet and government agencies falling all over us to get us the info we need."

"I know what you're thinking," Snelling said.

"Tell me." Clayton shook his head. They used to be friends a long time ago, before Snelling started thinking he was a cut above the rest of humanity. Morals, they were the death of a lot a good men. If you wanted to win the war you had to be willing to fight like the enemy. If that meant taking no prisoners, then so be it. A hundred of theirs for every one of ours. That's how Clayton thought. Men like Snelling shouldn't go behind enemy lines, shouldn't guard the wall of freedom. They're too soft.

"You're thinking this is the big one. If I'm willing to pay out a hundred thousand, then there must be a big pot at the end of a rainbow somewhere. You're thinking it's not fair for Old Paul Snelling to be scooping up the gold all by his lonesome. You want to come along with a forklift or something and pick that pot up for yourself. Am I right?"

"Not true," Clayton said. "I just want to know, that's all." He backed off the power, in preparation for landing.

"It wouldn't interest you," Snelling said. "It's a personal matter, but for your information, I'll tell you this, you couldn't be more wrong. There is no money here.

"Don't shit a shitter."

"I brought you into this because it had to be done outside the Agency. They're lending us the assets, but that's all. You held me up for a big paycheck, but it was within budget."

"What are you saying?"

"This is personal, as I said. Outside government. Outside the law in more ways than you can imagine. And I'm doing it as a favor. I wouldn't ask for money, not for this and don't you ask for anymore either."

"Who said I would?"

"I'm serious."

"A deal's a deal. I just wanted to know what we were up to."

"No good. That's all you need to know. Now why don't I give you a little quiet so you can get us on the ground in one piece?"

Clayton brought the plane onto final. The wind sock said there was wind blowing across the runway. He hated crosswind landings at night, was starting to hate Snelling. Soon he'd find out about the money. Then it was going to be a bullet in the back of the head for his dear old friend.

* * *

"It's beautiful," Nina gushed, running straight to a computer desk that took up a fair part of one of the walls in the homey living room. "Macintosh, what we have back home. Are you on line?"

"Connected day before yesterday," Malcolm said.

"Can I?" Nina swept him with a smile that would have melted the north pole with enough left over to melt the South Pole as well.

Joey laughed. She didn't think there was a man alive who could say no to that.

"Be my guest, Malcolm said."

She pulled out the chair, sat, the dog by her side, as if he wanted to see what magic she was about to work with the machine.

Joey, not interested in computers of any kind, turned to Dottie, "It looks like your dog has a new friend."

"He doesn't take to many people. Me, Malcolm, a couple others. Shows he's got good taste."

"Are all the cabins like this?" Joey swept her arm in front of herself, taking in the room with its early American style furniture. The cabin actually was built from logs. It was spacious, with a varnished hardwood floor covered with a large circular rug. It reminded Joey of a Western movie.

"No. The other three are like duplexes, a unit upstairs, one below. This is the owner's cabin, a guest bedroom downstairs, two upstairs. Would you like a tour?"

"Sure."

Dottie took Joey through the place with Malcolm in her wake. Each bedroom had it's own bathroom. The kitchen was done in cobalt blue tile with stainless steel sinks, stove and microwave. The only thing missing was a hole or two in the wall to stick a rifle out of to fight off the Indians. But they did have a week's supply of wood for the fireplace and emergency equipment—a powerful policeman's flashlight, a hurricane lamp, candles and lots of canned food—in case they got snowed in and the power went out.

"Our plan," Malcolm said, "is to rent the other cabins out to people who want a quiet, secluded and extended vacation. A month or more. We want to get to know our tenants, make friends."

"It sounds nice," Joey said.

"And you're going to be our first guests," Dottie said. "Non paying, of course."

"I can't thank you enough."

* * *

Clayton was so tired of being cooped up, he thought he might kill Snelling just for shits and grins, just to be rid of his sanctimonious face. They'd been snowed in the tiny hotel by the airport for three days. Three insufferable days. If he had a choice next time, three days stuck in a room with Snelling or three years in Attica, he'd probably take Attica.

He'd had to wait a whole day before Snelling took a walk in the snow, before he could get out the receiver and put up the antenna. The receiver told him the women weren't far, so they were probably snowed in, too. But he couldn't go for them, not without alerting Snelling. Fortunately the snow had finally let up enough for them to open the airport on New Year's Eve. And fortunately Snelling had a sister and a niece back in Scottsdale he wanted to hug and kiss at the stroke of midnight. Very fortunate indeed.

"You get a hit on one of those VISA cards, call me," Snelling said as he went out the door.

"Will do."

"You won't go off without me again?"

"No, sir." But of course he would, just as soon as it got dark.

* * *

Nina felt like her rear end had become glued to the chair, her eyes to Malcolm's big twenty inch monitor, her fingers to his keyboard. He'd allowed her the use of his Mac, told her she was free to surf the net. She'd spent over an hour the first morning just answering her e-mail. Because it was something she did every day back in Fortaleza, she'd never thought about how many yachties she'd made friends with, how many e-mails she sent all over the world every week. Then she e-mailed Joana and told her where she was. She'd almost told her about all the trouble she'd been in with Joey, but changed her mind, not wanting to worry her.

Then she discovered that she could hook the camera up to the computer and download her photos. She could print them out, too. Not only that, Malcolm had all the fancy programs, like Photoshop, so she could change the photos in thousands of ways.

"Sure you don't want to go with us?" Dottie said.

The snow plows had cleared the road and the three of them were going out to dinner to celebrate the New Year. Malcolm and Joey were already in the car. Dottie had come back in to make one last plea for Nina to go with them.

"No thanks. I probably have more e-mail to answer, plus I have to decide which photos to print, because the flashcards are all full."

"Child you shouldn't be alone on New Year's Eve," Dottie said.

"Dottie." Nina pushed her chair out from the computer, got up and faced the older woman. "I come from a poor Brazilian family. My mother died in childbirth and my father had three sons to raise, plus me, the infant that killed his wife. He got even by taking me to a certain place when I was eleven years old. I stayed there for eight years before a good person helped me and my best friend buy our way out. Do you understand the kind of place I'm talking about?"

"I think I do."

"Then you can understand that holidays have never been much fun for me. Sweaty men out for a good time."

Dottie put a hand up.

"You don't have to say it," Nina said. "I know they're not all like that. Still, the best way for me to spend a holiday, especially this one, is by myself. Just knowing that I don't have to do anything I don't want to is the best New Year's Eve I could ever have. Besides, I've got

Sherman to keep me company."

The dog, hearing his name, barked. Then trotted over to Nina's side. She scratched his head.

"I understand," Dottie said. Then, "He's really taken to you. It's almost like he's your dog now." She laughed. "Seven years, big guy, and you throw me over for a pretty face."

"You think I have a pretty face?" Nina said.

"Darling, I think you are just about as pretty as they come."

"Really?" Nina didn't know exactly why, but hearing Dottie say that made her feel good, really good.

Sherman barked again.

"We won't be back till late," Dottie said. "Oh, I almost forgot, Sherman has the sniffles, I think he's getting a cold, so don't let him outside unless it's to do his business, then make sure he comes right back in. Okay?"

"Dogs can get colds? I didn't know that."

"Yes, they can, and Sherman is a monster when he's sick. You have to wait on him hand and foot. It's no fun at all."

"Really?" Nina laughed.

"Really." Dottie laughed too. Then, "I left some sandwiches in the fridge."

"*Fridge*?"

"Refrigerator."

"Oh, yeah." She laughed as Dottie went out the door. Then she went back to the computer, logged on to her e-mail and was surprised to find one from Joana. She'd never received an e-mail from her. Then she laughed to herself.

Of course not. She'd been with her every day of her life since she was eleven years old, right up till she flew off to Trinidad in search of Mick.

Excited she opened the e-mail and read:

Nina,

I've been going sick with worry. I didn't know how to contact you and stupid me, I never thought about e-mail until I got one from you.

I feel so dumb. Listen, I mean, read this:

Mick was waiting when I got back home. He wanted his camera bag. When I told him I didn't know what he was talking about, he got this look on his face that could scare that wicked woman we used to work for out of all her money. He asked where you were and I told him I didn't know, but that I thought you'd be back later on.

He said he had some important pictures on a flashcard in that bag and a lot of money. He said he wants it back and if you know what's good for you, you'll hand it right over.

He told me he's very disappointed in you. The way he said it tickled the hair on the back of my neck. I hope you're okay. Stay well and stay away from Mick.

Love — Me.

Oh, yes, English, like we promised, aren't you proud of me?

What was she talking about, pictures on a flashcard? All of the flashcards were blank when she got them. She should know, she'd used them all. The bag was sitting next to the monitor. She picked it up. The only things in it now were the Jack Priest paperback, the pocket dictionary she'd bought at the mall, her compact and her lipstick. She dumped the bag out, then rifled through the pages of the Priest book. Nothing. The bag was empty for the first time since she'd had it. The lining was held on to the leather with Velcro. She pulled it apart and there it was, another flashcard.

In seconds she had the card in the camera, the camera plugged into the computer. She clicked on the card icon, opened up the first photo and saw a man and a woman engaged in sex. The woman was on her hands and knees, facing away from the camera. The man was mounting her from the rear, as if she were a dog. Dirty pictures? Pornography? She'd seen plenty of that in her life. So what? Mick liked porno, had some pictures, so did a lot of men. This didn't surprise Nina, didn't even annoy her.

She clicked on another photo. This was more interesting, because it was Mick with the girl, same position. This time the man in the first shot must be holding the camera. So Mick and some friends liked three way sex, still so what? In her life she'd had sex with two men on numerous occasions. She'd never liked it, but they seemed to. She didn't even think it was unusual. And from her experience, she'd learned that a lot of men like photos of themselves.

She clicked on a third photo and this time she gasped. This time the girl was on top, facing the camera.

"Oh my God," she mumbled, because she knew who the girl was.

So did everybody else in the world.

CHAPTER TWENTY

CLAYTON THOUGHT OF SNELLING, winging his way to his sister and niece, as he drove the Mercury Sable rental through town with the Yagi antenna unfolded on the passenger seat, the receiver in his lap. The Sable was a damn sight better than the Pinto. In fact, he'd caught a couple of the chicks that were between bars on this cold New Year's Eve giving him the eye as he slowly drove past. His shaved self, combined with the car, had them looking and it made him feel good. Almost good enough to stop for a drink, but not. He was a disciplined man.

Work first, pleasure later.

Still, the small town excited him. Because of the holiday, people were out, despite the weather. They said hello to each other with smiles on their faces, friendly. Whiskey Row, the main street, had several cowboy bars, the best kind of places in the world as far as Clayton was concerned.

"Hey, big guy!" A woman's voice. Clayton snapped his eyes away from the signal strength meter to the passenger in the Chevy pickup moving along next to him.

"What?" Clayton was gruff, but when he saw the woman he lit his face up in a grin.

"What are you up to tonight?" She wasn't as young as he liked them, but she wasn't over the hill either. And she was coming on to him, something that didn't happen too often.

"I got some business to take care of." He hadn't talked to a woman, window to window, while cruising a boulevard since 1963.

"Be done by midnight?" She was a redhead. Damn, and he'd let that nurse shave him.

"Yeah." Clayton grabbed a quick glance at the dashboard clock. It said 10:00. "I'll be finished by then, no problem."

"Wanna meet up at the Trap?" She said.

"Where is it?" He couldn't believe it. She was picking him up.

"Just there." She pointed.

"I see it and I'll be there."

"Swear?"

"Nothing short of death could keep me away from

someone as pretty as you."

"I can't wait." She waved and the girl driving stepped on the gas.

He was still smiling about his unbelievable good fortune as he followed the meter, whistling an old Kingston Trio song, something else he hadn't done since 1963.

The meter told him to turn left at Hungry Jack's Roadside Bar and Grill. Cars lined the street on both sides, the parking lot full. The restaurant, like the town, was hopping tonight.

The road he turned onto was a one lane, one car at a time affair, and it wound into the forest and the night. He turned off the lights and crept the car along, quiet as a snake. Soon he had his night vision, but he didn't need it to see the light coming from the cabin ahead.

He shifted into neutral. If he went any closer, they'd hear, but he couldn't leave the car where it was, blocking the road. He could pull over to the side, but anyone coming would see the car and wonder what it was doing there at best, remember it at worst. He had no choice, besides, it wasn't too far. He backed out, back to the highway. At the restaurant he drove into the parking lot, saw a car pulling out, took the spot and parked.

Okay, he told himself as he got out of the car, he had time. It was maybe ten minutes since he'd seen the girl. Fifteen minutes to walk up the road. That gave him an hour to do what he had to and a whole half hour to get back to the Trap. Piece of cake.

Cold ran through him and he rubbed his hands together as he tramped up the road toward the cabin. He wasn't dressed for the cold, but it was bearable. Just. Closing in on the cabin he saw there were three others, but they were all dark. There were no cars. So either no one was home, which made sense, because of the holiday, or no one lived in them. Either way, it worked in Clayton's favor.

There was no car at the last cabin either, but someone was home. He could feel it. He pulled the thirty-eight from a shoulder holster concealed by a sport coat that was way too light for the weather. He was about to walk up to the door and boldly knock when he remembered the dog. If that fucking beast was in there, knocking would be dumb, because it wasn't gonna be afraid of no gun, and if he didn't get it with the first shot, he would be fucked.

He stopped, tested the wind. So far it blew from the cabin to him. Upwind, the dog couldn't smell him. But he'd have to be quiet, fucking dogs could hear real good.

Close to the cabin, Clayton circled round to the back, keeping always upwind. There had to be a way to get whoever was in there to come out. He saw a building behind the cabins. A garage. There was a breaker box by the side door. He kept himself still, felt the wind. Yes, he could get to it without alerting the dog.

At the box, he pulled up the lid, slow, quiet. So quiet the devil himself couldn't hear, never mind the damn dog. Fucking dog probably wasn't even in there, he thought. But maybe it was. No sense taking chances. With the cover open he was confronted with a bank of switches. Too many for one cabin. Plus, most of them were off. The other cabins, had to be, this was the breaker box for all of 'em. Five switches were in the on position. He thought about turning them all off, but that might be obvious. He wanted it to look like the breaker tripped by itself.

He flicked one off.

And the dog barked.

* * *

"Quiet, Sherman," Nina said.

The dog stopped barking.

The lights had gone out, exciting the dog, her too. But the rest of the electricity was still on. She could hear the whisper quiet hard drive whirring in the computer. The monitor still showed Suzi Walcott, the daughter of the President of the United States, sitting astride a naked man, grinning wide, as if she'd never had so much fun in her life. Sherman lay down by the chair and Nina felt a shiver run through the dog's body as she scratched between his ears.

"It must be a circuit breaker," she told the dog. "It happens all the time back home."

* * *

Clayton was careful to stay upwind as he moved through the snow. The dog was in there, he knew that now, and he remembered what the fucker had done to him the last time they'd met. He tightened his hand on the gun. This time it would be different. He stood about twenty paces from the back door and waited for whoever was in there to come out to check that breaker. He was ready to shoot the second it opened if the dog came into view.

* * *

Nina got up, went to the kitchen, got the matches and picked up Malcolm's police flashlight. Back in the living room she lit the hurricane lamp. She'd seen the electric meter on the side of the garage several times during the last three days, but the soft light from the lamp was kind of soothing. The breaker, if that's what it was, could wait till Malcolm got back. Besides, men liked doing that kind of thing.

She went back to the computer and clicked on another photo. Again she saw Suzi Walcott engaged in what appeared to be happy sex. Another photo and Nina saw Suzi alone, posing nude for the camera. Another, Suzi masturbating. Another, Suzi still playing with herself. Another, another, another, more of the same, fifty-six photos in all.

How?

Nina felt her heart racing.

Why?

Then the answer came to her as if she'd been struck with a mallet. Blackmail. Somehow Mick was blackmailing Suzi. All of a sudden a shiver shocked through her. Not Suzi. Mick was blackmailing her father. He was blackmailing the President of the United States.

That's why Red Beard and the others were after them. They wanted the photos. Somehow they knew she had them. Impossible. Not impossible, they'd been onto them too fast. They knew where the photos were. How?

She turned an eye to the camera bag sitting to the right of the monitor. The Porno Suzi flashcard had been hidden in it. What else was in there? Slowly, like it was white hot, she reached for the bag, picked it up. It looked empty and innocent, but it had been hiding that flashcard. She pulled out the Velcro lining and cringed at the scratchy sound it made as it separated. Then she saw it. Gingerly, like it might bite, she picked it up. She didn't know what it was, and yet she did know. It had to be some kind of signal sending device. How far could it go? From the size of it, not very.

Could Red Beard have already found them because of the thing she was holding in her hand? No, she didn't think so. They hadn't used Joey's credit card and there was no way he could know where they were now, even if he took down the license plate number, because Malcolm said the car was registered in California. So they were safe.

But even so, it was like Joey said, spooky.

A cold chill seemed to run through the room.

Sherman growled.

"What is it boy? Do you see how nervous I am?"

She dropped the tiny electronic thing on the floor, stomped on it. There, at least Red Beard wouldn't be able to find them now.

Then she got up and went to Malcolm's CD collection. She had a lot of work to do and she wanted a musical background. She found one she liked. Bob Dylan's 'Highway 61 Revisited.' She had that at home. Joana played it all the time. She put the CD on, then went to the computer, logged onto a search engine and fed it Suzi Walcott's name. She wanted to learn as much as she could about the president's daughter.

The first two articles told Nina that Suzi Walcott was a nineteen-year-old junior at UCSB, the University of California at Santa Barbara. She lived in a little house in

Isla Vista, a small seaside college community just north of Santa Barbara and adjacent to the University. Suzi had picked UCSB, she said, because you can sail off Santa Barbara every day of the year. She was an avid sailor, her goal upon graduation was to sail around the world single-handed.

Avid, that word stumped Nina and she went for the English-Portuguese dictionary and looked it up. The hurricane lamp didn't make enough light for her to read the small print, so she used the flashlight. It was awkward, but possible if she held the flashlight in her right hand and manipulated the tiny book with her left. But no sooner had she learned the word, when she was stuck with another.

Damn. She had two choices. Skip the words she didn't know, or go out and see if the breaker was the problem with the lights, like it was all the time at the hotel back home. But she really only had one choice, she hated letting words sneak by. If she let her guard down like that, she'd never learn English like an American.

She got up, grabbed the flashlight and started for the back door.

Sherman followed.

"No, you have to stay inside. Dottie said."

"Woof."

"Don't woof me. Stay."

The dog sat and Suzi continued out through the kitchen toward the back. The door had a window in it and Nina peered outside. She was warm and didn't really want to go out into the cold, but she wanted the lights working, so she grit her teeth and opened the door.

* * *

Clayton was cold and it was killing his patience. Over ten minutes and no one had come out to check the breaker. He'd seen the lights go out, but he'd also seen the faint glow of firelight. Then Bob Dylan started screeching, wondering how it felt to be like a rolling stone. He hated Bob Dylan. He didn't like any left wing music, but Dylan was the worst.

One advantage to the music, he didn't have to be so quiet. No matter how good the dog's ears were, he couldn't hear nothing over that harmonica. He went back to the breakers, was about to shut the other two off when the back door opened.

Shit, his gun was back in the holster, he grabbed for it as he scurried around behind the garage. Now he had no shot. If that damn dog came charging out that door, he was fucked.

But it didn't happen. He heard the door close. Breathing a silent sigh, he peaked his head around the corner. It was Nina Brava. She was sweeping the air with a flashlight and the beam was moving right at him. He pulled his head back as she swept the garage with the light. She was coming for the breaker, after all. And now all he had to do was wait till she got to it.

* * *

Nina swung the light back and forth, lighting up the snowy pine trees. She sighed. This really was a Hansel and Gretel kind of place. A fairy tale world where maybe even Santa Claus could be real.

She paned the light through the trees and grabbed a quick breath when she saw a pair of eyes. She locked the light on it. A deer, frozen in fear as she stared into the light.

"I won't hurt you, little doe," Nina said. But apparently the deer didn't believe her, because she was quivering as if a mountain lion were stalking her fawn. "Really, it's okay, shoo." But the deer stayed where she was, stuck in place, grounded by her fear.

"Oh, stupid me." She moved the light away. Caught movement in the brush and laughed. It was the fawn. That was probably what Sherman had been nervous about, she thought.

She put the light on the electric meter and the breaker box beneath it. She walked through the slushy snow, never taking the light off her target. At the box, she raised the lid. "Heck," she said. There were a bunch of breakers in the off position. "Darn."

What to do? Should she just start flicking them on and hope for the best? Why so many? She turned the light toward them. Then she saw something she should have notice right away.

Footprints in the snow.

She spun around, swinging the flashlight like a lighted club. He was behind her, coming fast, gun in his left hand. She took it all in in less than a flash of a second. The cast on his forearm, the fat nose, the shaved head. That didn't fool her, she knew who it was.

Red Beard.

She thought he was going to pull the trigger, thought this was the end, but instead he tried to jerk his hand out of the way. He'd been caught by surprise. She connected with his cast, a loud whack, as if she'd been holding her racket, returning one of Joana's lightning serves.

"Motherfuck!" Red Beard screamed as the gun went flying into the snow.

Nina, swirled around to run, but Red Beard fisted a beefy hand in her hair. She jerked away as she swung the light at the cast again, hitting it with a solid thunk.

"Shit!" he screamed as he let go.

He raised his arm. She instinctively knew he was going to use the cast as a weapon and was back peddling away even as he was swinging it at her. She had the flashlight and it was a good weapon, but it was no match for that cast when he put his bear-like strength behind it. If he hit her with it, she'd be finished.

And he would have, but she slipped and fell, the swinging cast missing her head by millimeters.

"Cunt," he muttered. He started toward her as she moved backward through the slush, hands behind herself, legs bent in front of herself, ass bouncing on the ground. She was a scrabbling crab, slipping and sliding her palms on the slushy snow in a desperate effort to get away and in the background she heard Sherman barking like a raging mad dog.

Red Beard bent, grabbed her foot with his cast hand, trying to pull her from the ground. She lost the light, had no weapon now. She lashed out with her other foot, kicked at him, but her soft running shoes weren't hurting him.

"Whore!" he said as he tried to twist her so she'd be face down in the snow.

250

"I'm not a whore!" She was mad now, struggling to keep from going over on her stomach, where she'd be helpless.

Then she heard a crash, breaking glass, a roar that woke up the night, and all of a sudden he let go as Sherman ripped into him with his massive jaws. She pushed herself to her feet. Saw the light. It was still on. She picked it up.

"Back, Sherman!" she screamed.

The dog released the man. Now he was the one on his ass. He turned fierce eyes toward her as she swung the light like a baseball bat, connecting with his head.

* * *

Clayton came to in a cold sleep fog. He was being dragged. His left hand was screaming. His right arm felt like someone was beating on it with a red hot poker, but neither of those hurts came close to the blazing pain that shot up his legs from his frozen feet. He tried to scream, couldn't. There was something in his mouth. He was suffocating.

"I saw your eyes open, so I know you're awake," Nina Brava said.

Clayton tried to mumble something through whatever was in his mouth.

"You can't talk. I stuffed a rag in your mouth, then wrapped some electrical tape around your head so you can't spit it out."

Clayton darted his eyes around, but all he could see were stars and her face staring down at him, beautiful, but hard, too. He tried to move, couldn't. He felt panic welling up, tried to control it. There was a way out of this. There was always a way out. He just had to remain calm. Think.

"You probably think you're paralyzed or something, maybe frozen into a block of ice, but you're not. I found some rope in the garage and tied you up with it."

Clayton squirmed his body, tried to move his arms.

"You look like a snake when you do that."

"Take it off," he tried to mumble through the rag in his mouth, but it came out "Dake e oo."

"Don't even try talking, because I can't understand you. And anyway, it wouldn't make any difference if I could. So just relax and maybe it won't hurt so much." Then she was out of his sight, but he heard footsteps crunching in the snow.

"Mush, Sherman," she said and frozen pain bolted up his legs. It was as if someone had shoved swords through the arches of his feet and rammed them inside his legs up to his ass. He bucked like a scalded snake, but that only made it worse.

"Stop, Sherman," she said and then her face was overhead again, blocking out the stars. "I told you, stay still."

"Fuck, you," he mumbled. It came out. "Uck, ooo."

"I understood that. You're not very nice."

He raised his head a couple inches off the ground and what he saw sent frozen needles twirling up his spine. She'd tied him good, trussed him like a rodeo calf. And she had a rope from his feet to the dog, apparently secured to the beast's collar.

"That's right," she said. "I'm towing you away from

the cabin. It wouldn't be good for Malcolm and Dottie if you were found too close to their home. The police would come around and ask all kinds of questions. Maybe other people, too."

He stared up at her, she blazed ice back. How could he have misjudged her so?

"Okay, Sherman, go."

The pain was excruciating. His feet, legs, head burned with it as she dragged him through the snow and his hands now, especially his hands, as she'd tied them behind his back. They suffered the full weight of his body as the dog pulled him along.

"Maybe in the big plan of things you're one of the good guys. But even if you are. Even if you work for the President of the United States. You had no right to kill my baby. I didn't do anything except fall in love with the guy that took the dirty pictures of his daughter."

What was she saying? What pictures? Whose daughter? Then it hit him. Holy fuck! She's talking about the president, about Suzi Walcott. Mother of God! He had to get up. She had to let him go. This was big. The president was a millionaire, no a billionaire. He'd been right all along. There was money. A never ending supply.

"Stop!" he screamed. It came out, "Tomp!"

But she kept going and the pain kept hurting, on and on and he could do nothing except watch the stars and the tree tops overhead. His nose started to run. He swallowed snot, gagged. Stay calm, he told himself, and he tried, because he didn't want to drown in less snot than he blew out his nose in the shower every morning.

He took short breaths, fought to keep from choking.

She must have seen his difficulty, because she stopped. He heard music. It must be coming from that restaurant on the corner. A country band was doing Johnny Cash's 'Ring of Fire.' Clayton imagined he was going down into that burning ring, imagined the heat, but all the imagining in the world wasn't going to chase away the cold. He heard a car go past. They were at the highway. She was going to leave him here. Someone would see. He'd be free soon. He closed his eyes in painful anticipation. See how the bitch liked it then. The next time he got his hands on her, he'd snap her neck like a twig. Stupid cunt, never should have told him the secret. She signed her own death warrant when she'd done that.

But a part of his muddled mind wondered if she'd let him go at all. And still another part wondered what good the secret was without the photos. Then she grabbed him under the shoulders, started dragging him onto the sidewalk. Where was everybody? Couldn't someone see what she was doing?

"I've pulled you up against a fence by the sidewalk." She tucked him into the base of the fence, facing him outward. Then she started packing snow around him. "This is so no one can see you." She piled the snow all over him, leaving only a space for his face. "There, you're in the dark here, so I think you're hidden pretty good."

She had him trussed up good. He only hoped someone found him before he froze to death. He grinned in his mind, he wouldn't freeze, he had a lot of fat. He'd get free. He'd get her. There was no place she could go. No place she could hide. With the contacts he'd built up over the years, he'd find her. He'd find her fast.

254

"You look like the cat that swallowed the chicken. That's stupid. You must think I'm going to walk away. Dumb." She took the rope that was attached to his feet and he watched in horror as she tied it to the bumper of a pickup truck. What the fuck was she playing at? And then he knew as he watched her cover the rope with snow.

"Now I can go," she said when she'd finished. "Oh, one more thing, you never should have called me that name." Then she went, the dog too.

But she wouldn't get away with it. She had to have left a trail a blind man could follow when that fucking dog dragged him through the snow. In fact, someone would probably see it, would follow with their eyes and find him snug up against the fence. He only hoped they wouldn't think he was a homeless person. Then even that hope was dashed as it started to snow. There would be no trail. No help.

"Come on, Stacy, get a move on or we'll miss your date." A woman giggled. Clayton strained his eyes through the snow, saw two woman going toward the pickup. He tried mumbling through the rag. If he heard them over the band then maybe they'd hear him.

But they didn't.

"Okay," the other woman said. "Let's go to the Trap and see what I'm gonna let catch me."

It couldn't be. It was. The redhead. His date. Stop! Did he shout or only think it?

They got in the truck.

Stop!

He heard it start.

Stop!

Then the truck roared away from the curb, snow tires spinning in the slush. He screamed when the rope jerked him from his hiding place, wailing through his gag as his body shot across the sidewalk, then his head smacked against the curb and everything went black.

CHAPTER TWENTY-ONE

THEY DIDN'T GET BACK to the cabin till well after 1:00. Joey and Malcolm had wanted to call it a night earlier, but Dottie wanted to bring in the New Year with a crowd. So they hung in there and squeezed into a bar called the Trap.

The hour came, everybody cheered, drank their champagne and sang 'Auld Lang Syne.' After the song they pushed their way out of the bar only to find a scene straight out of a horror movie right in front of the bar. A skinhead had been tied to the back of an unsuspecting woman's truck. Unwittingly she'd dragged him through town. It was a miracle he hadn't been killed.

Joey didn't want to hang around, but Malcolm had had some medical training in his past and had tried to assist the poor devil until the paramedics came and took him away. Joey didn't like skinheads and their Nazi-like philosophy, so like her father's, but nobody should be able to do that to another human being. If you lynched the lynchers, then that made you just as bad as them.

Nina was still up, still playing with the computer, surfing the net when they came in the front door. She said hello, then listened while Dottie and Joey told her about their night and the battered and almost dead skinhead.

"It was Red Beard." Nina was still at the computer. "He called me a whore."

"What?" Dottie said.

"He shaved himself, probably so we wouldn't recognize him. He called me a whore, so I tied him to the back of a pick-up truck. I hope he dies." She turned back to the computer, turned it off.

"What are you saying?" Dottie pressed.

"We have to go to California first thing in the morning. It's the only way we can make them stop."

"You're not making any sense," Dottie said.

Then Nina told them everything, from when she discovered the Suzi pictures, till she tied Red Beard to the back of the pickup. After the telling she took them to the back door and they saw where Sherman had jumped through the window. "But he's going to be okay," Nina said. "He got a couple cuts, but the bleeding's stopped. I'm sorry about him getting out, but he seems okay, I don't think it hurt his cold."

Dottie looked down at Sherman, curled up next to Nina's chair.

"There," Nina parted the fur on his head. "That's the biggest cut. I cleaned it and I don't think it'll need stitches, but you might want to take him to the dog doctor."

Dottie looked at the cut. Sherman opened his eyes, licked her hand.

"I swear," Dottie said, "if dogs could smile, I'd say he's smiling."

"He is," Nina said.

"So why do we have to go to California?" Joey said.

"Because Suzi Walcott goes to college in Santa Barbara. We have to go to her and give her the flashcard with the pictures on it. Once she has that, there won't be any reason for those people to keep coming after us. It'll be over and we can get on with our lives."

"You think?" Joey was impressed with her logic.

"She lives in someplace call Isla Vista and has a boat called *Babycakes* in the Seaside Marina."

"How do you know this?" Dottie said.

"Simple, the net. It's been in the newspapers, all you have to do is look it up."

"I've read about *Babycakes*. She wants to sail it around the world when she finishes college. She wants to go to all the small islands where nobody knows her so she can just be herself." Joey certainly understood that. That's what she'd wanted to do, but it wouldn't happen now. *Satisfaction* was Mick's boat and she was through with him.

"Right, that's why she's going to school in California, so she can sail every day."

"That's it, that's the answer," Joey said. "We can call the newspapers and tell them what's going on. Then we'll be safe. They wouldn't dare touch us after the press gets a hold of the story."

"No, we can't do that," Nina said.

"She's right," Dottie said.

"Why not?" Joey said.

"Because," Dottie said, "if you did that, then the story about the pictures would come out and the whole world would know about the president's daughter. And that wouldn't be right, because probably none of this is her fault."

"Then she shouldn't have had sex with Mick," Joey said.

"If you saw the way she looked in those pictures you'd understand," Nina said. "She looked doped up. I bet she didn't even know what she was doing."

"Oh, my God." Joey remembered what had happened to her in Trinidad.

"Let me make some phone calls," Malcolm said. And he did. When he finished he said, "I've booked you a flight to Los Angeles, leaving Phoenix at 6:00 in the morning, connecting to Santa Barbara at 10:00, arriving at 11:00. So we have to get a move on if we're going to get you down to Phoenix in time."

"What about the roads?" Dottie seemed reluctant to let them go.

"They're clear," Malcolm said.

Four hours later Dottie hugged them goodbye.

"It seems like we were a big disaster in your lives," Joey said. "You wrecked your car, your window's broken, Sherman got cut up. We're really sorry about all that."

"Nonsense," Dottie said. "None of it was your fault."

"If these are the kind of people I think they are," Malcolm said just before they went through the boarding gate, "then Dottie and I can expect a visit soon. Maybe I can do something to make them back off."

"Be careful," Joey said.

"Don't worry about me," he said. "I'll do what I can. It might help." Then he hugged them, too. Dottie hugged them again, then they had to go.

* * *

It was an hour before noon on New Year's Day when they caught the taxi in front of the airport in Santa Barbara. There were some college kids on the plane, coming back from their Christmas vacations. And like Joey and Nina, they were dressed casually with jeans, T-shirts or sweatshirts and backpacks. Nina was proud of herself for the clothes she'd chosen for them. They fit right in.

"Well, what do you say, think we should catch a taxi to this Isla Vista place and try to find her house?" Joey said.

"I've been thinking about that, and I don't think it's a good idea. There's probably Secret Service people watching the place. We wouldn't even get close."

"I don't know. I bet she's got lots of college friends that come over."

"What if Red Beard was a Secret Service agent?"

"He didn't look like any Secret Service agent I ever

saw."

"When's the last time you saw a Secret Service agent?" Nina laughed. "In the movies?"

"Well, yeah."

"If she has someone protecting her, they'd have to fit in. It could be anybody. We have to be careful."

"Yeah," Joey said. "But Red Beard wouldn't fit in anywhere. He wasn't any agent. But I agree. We have to be careful."

"We should go to the marina. The articles I read said she goes sailing alone. She's practicing for when she finishes school and takes off on her solo sail."

"Okay," Joey said. "The marina it is. Then we play it by ear."

"What?" Nina fiddled with her ear.

"It means—"

"I know what it means. I was just kidding."

* * *

Paul Snelling got off the elevator on the fifth floor, checked a room number, then turned left. For the second time he was visiting Clayton in the Mariposa Hospital. Only this time it was serious. He'd been medivacked down to Phoenix during the night and was not expected to live.

He found the room, entered. Clayton's eyes were open, but Snelling didn't think he was seeing anything.

"You look horrible." Snelling shook his head, moved close to the bed.

"Are you the one I've been waiting for?"

Snelling turned toward the voice, found an old man,

thin, head a few sizes too large for his body. He was dressed in Dockers and a yellow Polo shirt with brown loafers on his feet. He looked well off, like a doctor, but instinct said he was no doctor.

"And you would be?" Snelling said.

"Morrison."

"Ah, the '56 Ford."

"The same," Morrison said.

"Did you do this?" Snelling turned back to Clayton. There was an IV drip, but other than that no extraordinary measures were being used to save his life. Clayton had no living relatives, but had left written instructions with Snelling and a few others years ago that he didn't want life support, no machines keeping him alive. His wishes were being honored.

"No, my wife's dog had a hand in it, but mostly it was one of the girls you've been chasing." Morrison pulled a pack of Marlboros out of his shirt pocket, put one to his lips and flicked a Bic.

"Hospital, No smoking."

"You guys been going to an awful lot of trouble, chasing two little girls to hell and gone," Morrison said, ignoring the remark about the smoking. "I gotta think you got a good reason for that."

"We do."

"Dirty pictures of the president's daughter ain't no good reason. Tell me it's something more. Something that makes sense. Tell me they're carrying secret microfilm that endangers the free world as we know it. Or tell me one of 'em's sick with a virus that's gonna wipe out the planet if we don't catch her and cure her. Can you tell me something like that?"

"No."

"So it really is about some dirty pictures. Kind of makes you feel soiled, doesn't it?"

"Mr. Morrison, why don't you tell me what it is you came to tell me."

"Your man's gonna die today. You lost another in Tobago, I hear."

"Mr. Morrison, unless you want to be charged with obstructing, maybe even murder," Snelling nodded toward Clayton, "you better tell me what I want to know and you better do it quick."

"Look at me, young man." Morrison took a drag on his cigarette. "Look into my eyes. Do you really think I'm the kind of man you can bully with words?"

"I can make good my threat."

"Then let me make one of my own. As we speak a friend of mine has his finger on his keyboard. If anything happens to those girls, or me or mine, then he sends a photo to about a million sites on the internet."

"You would do that, put an innocent girl's pictures out there like that?" Snelling fought to contain his temper. "She didn't know what she was doing. She was drugged!"

"Not hers. Yours." Morrison took another hit from the cigarette, then dropped it on the clean floor, stepped on it. He was a neat man. Not the kind who would dirty something without reason. He was sending a message and Snelling was afraid he understood it.

"What are you saying?" Snelling said.

"We took your picture when you entered the

hospital."

"Not possible," Snelling said, but he knew it was. "You would have had to take hundreds to make sure you got one of me."

"Digital camera, lots of flashcards. No problem."

"I see."

"So here's my threat. The message with the photo reads something like, 'Do you know this man? He raped my daughter. Any information held in confidence.' Then there's an e-mail address. Someone will answer. You hurt those girls, I hurt you. That's the deal."

"Did you think that would frighten me? It's the kind of threat people like me live with all our lives."

"There's more. You got family, I'll find 'em. What you do to those girls, I'll do to whoever you hold dear."

Snelling stared into Morrison's eyes. The old man was calm as a flat sea. Not a shake. Not a shiver. He had balls and he would do what he said.

"And Mick Sapphire? He married them both, you know. What about him?"

"Him, you can kill." Morrison took another cigarette from his pocket. "But don't do it to protect the world from some dirty pictures. Kill him because he needs killing."

"About the pictures?"

"I've said all I came to say." The old man stooped over, picked up the butt, started for the door.

"You seem like a decent man. Tell me where the pictures are, so no one else gets hurt."

"I wish I could, but I'm not a snitch." He laughed. "Besides, it looks like your side's the one taking all the hits." He walked to the door. "Call me when it's over, maybe we'll have a beer. You can pet the dog." Then he was out the door and gone.

Snelling thought about going after him. But decided against it. He knew where the girls would go next. They'd found the pictures. They'd go to Suzi. They'd want to give them back, because basically they were like that old man. Good people. It was the bastard husband he had to worry about. He was still out there.

The jet would have him in Santa Barbara in about an hour-and-a-half. It was a good thing he'd gotten a new pilot as soon as he'd heard about Clayton.

* * *

The marina wasn't what Nina was used to. Of course she'd only been to two. The one back home and the one where *Satisfaction* was in Trinidad. This was different, it was a marina for people who didn't live on board. There was no hotel attached, no bar. There was no frantic activity on the dock. No dock workers busy with varnish work, deck work or spit and polish work. No cabinet makers, sail makers or diesel mechanics. No boat work at all. Just boats rocking gently in their slips.

The boats, mostly sail, came in all sizes from twenty up to seventy feet. Nina had learned how to tell the rich boats from the poor boats. These were mostly rich boats. Not boats, Nina thought. Toys. These were rich men's toys. She looked over the marina and saw no wind generators, solar panels or SSB antennas mounted on the stern of any of the boats she could see. Essentials for most cruising boats and noticeable in their absence from these boats that never strayed very far from their home port. She did however see quite a few radar antennas, then she remembered reading about the California fog.

"It must be nice to be rich," Joey said.

"I was just thinking the same thing," Nina said.

"There it is," Joey said. "*Babycakes*"

"So small."

"Twenty-one feet."

"And she's going to sail it around the world. She must be pretty brave."

"Yeah," Joey said.

"Ladies, what a surprise." It was Mick. He was barefoot and was wearing a neon green, baggy bathing suit with a bright yellow windbreaker. It was almost like he was crying out to be noticed. Then Nina realized that he wasn't standing out, he was blending in. Anyone who didn't belong here, wouldn't dress like that.

"What are you doing here?" Joey said.

"Just move along," he said. "I've got a pistol with a silencer under my jacket and it's pointed at Nina's belly. Be a shame to hurt the baby."

"The baby's dead," Nina said.

"You could be too if you don't move along." Nina couldn't believe it. He didn't bat an eye when he heard. He didn't care.

"What if I scream?" Nina said.

"Then I'll shoot you right here."

Nina took a quick look around. She saw a man way down at the other end of the dock. Too far. Mick could shoot her and push her into the water in an instant.

"Come on, Nina. Let's see what he has to say for

himself."

"Smart, Joey." He led them away from *Babycakes*, down the dock. "Stop here, the old raceboat, get on."

Joey climbed aboard a forty foot boat. Nina followed her up. Mick came last.

"Now what?" Joey said.

"Let's go below." He motioned toward the companionway with the gun.

Below, Nina saw that whoever owned the boat was rebuilding it, making it new again. There was a settee on both sides of the salon, a separate area for eating, a new stainless steel sink in the galley. He had them take off the backpacks, then picked up some meter long lengths of rope that were on the starboard settee next to a dive tank, mask, fins and a buoyancy control vest. "You're good with knots, Nina," he said, "so tie Joey's hands behind her back." Nina hesitated and he added. "Go ahead, I'll shoot her if you don't."

Nina did as ordered, then he commanded Joey to sit on the floor in the middle of the salon, had Nina turn and he tied her hands, then he had her sit, too. Then he tied her back to back with Joey, hands and arms bound together. Nina was good with knots, he was better. The ropes were good and tight. Nina was afraid it would cut off the circulation to her hands.

With the girls secure, Mick went through the packs, dumping out the contents. Joey's first, then Nina's where he found the camera bag.

"When I saw you two, I knew you'd found the pictures. There was no other reason you'd be here. He took the camera out, put his eye to the viewfinder and previewed the photos. "I don't need them anymore, but they'll be nice souvenirs." He seemed satisfied with himself.

"What do you mean, you don't need them anymore?" Joey said.

"Little Suzi Sailor is going to give me two million dollars today." He looked at his watch. "Pretty soon now."

"They'll come after you," Joey said.

"They don't know who I am and Little Suzi ceases to be a problem at exactly six o'clock."

"What do you mean?" Nina said.

"I'll have the money, so she won't be a problem."

"I don't understand," Nina said.

"She doesn't remember me." He went to the refrigerator, took out a steak, then went to the galley, lit the burner, then turned back to the girls.

"When did you start eating meat?" Joey said.

"Sometimes I'm a vegetarian, sometimes I'm not. Depends on who I'm with." He pulled a cast iron skillet out from a cupboard next to the stove, put it on the burner.

There was something wrong with him, Nina thought. Only a crazy person could tie two people up, then calmly cook a steak. In a few seconds the pan was hot enough and he dropped the meat on it. "T-Bone," Mick said as he opened a can of spinach.

"My plan's really beautiful in it's simplicity. I got Suzi Walcott's private e-mail address the night we took the pictures. I had her get the money and hold it till I e-mailed her again. Then I e-mailed her this morning and told her what to do. She's gonna take the cash and sail out from the marina due west for one hour, then she's gonna turn around and head back. I'll stop her somewhere along the way and she'll hand over the money."

"And you're going to wear the dive mask so she doesn't recognize you?" Nina said.

"Something like that."

"That isn't right." The steak smelled heavenly to Nina. She'd only picked at the food on the plane and was hungry now.

"Jesus, Nina, grow up." He turned it and the sizzling sound had her salivating. Then he dumped the spinach in with the steak. Nina squirmed against the rope as Mick emptied the skillet onto a plate.

"I don't get it," Joey said. "Your family's rich. You can have anything you want. This doesn't make sense."

"My family," he said. Nina heard the disgust in his voice. "If it wouldn't have been for the inheritance left me from my grandmother, I wouldn't have had the money for *Satisfaction*. I wouldn't have been able to live the last five years."

"You're not rich?" Joey said.

"My father's rich. He doesn't plan on letting me have a cent till he dies. Maybe not even then if he doesn't think I measure up. And I won't. I've got two sisters and an older brother, all lawyers following in Daddy's footsteps. Brown nosers. They'll measure up."

Brown noser, that was a word Nina knew. "So you doped up Suzi, took those pictures and are going to steal money from her so you don't have to brown nose? I'd rather be married to an ass kisser than someone who would do that."

He laughed, then ate his meal, slurping the spinach through his gleaming teeth. Finished, he looked at his watch, got up from the table and started toward the companionway.

"She should be pulling away from her slip about now." He went up the steps, stuck his head out the hatch, went up another step, till he was out of the boat from the waist up.

Nina thought he was going to leave them there, but he didn't. From her position on the floor, looking up at him, she saw the calluses on his feet, thick, pad like, like a dog. She used to admire him because of his tough feet, but she'd never really looked at the ugly calluses that gave him the power to put out a cigarette with his naked heel. Seeing him now, she saw there was a lot of ugliness about the man she'd allowed herself to love.

"Turn a little to your right," Joey whispered.

"What?" Nina whispered back.

"I think I can reach the pocket knife in my front pocket."

"Okay." Nina had forgotten about the Swiss Army knives. Dumb. It had been her idea to buy them. She turned and Joey tried to snake her hands around her side to get them in her pocket.

"I can't reach, turn some more."

Nina turned some more and now the women were sitting side by side, but, with their hands tied together, Joey could only get a couple fingers in her pocket.

"My pants are too tight. Can you get yours?"

"Yeah," Nina whispered. How come she hadn't

remembered her knife? Stupid.

"Hurry!" Joey's whisper was urgent.

Nina didn't quite fill out her jeans as Joey did and she was able to get her hand in the pocket, close her fingers around the knife. She pulled it out as Mick started back down the ladder. She wrapped her hand around it even as she scooted back to her original position and they were back to back again.

He came down the hatch, crossed the salon to the nav table, picked up a pack of Camel Lights. He tapped one out, turned to the girls. "She left right on schedule."

He started back to the companionway and Nina remembered that he didn't smoke below on a boat. A mortal sin, he called it.

"You're not going to hurt her, are you?" Joey said.

"What? Me?" Mick stopped, went back to the nav station, dropped the cigarette.

"You're not, are you?" Joey said again. This isn't the time for conversation, Nina wanted to shout. Let him go outside and smoke. But Joey kept on. "Because if you did, they'd never stop looking, they'd find you."

"Nobody's getting hurt," Mick said. Then he flopped down on the port settee and picked up a book.

"You're not going to read and ignore us?" Joey said.

"Yes I am. I've got a little time to kill and I'm at a good part." He propped a pillow against the back of the settee and laid back with the book on his chest as if he were at home by a fire, stretched out on a couch. "Close your eyes, get some rest." He opened the book, started to read.

But Nina knew that the slightest movement on her

part and he'd be off the settee in a flash of an instant. There was nothing she could do, not till he went topside to smoke.

CHAPTER
TWENTY-TWO

SUZI WALCOTT INHALED the salty air as she approached the channel buoy. It was 4:30, the yellow sun was already turning orange as it started its slide out of the sky. She passed the buoy, laughed at the seal sunning herself on it as it rocked back and forth with the gentle waves.

"Real cool, Suzi," she mumbled to herself. "You're going out to meet a blackmailer and you can still laugh."

She thought about her mother, who never laughed anymore and she remembered how it used to be. She'd been five years old when her mom married the junior senator from the smallest state in the union. Her real father had been killed by a drunk driver before she was old enough to remember him. Jason had been the only father she'd ever known. He'd adopted her, treated her as if she were really his and she loved him more than anything in the world.

And that was why she was out here now. When she'd gotten that e-mail with the horrible pictures on it, she went straight to her mother, who said they had to pay, had to do anything to keep the press from finding out and ruining her father's re-election. And above all, they had to keep it from him, because he was the type of man that would quit the presidency in an instant to protect his family. Suzi had to agree with her mother, Dad would call out the Army, Navy and the Marines, waste the blackmailers, quit the job and damn the consequences.

The blackmailers had wanted her to take two million dollars to her Isla Vista home and wait for further instructions by e-mail and that's what her mother told her to do. Fortunately Gwendolyn Walcott came from money, had plenty and could afford to take two million dollars out of the bank without missing it. However Suzi thought that her mom must be doing something behind the scenes, because not only was Gwen Walcott a manipulator, she really, really liked her money.

The seal barked again and Suzi realized she was too close to the buoy. For a second it looked like it was going to hop in the boat, but she pushed the tiller a bit, giving the channel marker a wider berth. Past the buoy, she pushed the tiller to port and set a heading of two-four-zero.

For the thousandth time she wondered if the men with the pictures meant her harm, but as she had all those thousand other times, she shrugged it off. Whoever they were, they just wanted the money. They'd gone to too much trouble to keep it quiet, out of the press and away from the police. The world would never rest if they harmed the president's daughter.

Besides, they were getting away with it and it chilled her to think about it, as did the breeze that was picking up. She had the city at her back as she turned to starboard, into the wind, to raise the main. She'd sailed out of the channel under headsail alone, as usual. With the boat in irons, she went to the mast, took the main halyard off a cleat and hauled up the sail, then cleated it off.

This was what she lived for, to be on the water. She looked out at the boats at anchor, live aboards mostly, and envied them. She saw a Spanish flag, a French one too. Small boats, bigger than *Babycakes*, but less than forty-five feet. International cruisers, today's hippies, sea going gypsies that had given up the air-conditioned mall, the oh so wonderful smell of a new car, beer and hot dogs at a major league ball game—she smiled, or in their cases, a soccer game. They'd walked away from a hundred channels on the TV, the latest electronic gadgets and a new computer every year. God, how she longed to join them.

The flapping sails snapped her out of her reverie and brought her to the task at hand. If she had to be on the water, she might as well enjoy it. The wind was coming out of the southwest, a close reach. She went back to the tiller, turned her face into the wind and sniffed the breeze, then she pushed the tiller and adjusted the main as *Babycakes* heeled over, picked up speed and sliced through the sea. Spray splashed over the side and Suzi tingled the way she did every time she was on the water.

* * *

It took fifteen minutes for the nicotine urge to get Mick to put the book down. It was 4:45 by the shipboard clock next to the barometer above the chart table. Nina thought her hands were going to fall off they were so numb. She watched with wary eyes as he picked up the cigarette and headed for the companionway. He didn't even tell them to be quiet while he was on deck. Not a word to them, not a glance. It was as if they weren't there. As if they were roaches, unseen, unwanted. He was crazy. He was cold, too. How could she ever, ever have let him touch her, make a baby?

The second he was through the hatch, she went to work at the knife, but her hands were slippery with sweat and she couldn't get it open. She tried digging her thumbnail in the tiny groove in the blade, but still she couldn't open it.

"Let me try," Joey whispered and Nina slipped the knife into her hands. And from the frantic way she was jerking those hands behind her back, Nina guessed Joey was having the same problem.

"Can you get it?"

Mick started to come back down. No, Nina wanted to scream. It was too quick. He couldn't possibly have smoked the whole cigarette by now.

"How's it going today?" some man up above said, talking to Mick.

"I've been better," Mick said to the man. "Been worse too." He went back up on deck.

"Come on, Joey!" Nina said.

"Got it."

"Hurry!" Nina heard the blade flick open.

"I'm hurrying!" Joey had the blade open now and Nina felt the blood rush to her hands the instant Joey cut the rope. "When he starts to come back down the ladder, grab him by the foot and jerk."

"Okay." Nina didn't spare a second to question Joey. She had no time, because Mick was coming back down even as she pushed herself up from the floor.

"What?" he said when Nina grabbed his calloused foot. "Fuck!" he said when she jerked him on down. He fell to the floor with a crash, arms and legs akimbo. But he righted himself instantly, like a jaguar. And like a jaguar, he was about to pounce on Nina when Joey smashed him in the head with the heavy iron skillet.

He sank back to the floor with a thud, but he pushed himself back up as quick as a feline recovering from a cat hater's kick. His face, formed by rage, was wolf-like in it's fury. He was going to kill them and he was strong enough to do it. But Joey didn't give him a chance, she whacked him again and this time the pan echoed with an almost bell ringing sound as Mick fell back to the floor. Again he tried to get up, blood covering half his face now, slower now, but just as menacing and Joey leapt toward him, swinging the pan like Joana's wicked tennis racket, connecting with the side of his head. Once again that horrible bell ringing sound and once again Mick thudded to the floor.

But this time he didn't get up.

Joey was breathing like a race horse.

Nina was holding her breath.

Mick wasn't breathing at all.

"Is he dead?" Nina took a breath at last.

Joey waited a few seconds and Nina saw that she was catching her breath, then she reached down and felt the side of his neck.

"Yeah, he's dead."

* * *

Paul Snelling called Gwen Walcott, the First Lady, from the jet and got the cell number for Claudia Dowling, Suzi Walcott's Secret Service agent. He had wanted to keep the Service out of it, but the play was now moving to Santa Barbara, too close to the president's daughter for comfort.

Dowling told him that Suzi was safe in her home. Paul said to make sure. Dowling did and reported back that Suzi had pulled a switch with a girlfriend, Linda Drummond. Under Dowling's angry questioning, the Drummond girl had admitted to helping Suzi elude Dowling in the past.

Dowling agreed to meet the jet when he arrived in Santa Barbara.

* * *

Suzi checked the time on the GPS mounted on the binnacle, 5:00, thirty minutes till she was supposed to turn around and start sailing back. She sighed. Alone on the water, headed out to an uncertain fate, she wondered if she'd done the right thing. She sighed again.

"Oh well, Suzi. Too late to back out now."

* * *

"Dead," Nina said. "Now what are we going to do?"

"We have to get this boat to sea, now!" Joey thought she knew what Mick had done and she was afraid.

"What about him?"

"We don't have any time for him. We've got to get Suzi Walcott off *Babycakes!*"

"I'm sorry," Nina said. "But I'm more worried about us right now. Mick's dead, so he's not going to go after her. She can keep her money and live her fairy tale life. But we've got him," Nina nodded towards Mick's body, "and Red Beard to answer for. We're the one's in trouble, not Suzi Walcott."

"No, she's the one in trouble!" Joey was breathing hard. She slowed it down, caught her breath. "I think there's a bomb on her boat and it's going to go off at six o'clock."

"What are you talking about, bomb?" Nina said.

"See that?" Joey pointed to the diving gear on the port settee. "He was a Navy Seal, a demolition man."

"I don't understand," Nina said.

"A Seal is like a commando, you know, like Rambo. A demolition man is a bomb expert."

"Now I understand." Then, "He said Suzi wouldn't be a problem after 6:00. You think he put a bomb on her boat?"

"Yeah, I do."

"We should call someone, the police."

"Nobody's gonna believe us, not after they find out about Mick. Once they know he's dead, they won't listen to a word we say, especially after they find out we're in the country illegally."

"He said she was going to sail due west for an hour, then turn around. Can you sail this boat? Can we get to her in time?"

"Mick thought he could, so we probably can. But we have to go now. We can't wait around."

"So, let's go!" Nina looked up at the time. It was 5:15. "Let's go now!"

* * *

"Agent Dowling, I presume." Snelling checked his Citizen as he deplaned, it was 5:20. Then he took her in with a quick glance. It was easy to see why she had been picked for the Dolphin detail. She looked like a college kid herself. Snelling wondered if she attended all of Suzi's classes with her. Was Dowling getting a second college education at the government's expense?

"And you're Paul Snelling. Your reputation precedes you."

"I don't have a reputation."

"My mother worked with you." She was walking fast, trying to keep up with his long strides as he headed for the terminal.

"Your mother?" He stopped on the tarmac, looked her in the eye. "Who?"

"Lily Nuygen," she said and instantly he was

transported back to a rainy morning in a green jungle. He was behind enemy lines, a bullet in the thigh, death above in the form of a Russian pistol in the NVA's hand. The soldier in black pajamas squinted his eyes closed and Snelling knew it was all over. He was about to learn the answer to the ultimate question. Then out of nowhere the silent wraith that was Lily Nuygen flew at the NVA. She snapped his pistol away with her right hand, even as she was slitting his throat with the knife in her left.

"You're Vietnamese? You don't look it." Maybe a little Eurasian, he thought, but even with his eye, he'd've missed it if she hadn't spoken up. "You're small, but otherwise you look as American as the next person."

"I don't know if I appreciate your attitude."

"Oh, stop. I'm too old to be politically correct. I was just stating the facts as I see 'em. Besides, I'm the one that's supposed to have an attitude here."

"What do you mean?"

"You lost your charge."

"Now you stop. I'm one agent. I can't do anything without Suzi's whole hearted cooperation. She ditches me all the time. There's nothing I can do about it and you should know it."

"How is your mother?"

"She died last year."

"I'm sorry, I didn't know." He wondered how much she knew about her mother, decided to say something. "She saved my life one night a long time ago."

"I know all about it."

"I never got a chance to repay her."

"You got her on that helicopter. You're the reason she

made it to America and met my dad."

"I didn't think she knew about that."

"My mother knew a lot more than you guys ever gave her credit for. I do too."

"What are you saying?"

"I know that Suzi's in trouble and that somebody is letting her twist in the wind. I know she should have ten times the protection till this is all over, whatever it is. But I'm glad they at least sent you."

Snelling thought for about a half a second, then said, "Remember Trinidad? Suzi and the first lady were there for that sailboat race."

"Yeah."

"Remember Suzi snuck out?"

"She does that a lot."

"I'm not saying it's your fault, but that particular night Ambassador Atwood's kid, along with Harry Sapphire's kid, drugged her and took dirty pictures." For a quick second he thought about telling her about Atwood's death and the fate he had planned for Sapphire, but candor only went so far, no matter who her mother was.

"Oh no!"

"They didn't think we'd figure out who they were and they sent a crazy ransom demand. Have Suzi bring two million dollars to California and wait to be called. Someday they'd ring her up and arrange for an exchange, pictures for the money."

"And her father's going along with it?" She glared up at Snelling with the fieriest black eyes he'd ever seen.

"No. It's his wife, she gave your Dolphin the money.

She doesn't want the president to know. She doesn't think he's capable of making a sound judgment where Suzi's concerned, thinks he might do something that'll cost him his job.

"What a bitch," Dowling said.

"You are your mother's daughter. She said what she felt and damn the cost. It got her in a lot of trouble sometimes."

"Usually I hold it in, but I'm pretty pissed off right now and I'm getting madder by the second."

Yeah, he thought. She may not look Vietnamese, but she had the temper. Little as she was, he didn't want to get on her wrong side. He looked around the tarmac, heard the whirling blades before he saw the Coast Guard helicopter. "That for us?"

"Yeah, we better go."

"We need it?" He didn't want to get in another helicopter.

"Her boat's not in her slip. She's at sea somewhere."

"Christ." It was going down, the exchange. Mick Sapphire was a Navy Seal, he was doing it at sea, his element, where he thought he'd be safe. Well, he wouldn't be safe. Snelling started for the helicopter at a full run. To his surprise Dowling matched his speed.

"Go!" she said as she hopped on board after him. The pilot lifted off. There were three guardsmen beside the pilot aboard and they looked like they were prepared for an air-sea rescue. He hoped it wouldn't come to that.

* * *

At 5:30, after Suzi had sailed the required hour, she

started to tack around to a course of zero-nine-zero, due east. It was somewhere on this reciprocal that she expected to meet the man who had taken the photos. Though she didn't now who it was, not for sure, she suspected it was David Atwood's friend. She didn't remember much about him, not even his name, but she could almost picture his face. He'd been good looking. She remembered that. But try as she might, she couldn't remember anything more from that evening.

She completed the tack and now she had the wind at her back. She'd make better time heading home than she had going out. Home, she thought, where exactly was that? The mansion in Providence, the White House, her apartment in Isla Vista, or *Babycakes*? She spent more time on the small boat than she did any of the other places, planned on spending five to seven years on her when she sailed her around the world. And she would do that, no matter what her mother said. She'd forced her into going to college first, but the very instant she graduated, she was gone, even if her dad did get elected to a second term and was still president. She'd change the name of her boat if she had to, dye her hair, whatever, but she was going to go.

Ever since she was a little girl she'd been a collector and reader of charts. She grew up sailing small boats and loving the sea. Her daydreams had been about being there, sailing there. And *there* was wherever the wind took her. South America, Africa, the South Pacific, she wanted to see it all, sail it all.

The on shore breeze had died down, the seas were calm. *Babycakes* was sliding through the water the way only a monohull with a deep keel could, steady, with a quick response to the tiller. Suzi's hair was blowing around her face as she watched some clouds move in. Maybe the wind might pick back up, after all. Maybe she'd even get some rain. Ordinarily that would get her heart pumping, as she loved sailing in weather, but not today. Today she wanted calm seas, so she could sail alongside her blackmailer's boat, toss the sail bag to him and be on her way and have this chapter of her life finally over.

* * *

Nina jumped off the boat to the pier, pulled the dock lines off the cleats as Joey started up the engine. She heard the diesel rumble to life as she noticed the name on the bow, *Reaper.* She tossed the lines on deck, was climbing aboard as Joey backed the boat out of the slip. What they were doing was crazy. Two fugitive women chasing after the president's daughter with a dead man on board. Craziness. Was that a word? She thought so.

On deck Nina jumped into the cockpit as Joey spun the wheel while looking back over her shoulder. The boats were packed in tight, sandwiched close together like those little silver fish in a flat can.

"You're going to hit the boat on the left." Nina felt like she was going to pee her panties.

"I'm not gonna hit anything!" Joey seemed so sure of herself.

That was good, Nina thought, then she heard the crunch.

"Oops," Joey said.

A head popped out of the boat they'd hit. He looked to be in his fifties, like one of those American country and western singers. Silver hair, not hair, more like a great horse's mane. Silver beard, trimmed like they do in a beauty shop, but no cowboy hat, instead a Chicago Bulls baseball hat.

"What the faaa—" He saw the two women and didn't finish the word.

"We'll take care of the damages when we get back," Joey said. Though they were still going backwards, they were only a few meters apart.

"No problem," the man said. He pulled off the hat, swept his arm in front of himself. Old guys like to do that kind of stuff, Nina thought

"How do you get outta here?" Joey said.

"Go straight, maybe a quarter mile, make your first right, it's the channel to the open water. Can't miss it."

"Thanks." Joey shifted gears and they started to move forward.

"Anything for a lady," he called out as they started to move away. Then "Any chance we might get together later? Have dinner or something?" Now he had to shout as they were farther away.

"No chance at all," Joey shouted back. Nina heard the man laugh.

"Why do they call them baseball hats if basketball players wear them?"

"What?" Joey said.

"You know, the man, he had a Chicago Bulls baseball hat on. The Bulls are a basketball team."

"How do you know that?" Joey said.

"Joana and I watch NBA basketball."

"Really?"

"We get basketball in Brazil."

"That's not what I meant. I meant it's unusual for girls to be interested in sports."

"Good looking men, strong bodies, lots of sweat. What's so unusual about that?"

"Nothing?" Joey laughed. Then, "I don't know about the hats. Maybe it's because baseball players had them first."

"What's *Reaper* mean?"

"You really are the question girl, but now isn't the time. We have to get to Suzi Walcott's boat before she goes boom."

"Just this last question. What's it mean?"

"I don't know. I think it must be like a sickle."

"What's—"

"I know, what's a sickle? A sickle is like a long curved blade attached to a pole. You use it for harvesting grain, like wheat." Joey turned the boat a fraction. They were motoring through a narrow channel, boats were docked on both sides of them. Some longer than others. To Nina it looked like threading a needle, but Joey didn't seem to be having any trouble. "Then there's the Grim Reaper."

"I don't like the sound of that."

"Yeah, the Grim Reaper is death."

"It's also the name of this boat."

"Swell," Joey said.

Then the engine died.

CHAPTER
TWENTY-THREE

"**NINA, COME BACK HERE** and steer the boat!" Joey tried not to shout, but couldn't help herself. The GPS said it was 5:35. If she was right, they had less than half an hour to find Suzi and get her off that boat before it blew up. An impossible task, but they had to try.

"I don't know how!" Nina's long hair was blowing in the breeze. Her hazel eyes were intense. She reminded Joey of the fox running from the hounds, the odds against it huge, but it keeps running.

"Just keep it pointed the same direction we're going.

It's not any harder than driving a car, you turn the wheel and the boat turns."

"I told you, I've never driven a car."

"Oh, yeah." Joey looked at the boats in their slips to the left and the right of them. The channel between them was narrow, one little slip up and they'd be scraping hulls. And all those boats looked expensive. To Joey's eyes it seemed Americans were all rich. "Come on, Nina, we don't have time to argue."

"Coming." Nina moved behind the wheel.

"Make little turns. Treat it gentle," Joey said.

"Okay." Nina grabbed the big wheel with both hands. "I'm ready."

"Stay cool," Joey said, "because we gotta keep it together." Joey was talking as much to herself as she was to Nina and she knew it.

"Cool as a big pickle."

"Right," Joey said. Then, "I'm gonna unfurl the jib." She turned her face into the breeze. It was coming from the southwest, they were headed south. They could sail forty-five degrees to the wind. Thank God.

"What are you doing?" Nina said and her voice reassured Joey. Answering the girl's questions as she worked was a good way to keep her mind focused and if she'd ever needed to be focused in her life, now was the time.

"Taking off the lazy sheet." Joey took the line off the big winch.

"What?"

"The rope on the starboard side that holds the headsail rolled up tight." Joey held the line up in her hand for Nina to see, then she dropped it so that it could run free. "Now I'm gonna winch in on the port side till the sail starts to unfurl and the wind takes it, then I'm going to crank it in, till we get the best angle of attack."

"Whatever you're going to do, hurry!" Nina said.

"Yeah!" Joey slapped a winch handle in the winch and started grinding. She got the sail about a quarter of the way off the roller when the wind took it and it unfurled, billowing out with a whoosh, a full genoa. Good, Joey thought, because she was going to need lots of sail to get the boat moving in the piddling wind they had inside the harbor. Joey didn't know the boat, but *Reaper* was a fin keeled sloop and she looked fast. She wouldn't be surprised if her owner raced her. She looked over the deck, took a good look at the condition of the line, the rust starting to creep around the stanchions. No, the owner didn't race her. Whoever he was, he apparently didn't have enough time for the boat. Once started, if left alone, rust moves pretty fast. It never got a chance on *Satisfaction*, Joey saw to that.

"How we doing?" Nina said.

"It'll be a second," Joey said. Once they were out in open water they'd fly, but would they be in time?

"Okay, we're moving," Nina said as Joey cranked the jib in tight. "Now what?"

"In the best of circumstances we should have the boat aiming into the wind to get the main up, but the wind is light, so I'm gonna try it."

She went to the mast. If she had the time, she'd wait till they were out of the channel to bring up the main, but they had no engine and were in a hurry.

She took the main halyard from its winch and started hauling the sail up. The wind, light as it was, took the sail when she got it about a third of the way up the mast. Halfway up and it was harder to pull on the line. Sweat ran down her forehead, into her eyes. It was dripping under her arms, sliding down her side, cold sweat, chilling her.

She dropped to the deck, wrapped the halyard around the winch, snugged it into the self-tailing jaws and started grinding. Hard work, but she struggled it up.

"Joey!" Nina side swiped a boat with a crunch.

"Hey!" an angry owner shouted.

"Back in hour. Have insurance!" Joey yelled.

"You're not going anywhere!" the man shouted. "He was a young blond man, shirtless, rippling muscles accented by a butter-basted tan. He reminded Joey of those chickens you see roasting on a spit in the supermarket.

"An hour," Joey said again as they steadily moved away.

"I'm calling the cops!'"

"Go fuck yourself!" Nina called back.

"That did it." He went below, to make good his threat Joey was sure.

"Go fuck yourself?" Joey said as she jumped down into the cockpit.

"I know American swear words."

"Nina, you made him mad. He's calling the police."

"Why, because we hit his boat?" She turned the wheel to avoid another screeching side swipe. "How much more trouble can we be in?"

"Good point." Joey adjusted the mainsheet. "Okay, I see the channel. We're gonna have to tack."

"Tell me what to do."

"When I tell you, turn right ninety degrees and drive the boat right down the center of the channel."

"I can do that."

Joey got the jib sheets ready, took the port sheet out of the self-tailing jaws, held it snug on the winch. "Now!" She took the sheet off the winch, let it go, wrapped the starboard sheet on its winch, hauled the sheet in with a frantic effort while Nina swung *Reaper* to port.

The headsail came across, as did the main. Both sails caught the wind and again they were sailing forty-five degrees off the wind, only now it was coming off the port side, and there was more of it in the channel. *Reaper* picked up speed.

"Okay," Joey said as she stepped back into the cockpit," I'm gonna go below and see what's wrong with that engine."

"I already know," Nina said.

"What do you mean?"

"There's two gas gauges." Nina pointed to the engine gauges. "One of them says empty."

"Diesel," Joey said, looking at the gauges. "Boats run on diesel."

"So what are you going to do?"

"Go down and switch tanks." Below deck Joey tried not to look at Mick's body as she made her way to the engine room. She saw the fuel filters and the tank cock next to them. She flipped it from the left to the right tank, then went back up on deck.

"We're moving now!" Nina was bobbing up and down on her feet, hair blowing in the brisk breeze. They had wind in the sails.

"I'll take over." Joey moved behind the wheel. They had the wind, but she didn't want to depend on that alone. She checked the engine gauges. *Reaper* had an ignition button, no key. She pushed it and heard the starter grind, but the engine didn't start. There was air in the lines. She should have looked for tools below, bled it out, but she didn't have the time. She pulled her finger off the button.

"Do you know where west is?" Nina had remembered what Mick had said.

"Yeah," Joey said as they passed a seal basking in what was left of the sun on the marker buoy. "West is a course of two-four-zero." They weren't too far off course and Joey turned to two hundred and forty degrees as soon as they passed the buoy.

"Look!" Nina pointed up, but Joey heard the helicopter before she saw it.

* * *

Snelling scanned the sea below. It was a clear day and apparently a good day for being on the water, because it was 5:45 and several of the boats under sail down there weren't showing any sign of heading back to harbor.

He checked out the boats at anchor as they flew over and wondered what it must be like to live on a sailboat. Going where you wanted, when you wanted. A chill tingled up his spine, they'd have no government, international sailors. No respect for the police. If they were unhappy in one country, they'd simply pick up and sail on to the next. They probably didn't pay taxes, didn't send their kids to school, didn't vote or go to church. That tingle pricked him a little more. They must think themselves above the law. Hell, as long as they didn't kill anybody, they probably were. He sighed, because he envied them.

"Can you tell which one is *Babycakes?*" He squinted his eyes against the blast of wind coming in the open door and had to talk loud to be heard above the rotors.

"From up here they all look the same!" Dowling's voice didn't carry like his, she was shouting. "Can you take us down some?" she said to the pilot. Then as he brought them lower, "We're more interested in the boats on the move. She won't be at anchor."

She was right, Snelling thought, they did all look the same, dozens of triangular white sails slicing through an azure canvas. The sea was gentle today, no hint of the kind of storm he'd experienced the last time he was in a helicopter searching for a sailboat. Could that have only been a few days ago? It seemed a lifetime.

He looked back toward the land. High mountains, dark shades of brown and green in the distance, jagged peaks reaching to the evening sky, a majestic contrast to the flat sea below. Soon it would be dusk, but it was a diamond clear day and he could see snow topping the mountains in the far distance. He thought of the snow in Prescott where Clayton had died, then he journeyed his mind back to Trinidad and Tobago where one of the local policemen he had hired had died. From the beginning, with the killing of David Atwood, he'd handled the case badly. Atwood had to die, but not that way. He should have consigned his body to the deep as Joey Sapphire had done. But he had to get cute. He looked away from the mountains, but in his own defense, how could he have known those women would be so resilient, so resourceful, so dogged in their determination?

Well, finally, he was ahead of them.

"There's a boat leaving the channel, too big to be *Babycakes*," Dowling shouted. She was looking down at the ocean through the open door of the chopper, straining at her harness, as if even a few more inches would enhance the image she was seeing of the boat below through her binoculars.

"Why that boat?" Snelling said.

"It's too late for someone to go out for a day sail," she said. Then, "Never mind, false alarm. The boat's crewed by two women."

"What?" Snelling shouted.

* * *

The helicopter dropped out of the sky like some kind of prehistoric beast. One second the sky was clear, the next the giant machine was blocking out the sun's rays, its rotors stealing the sounds of the gulls overhead, the barking seal, the waves splashing against the hull.

There were binoculars hanging off the binnacle. Keeping one hand on the wheel, Joey grabbed them, put them to her eyes and saw him, staring out of the giant open door, him, the man she'd seen from underneath that restaurant in Tobago. The man she'd seen illuminated by a lightning blast when she'd done battle with a helicopter.

How?

Then it hit her as she rehung the binoculars. The president's daughter. Somehow he knew about Mick, knew about the pictures and was trying to stop Mick from blackmailing Suzi.

"What do they want?" Nina said.

"They think we're working with Mick," Joey said.

"What are we going to do?" Nina was looking up at the helicopter. "If we give up, maybe we can tell them about the bomb? Maybe they can get to Suzi faster then we can."

"There!" Joey pointed. She saw *Babycakes* in the distance. They were on a collision course. She looked at the time, it was 5:47. "That's her."

"You're sure?" Nina shouted to be heard over the roar of the helicopter.

"Yeah." Joey couldn't believe it. This helicopter was so much bigger than the one that man was on the last time.

"How much time do we have?"

"Thirteen minutes." Joey looked at the helicopter. "I don't think that's enough time to give up and convince them about the bomb." She pushed the starter button again, heard the starter grind again, but she kept her finger on it. Please, Lord, please let it start. It did, with a cough of black smoke.

"Can we make it? Can we get Suzi off her boat?" Nina said.

"Maybe, the engine will give us more speed."

"You want to go for it?" Nina said.

"Yeah, I do."

"I do too. Let's go get her!"

"Okay, take the wheel. I'm going to tighten sail."

"Aye, aye, Captain." Nina moved behind the wheel.

"He'll try to block us," Joey pushed the throttle full forward. "Whatever you do, don't turn. Keep the boat pointing toward *Babycakes* at all costs. If he makes us turn, Suzi dies and maybe us, too."

"Got it," Nina said. "I won't turn."

And as she said it the giant helicopter flew off and moved to block their path. They'd seen *Babycakes*, too.

* * *

"You're sure that's Suzi's boat?" Snelling said of the boat in the distance.

"I am," Dowling said as the pilot moved to block the boat below. She must have instructed the pilot to protect the president's daughter.

"No, don't do this. Move away," Snelling said.

"I'm sorry, sir," Dowling said. "But I'm in charge now. Suzi Walcott's safety is an issue. That's Secret Service business."

"Move off!" Snelling told the pilot.

"She's in charge, sir," the Coast Guard pilot said. "We're going to stop *Reaper* and order her to heave-to."

"*Reaper?* What's *Reaper?*" Snelling said.

"The boat below. That's her name," the pilot said.

"Jesus," Snelling said under his breath. Then he shouted, "She's not gonna stop!"

"She will!" the pilot shouted back.

"If she runs that mast into your blades, what happens to us?"

"Won't happen," the pilot said.

"Listen to me," he said to Dowling. "I've been here before. I was in a chopper above that woman only a few days ago. She was in a small boat. We tried to stop her. The pilot tried the same thing we're doing here."

"What happened?" Dowling said.

"She drove that boat straight at us. Missed us by inches."

"Don't worry," the pilot said, talking loud now, not shouting. "We've done this dozens of times. She'll heave-to. They always do."

"She won't," Snelling said.

* * *

Suzi saw the Coast Guard helicopter flying above *Reaper* and shivered. Her first thought was that there was a rescue in process. She knew Tom and Betsy Reaper. They were older, in their middle sixties and Betsy had a heart condition. She remembered when they renamed the boat, giving it their last name. They'd said it was the child they'd never had. She was afraid that Betsy had had a heart attack at sea.

Then she remembered that Betsy had told her something about leasing the boat out for a couple of months to a young man from Texas. What was it she'd said? A writer doing a horror story that took place on board a sailboat. So it wasn't Betsy on board. She wasn't having a heart attack. It was that writer.

All of a sudden the helicopter moved to block *Reaper* from continuing on her course. What was that all about? Had someone stolen Tom and Betsy's boat? Was the writer some kind of criminal? "Oh no!" The flash of truth burned through her. No writer had leased *Reaper*. The helicopter wasn't effecting a rescue. Her blackmailer had rented the boat, that's why she hadn't seen him. And now he was on his way out to collect his dirty money and somehow the Coast Guard had found out.

How?

Who?

The Secret Service had to be involved. That meant Claudia. Damn.

* * *

Joey tightened the mainsheet, then winched in on the headsail, tightening it, too. It might not do them much good right now, the way the helicopter was playing havoc with their wind, but once Nina chased it away, they'd scoot. She looked up at the flying machine, they were seconds away from collision.

"Joey, he's not moving."

"Hold steady," Joey said.

"Joey!" Nina screamed.

"Hold your course!"

"I'm holding!"

Now either they were going to hit the helicopter and they'd all be dead or the bastard would pull up. The sound of the rotors was deafening, louder than a West Indian jump up, louder than the inside of *Satisfaction* during a gale, louder than anything she'd ever heard. Loud and deadly. Any second the mast was going into the blades.

"Joey!"

300

"Fuck him!" Joey flashed the finger.

* * *

"Pull up!" Snelling screamed and the pilot obeyed. He'd seen the finger, too, knew what it meant. She was going to take the boat into the chopper and damn the consequences.

"Jesus," Dowling said. "Those are gutsy girls."

"You don't know the half of it," Snelling said.

* * *

Suzi had one hand on the wheel, the other was holding binoculars to her eyes. Two girls on *Reaper* and they'd almost rammed the Coast Guard helicopter in midflight. So it wasn't the horror writer. But why would a couple of girls risk death by sailing into the blades of something like that? She trained the binoculars on the chopper, saw Claudia through the open door.

Had her mother told the Secret Service? Had she warned Claudia? Did Claudia know about the pictures? The blackmail? No, Claudia must have found out all on her own, because her mother never would have told, she didn't trust the Secret Service. Maybe Claudia was somehow tuned into her e-mail, whatever, it didn't make any difference how. The fact was, she was out here now, trying to keep that boat away from her. Why?

Certainly they weren't the blackmailers. Not girls. Especially not those girls, they braved that helicopter to try and intercept her and they were still coming. They had *Reaper* heeled over, sailing her the way she was meant to be sailed, like Tom and Betsy had never sailed her.

Suzi made a decision. She tightened sail, picked up speed. For some reason those women wanted to talk to her badly enough to risk the wrath of the Coast Guard and the Secret Service. And they were sailors. If they wanted to say something to her that bad, then she was going to listen.

Now the helicopter was heading her way. In seconds it was directly overhead.

"Suzi, this is Claudia. Change course." Claudia's voice boomed over a loud speaker, so loud it drowned out the sound of the rotating blades.

Suzi waved the chopper away.

Reaper was getting closer.

* * *

Joey glanced at the time as the helicopter stopped hovering over *Babycakes* and came back. Four minutes to six. Not much time left. All she could do was try, but she didn't see how they could possibly get Suzi off *Babycakes* in time. It all seemed so futile, so stupid. A desperate attempt at the impossible. And at the end of the line there was nothing for Joey and Nina but a long term in prison. She wondered if they had the death penalty in California and if so, what was the instrument of killing, the hangman's noose, the bolt of juice or the cyanide pill in the iron chamber?

"They're going to try to kill us," Nina said.

"What?" Had the girl been reading her thoughts.

"There's a lady up there with a gun and she looks like she's going to use it." Nina had the binoculars to her eyes, was looking at the helicopter as once again it dropped out of the sky on top of them, hovering.

"Duck!" Nina shouted.

Joey dropped to the deck as three quick gunshots rang out.

* * *

"What the fuck was that?" Snelling grabbed the pistol from Dowling's hand, flung it through the open door. Christ, he couldn't believe it. Give a girl a gun and she had to use it. What was the world coming to?

"What are you doing?" Hot anger made her scream seem primeval. She sounded like she'd rip his heart out if he gave her half a chance. He wouldn't do that.

"No shooting!" He cut into her glare with one of his own. "They haven't done anything wrong!"

"I'll have you up on charges!" Dowling shouted. Then to the crew, "Do you have weapons on board?"

"No ma'am," the guardsman in the copilot's seat said.

"Give me your weapon, Snelling, That's an order!"

Snelling pulled his Glock from his shoulder holster, tossed it out to join her weapon at the ocean bottom. "No shooting!"

CHAPTER
TWENTY-FOUR

JOEY HUDDLED ON THE DECK, a hand still on the wheel. She'd heard the shots, felt the explosions from the gun as she'd never felt thunder. And she'd heard the unmistakable sound of bullets slamming into the deck. Those people up there really didn't want her and Nina to meet up with the president's daughter. They'd tried to warn them off by blocking their path, now they were shooting. Shit.

"Some guy up there grabbed her gun and threw it out!" Nina shouted. Like Joey she was on the deck, huddled in front of the binnacle, trying to make herself a smaller target, but it was futile, there was no place on deck to hide from the gunman overhead.

"What?"

"Come on, get up, I don't think they're going to shoot anymore."

"Shit and double shit." Joey, still holding the wheel, used it to pull herself up. A look at the GPS. Two minutes to six. She looked toward *Babycakes*, she was maybe two minutes away. Joey had hoped they'd have time to both turn into the wind. Side by side in irons, Suzi could have stepped over and they could have sailed off. No time for that now.

"We're gonna have to jibe and somehow we're gonna have to tell her."

"What do you mean?" Nina said.

"We're gonna turn right with the wind at our back. It won't be so hard for us, because we don't have to turn through the wind, so the boom won't come across. But she has to jib through, so her boom is gonna come across the deck. I hope she can handle it."

"She's a sailor. They used to talk about her on television all the time." Nina had to shout again, the helicopter was back, its giant rotor again wreaking havoc with their hearing.

"Yeah, that's right."

"So what do you want me to do?"

"Go up front and point to the right. You have to let her know we're turning. Also you gotta get the message across that we want her to turn, too."

"I can do that."

"Go."

"I'm going."

"Nina!" Joey called out.

"What?"

"Be careful, especially when I start the turn, don't get thrown off."

"Don't worry, I'm going to hang on!"

* * *

And Nina meant it. She was going to hold on for all her life was worth. She stepped out of the cockpit, thought about crawling up to the front of the boat, but the time was too short to waste, so she grabbed onto the boom, used it for support as she worked her way to the mast.

That helicopter was right on top of her, those spinning blades going whack, whack, whack, like the ceiling fan above her bed back in Brazil, only about ten million times louder. Whack, whack, whack. How could she think?

At the mast, she grabbed onto it for a second and snuck a quick look up. The giant helicopter was right on top of them, the door open wide, a window into the belly of the beast. And in the machine beast's belly she saw the woman who'd shot at them. She seemed so small, hair running wild around her face because of the wind blowing into the doorway. Next to her she saw the man that had taken her gun away and tossed it into the ocean. Also she saw some men that looked like soldiers. She saw all this in a flash of a second, then she looked away and dashed up to the front of the boat. The big sail was cracking in the wind, almost as loud as the whacking blades.

She had to get in front of the sail. Had to make Suzi see her. Otherwise everything they'd done was for nothing. She grabbed onto the front of the sail, moved around it, now grabbing onto the bow pulpit. As secure as she was going to get, she trained her eyes forward and gasped.

Babycakes was so close. It looked like they were going ram into each other. She had to signal her and there was no way she could do it without letting her hands go.

The wind was blowing strong now, or was it her nerves.

"I'm not afraid!" she screamed to the heavens. It was a lie. She was terrified. But she stood up anyway and let go her hands.

* * *

"Holy shit, girl," Suzi told herself. "Those ladies want to talk to you mighty bad." A ripple of fear ran over her skin, electrifying her body in a way that wasn't good. Claudia had no business shooting at those girls.

But maybe she did.

Maybe she knew something Suzi didn't. Maybe they were terrorists of some kind. Maybe they were on a suicide mission to kill the president's daughter. For a second she thought that maybe she should do what Claudia had said, turn course, run away. *Reaper* was a bigger, faster boat, but Suzi was a sailor, she could give them a run while Claudia slowed them down, or stopped them.

No, she told herself. She'd never heard of girl terrorists. She'd never heard of terrorists that could sail.

And she'd never heard of terrorists that were brave. Those girls were no terrorists. Somehow Claudia had got it wrong.

But they were on a collision course. She was going to have to turn and do it quickly or there was going to be one hell of an accident at sea, and that wouldn't do anyone any good. Especially her, the last thing she wanted was to be the feature story on the seven o'clock news.

The helicopter hovering over *Reaper* reminded her of the gunship helicopters she'd seen with her father on their trip to the Marine Corps Air Station at El Toro and for a brief second she thought they might start shooting again. *Reaper* was getting ever closer, so was the chopper and it was ungodly loud. That alone was enough to get her on the news. She was going to have the press crawling all over her. Her privacy was going to go out the window.

Didn't anyone care?

Eyes away from the helicopter, back on *Reaper*, Suzi saw the girl on the bow. She looked like a waif, beautiful, but small. Was she crazy? Now she was in front of the big sail. The boat lurched, she almost fell. She bent down, grabbed onto the bow pulpit as *Reaper* sliced through the sea. Then she let go, stood up straight as if she were riding a great white horse bareback in the circus. She waved.

What the hell?

Suzi waved back.

Then the girl pointed, stiff armed, ninety degrees to her starboard, Suzi's port. She was signaling a turn.

Suzi flashed the thumbs up sign.

The girl pointed at Suzi, then pointed to her

starboard again. She wanted Suzi to turn, too.

* * *

"My God," Snelling muttered when he saw what Nina Brava was doing. Such courage. She was as brave as her name. He'd go to battle with her anytime. What a soldier she'd make. Soldier, the thought rifled through his mind, exploding sure as if he'd been shot. Mick Sapphire was a soldier, more than a soldier, a Navy Seal. A demolition expert, like Clayton. A bomb man. "My God!" he said again. He wasn't muttering now.

"I don't get it," Dowling said. "What's she doing?"

"Pull up!" Snelling shouted.

The pilot, acting on instinct, obeyed, pulling the chopper a hundred feet higher in an instant. "What?" he said.

"There's a bomb on Suzi's boat. Probably gonna to go off any second. Those girls are trying to save her."

"What are you talking about?" Dowling was shouting now.

"It's the only thing that makes sense." Snelling had his mouth to Dowling's ear. He grabbed her hand, squeezed. Please, God let it not be too late. "We've chased them, tried to block them and shot at them, but they kept going. And now that girl is standing on the front of that boat down there, risking her life to get a message to Suzi. They're not doing it so they can swap some dirty pictures for dirty money. Jesus Christ, they're trying to save her."

"You're crazy!" Dowling said.

"That girl's husband down there, the one driving the boat. He's the blackmailer. He was a Seal, a bomb guy."

"Aw fuck," Dowling said. Now she believed, too.

"Yeah," Snelling said.

"We should try and get her off," Dowling said.

"The way those girls have been fighting to get to her, I don't think we have time." He looked at his Citizen. "He probably set it to go off on the hour. It's about a minute to six."

"Aw no!" Dowling leaned forward against the harness, looked down.

"Better take it up another hundred feet," Snelling said.

"Sir, we should be safe from the blast here." One of the crew had overheard.

"It's not us I'm worried about," Snelling said. "It's them, we're a distraction they don't need right now."

"Take it up!" the crewman shouted.

* * *

"Get back here, Nina!"

Nina dropped to her hands and knees and crawled back to the cockpit, slipping and sliding on the damp deck worse than she did on the snow up in the Arizona mountains.

"Take the wheel!" Joey pulled the shift lever into neutral as the chopper pulled away.

"Coming!" Nina scooted behind the wheel. "Just tell me what to do!"

"When I shout, 'Jibe,' turn right ninety degrees and hold your course. If she understood, we'll let her come alongside and I'll adjust the speed with the sails."

"You shout and I turn, got it!" Nina clutched the

wheel as Joey played the lines. She took one off a winch, held it in her hands, turned to Nina and gave her a look she'd never forget. Desperation, fear, sadness, it was all there in her eyes. Nina looked at the time. A minute to six.

"Get ready!" Joey shouted.

* * *

Suzi saw the girl scoot back to the cockpit and take the wheel, they were so close and closing fast. She looked down at the sail bag sitting in the middle of the cockpit floor. Two million dollars. Herself in dirty pictures. What was the world coming to?

And she was going to have to do an uncontrolled jibe, no time to tighten up the main. Nothing for it but to let the boom slam across the deck. A problem *Reaper* wasn't going to have as they weren't going to have to jibe through the wind as she was.

It was time.

Suzi spun the wheel to the left and *Babycakes* slid into a quick turn to port.

* * *

"Jibe!" Joey screamed.

"Turning!" Nina cranked the wheel to the right. She saw sweat raining off Joey's rippling muscles as she hauled on the rope. She had arms like an athlete. Heck, her whole body was athletic and she looked like a wound up spring ready to pop.

"Okay, you're there!" Joey was panting. "Hold it steady!"

"She's turning too. She understood!"

"All right! Keep her steady!" Joey said as *Babycakes* slammed into their side with a thunder-like boom and a scraping screech that sent quivers icing up her back. For a second Nina thought the boats were going to become tangled up with each other.

"Bomb!" Joey shouted.

Suzi Walcott grabbed a bag, stepped out of the cockpit, took two quick steps and jumped from *Babycakes* onto *Reaper's* deck. She was a girl that didn't have to be told twice.

"Kick in the gas and turn, turn!" Joey wailed.

Nina shoved the throttle forward and cranked the wheel, desperate to get away from *Babycakes* now.

"Suzi duck!" Joey shouted.

Still turning the wheel, Nina and Joey could only watch as Suzi dropped her bag and fell on it as the boom slammed across the deck, missing her by centimeters. Then the sail filled and *Reaper* picked up speed, as the wind was at her stern now.

"Are you okay?" Joey hopped out of the cockpit, helped Suzi up.

"I'm stupid, is what I am," Suzi Walcott said. "I'm a sailor, I shoulda been ready for that jibe."

"I should've been on the mainsheet and controlled the boom."

Then a thunderous sound shook the air. The loudest noise Nina had ever heard.

* * *

"Jesus wept!" Dowling said as the helicopter jerked and

bounced in the air.

"Everyone all right?" the copilot said.

"We're fine," Snelling said. But he didn't know about the chopper. "How's the plane?"

"Okay!" the pilot shouted and in seconds it was.

"I can only imagine what would have happened if we'd've been right on top of them," Dowling said. She didn't seem so sure of herself now and that was a good thing, Snelling thought. It was never good to be too sure of yourself.

"That was a good call, sir," the copilot said.

"Luck," Snelling said.

"Well you were right," Dowling said. "The girls were trying to save her."

The pilot, in control now, started to bring the helicopter back down.

"No," Snelling said. "Climb higher, but keep them under observation for a bit."

"What are you up to?" Claudia Dowling said.

"Those women have been through more than you can imagine," Snelling said. "And most of it's my fault. I'm not going to cause them any more grief."

"The president's daughter is down there."

"They just risked their lives getting her off that boat. I hardly think they're going to hurt her."

"Miss Dowling?" the pilot said.

"Do as he says," Dowling said.

* * *

"Holy shit!" Suzi said, staring at the pile of rubble that had been her boat.

"Yeah, holy shit." Nina was shaking and glad to see the helicopter getting smaller as it rose in the sky.

"I'd say we were some pretty lucky ladies," Joey said.

"I'm so scared, I think I'm gonna pee my pants," Suzi said. "I'm going below."

"Me too." Nina hadn't thought about it before, but she had to go now, bad. "I feel like my bladder is about to bust."

"*Burst*," Joey said as she moved behind the wheel. "We say *burst*."

Nina started for the companionway and the head below.

"Watch out for Mick," Joey said.

"Uh oh, I forgot about him," Nina said.

"Who?" Suzi said.

"Dead guy, below," Joey said. "My ex-husband. The one who took the pictures. Also the guy who planted that bomb." Then, "What's in the sail bag?"

"Two million dollars."

"Better take it below," Joey said.

"I'll help." Nina picked up the sail bag. It was heavy with the feel of freedom. She dropped it through the companionway. Then she followed it down.

"Holy Smokes!" Suzi Walcott said when she came below.

"Holy Smokes?" Nina said. "That doesn't sound like swearing."

"It's not," Suzi said. "Force of habit. When your dad's the president you don't get to swear too much." She went over to the body and went to her knees. There were some flies buzzing around the staring eyes. She brushed them away. "It's the face I remember. God, he was handsome."

"Even out here death brings the flies," Nina said. "How do they know?"

"I don't know." Suzi stood. "They just do."

"He was a fucking shit. That's how you swear." Nina crossed her arms in front of herself. "He didn't deserve any better." She looked at the stuff she and Joey had bought in Arizona, strewn about the floor where Mick had dumped it when he emptied their packs. She picked up the backpacks.

"You're not from here are you?" Suzi said.

"You can tell? Damn, I've been working real hard at sounding American. I was doing it for my baby." She rubbed her stomach. She felt hollow. "But I guess it doesn't matter how I sound anymore."

"So where are you from?"

"Brazil."

"And your friend, she sounds South African?"

"She is."

"How do you know Tom and Betsy?"

"Who?"

"The owners of *Reaper*."

"What? Oh, the boat. We don't know them." Nina picked up the sail bag.

"You stole the boat?"

"I don't know. He had it when we killed him. Then we figured out about the bomb." Nina opened the sail bag, dumped the money out on the settee, then started stuffing it in her backpack.

"What are you doing?"

"Taking the money."

"You can't do that," Suzi said.

"What are you talking about?" Nina whirled on her. "You let some creeps take sexy pictures of you and because of it horrible men came after me and Joey. They hurt me. They killed my baby." She stopped, mad enough now to spit fire, rubbed her stomach again. The hollow feeling would never go away. "You're fucking asshole right I'm taking the money."

"Now that's swearing," Suzi Walcott said.

"God damn right." Nina stuffed more packets of bills into the backpack.

"Let me help." Suzi picked up the other pack, started stuffing money into it. When they were finished, they cinched them up.

"That helicopter is still up there," Joey said, coming down the companionway. "But it's way up there now. I don't get it."

"Who's driving the boat?" Nina said.

"Autopilot," Joey said.

"Like on an airplane?" Nina put on her pack.

"Exactly," Joey said.

"Put this on." Nina held out the other backpack.

"Why?" Joey looked around the room, running her eyes over their clothes still on the floor, stopping her gaze at the empty sail bag. "The money?"

"God damn right," Nina said.

"Put it on," Suzi said.

"Okay, okay." Joey put on the pack.

"The head's up front?" Suzi asked Joey.

"Yeah, I think so."

"Sorry, I don't know your names."

"I'm Nina." Nina held out her hand the way Americans do and Suzi shook it.

"I'm Joey."

"I'm Suzi, but I guess you know that." Then, "Be right back." She went up front.

"So we're taking the dirty picture money?" Joey said.

"Yes."

"They'll never let us get away."

"We're going to try," Nina said.

"I guess we can't get in any more trouble than we're already in. But it doesn't seem right."

"I told her they killed my baby, she understands. And if that isn't enough, how about this, they turned us into killers. How about that?"

"She's right," Suzi said, coming out of the toilet. "You guys should have the money, even if only for saving my life, you've earned it."

"My turn." Nina went to the head.

"So, you got any idea how we can get away?" Joey was saying to Suzi when Nina rejoined them.

"Not a clue," Suzi said. "That's the Secret Service up there. There's no way they're ever gonna let this boat out of their sight, especially after *Babycakes* blew up like that." Suzi looked down at the body. "I feel like kicking the bastard. He killed my boat. Me and *Babycakes* were gonna sail around the world together."

"Kick him," Joey said.

"Yuck." Suzi brought her foot back to do it, stopped. "I can't."

"Think they'll put us in jail?" Nina could barely hear the helicopter now. It had gone even higher, but it was still there. Suzi was right, it wasn't going away. The police would be waiting for them when they got back to the marina.

"I don't think so," Suzi said. "Not after what you did, saving my life and all. But you never know. If I were you and could get away, I would."

"And how are we going to do that?" Joey said.

"I don't know, but it looks like he had a plan." Suzi nodded toward the scuba tank. "Too bad there's not another set of diving gear. You guys could just slip over the side when we got close to the marina and disappear. That's apparently what he was going to do."

"I don't know how to scuba dive," Nina said.

"There's only one tank so it doesn't make any difference," Joey said.

"You could get away," Nina said. "There's no sense both of us going to jail."

"No," Joey said. "We're in this together. I won't run out on you."

"One thing I don't understand," Suzi said. "If he was going to blow me up. Why'd he need the scuba stuff?"

"Maybe he didn't trust you. I mean, the Secret Service is on top of us right now," Joey said. "Maybe he was going to jump in the water the second the boat blew up, you know, when nobody was looking."

"What about us?" Nina said. "What was he going to do with us?"

"I don't know," Joey said.

"What are you talking about?" Suzi said.

"He had us tied up," Joey said. "So I guess if things would've gone as he planned, he'd be sitting here counting his money, and Nina and I would still be tied up back to back in the middle of the salon."

"I'm getting a bad feeling," Suzi said.

"There's another bomb," Nina said, calm, voice almost a whisper. "This boat's going to blow up, too."

"We're gone!" Suzi dashed up the steps, was through the companionway faster than Nina would have thought possible.

"Go, Joey!" Nina pushed her and Joey shot up the steps with Nina right behind.

"Faster!" Suzi was on deck. She grabbed Joey by the hand, jerked her out of the companionway, then she had a hand out for Nina. "Move your ass!"

"Over the side!" Joey shouted and they jumped.

The cold Pacific was like ice to Nina as she hit the water. In an instant she was under and going down. Wasn't she supposed to float right up? She wasn't a great swimmer, but she knew how. She struck out for the surface, was constrained by the backpack, but not for a second did she think about taking it off. She had half the money on her back. A million dollars. No way was she going to throw it away. Joana and her would never have to work again. All she had to do was get it back to Brazil.

Again and again she flayed toward the surface, finally broke through. She gasped in a breath, coughed it out, sucked in a great volume of air, filled her lungs, blew it out and started treading water.

"Are you all right?" Joey shouted.

"I'm okay," Suzi shouted back.

"Me too," Nina shouted.

"It's fucking cold," Suzi said.

"The boat didn't blow up," Joey said as they watched it sail away commanded by only the autopilot.

"Maybe we were wrong," Nina said.

Then the terrifying sound of thunder boomed across the water and *Reaper* was blown into a mass of wood and fiberglass splinters.

CHAPTER TWENTY-FIVE

THE EXPLOSION SHOCKED Claudia to the core. One second she was looking down at Suzi as she and the two other woman sailed back toward the marina. The next, they were diving overboard. Then the boat blew up.

"Take it down, now!" Claudia shouted.

"Yes, ma'am," the pilot said.

"You said she'd be safe!" Claudia rounded on Paul Snelling, the CIA man next to her. "You said those women had saved her life. You were wrong! They were part of the blackmail scheme all along and they just about killed her!"

"You don't know that!" Snelling said.

"They're all in the water. They look okay!" the copilot said.

"We let her go out on the ocean in a small boat with two million dollars, how stupid?" Claudia said.

"Calm down," Snelling said. "She's okay."

"No thanks to you! She turned to the copilot. "Can we get them up here?"

"No problem."

"Get the president's daughter first!" Claudia ordered.

* * *

Joey looked up at the helicopter hovering overhead as it seemed to drop out of the sky, a giant war bird backlit by the orange sun sinking into the sea. Something bumped her side and she screamed.

"Sorry!" Suzi Walcott shouted. "I didn't mean to scare you."

"It's okay!" Joey shouted back.

"Your friend's having a hard time! I tried to take the pack, but she won't let me. Talk to her! Tell her I'll give it back! She can't swim with it."

"You okay, Nina?" Joey had no problem swimming with her own backpack.

"Don't know." Nina was breathing fast.

"I'm a swimmer," Suzi said. "I can keep her afloat till they pick us up.

"I swim too!" Joey moved to Nina's left. "We'll do it together."

Suzi swam to Nina's other side, took her arm. "It's

gonna be okay," Suzi said. "We've got you."

"Sorry," Nina sputtered. "I don't swim so good."

"You'll be okay," Joey said. "Don't worry."

The helicopter dropped even lower, till it was right on top of them. It seemed almost close enough to touch.

Nina, supported by Joey and Suzi, pulled a hand from the water and pointed upward. "They're dropping a ladder."

Joey looked up as a diver jumped through the door. She kept her eyes on him till he splashed down less than twenty meters away. He swam toward them as welcome a sight as she had ever seen.

"Suzi Walcott goes first," the diver said, but Joey saw in his eyes that he'd figured out the situation.

"No," Suzi said. "She does."

"Right." The diver grabbed onto the hanging ladder. "Can you do it yourself, ma'am, or do you want me to go up with you?"

"I can make it." Nina grabbed onto the ladder, clawed up a couple of rungs, got a foothold. The diver signaled the copter and they pulled up the ladder.

"Suzi next, or it's my ass," the diver said.

"Probably already your ass if I know Claudia Dowling," Suzi shouted.

"She's a pistol," the diver said. He couldn't have been more than nineteen or twenty. He'd just jumped out of a helicopter and he was smiling, like he did this sort of thing everyday.

"You go next," Joey said. "I'll hang out here with him."

"You're Joey Ryder!" Suzi shouted. "I thought I

recognized you."

"Yeah," Joey said. It had been a long time since someone had used her maiden name and longer since someone had recognized her. Her gold medals were a fleeting fame, soon forgotten by all, except a few friends. To be recognized here, in the middle of the ocean, with a helicopter hovering overhead, by the daughter of the President of the United States. That was something.

"I was in Sydney. I saw you do it."

Then the ladder was back and Suzi climbed on.

"You gonna be okay, ma'am?" the diver said as they hauled Suzi up.

"You're all so polite!" A bolt of pure adrenaline mixed with joy charged through her. She'd saved a human life, the life of a good person. Maybe that didn't go all the way toward making up for what her father had done, but for her it was enough. She'd done her share, finally she could put his evil ghost away. She was finished with him.

"What?"

"Americans. You're all so polite. So nice."

"Not all of us." The diver smiled. "Hang around awhile, you'll see."

* * *

A wave of relief washed over Claudia when they pulled Suzi aboard. She grabbed onto her, hugged her. She couldn't help herself.

"I'm okay, Claudia." Suzi laughed. Was still laughing when they brought up the ladder with the diver and the other woman, Joey Sapphire.

"Okay," the pilot said, "we're outta here."

"I thought you were dead for sure," Claudia said fifteen minutes later, when they were on the ground. Then she hugged Suzi again.

"I'm really okay, Claudia. Thanks to Joey and Nina. I would've been dead if it weren't for them."

"So what do we do now?" Joey Sapphire said.

"If you don't mind house guests, Miss Walcott," Paul Snelling said, "I think we can prevail upon the Coast Guard to take you all to your place while Miss Dowling and I clean up."

"Clean up?" Claudia didn't like the idea of Suzi going anywhere without her.

"You know," Snelling said, and damn if he didn't have a twinkle in his eye, "make up a story for the press. Something like, Suzi was out sailboat racing, collided with another boat and there was a propane explosion, thank God nobody was hurt. Something like that."

"Lie?" Claudia said. "I like it."

"But somebody was hurt," Joey Sapphire said. "My so called husband was below. He didn't get off."

"What?" Snelling said.

"He was kind of dead, so he couldn't exactly jump overboard," Joey said.

"Who did it?"

"Isn't there some kind of rule about incriminating yourself in America?" Nina Brava said. "I've seen it on television and in the movies."

"I think what I'm trying to say," Joey said. "was that my husband was accidentally killed in the explosion as he bravely helped Suzi off the boat. It was a horrible shame. And by the way, his camera and all the pictures he'd taken were destroyed, too."

"That's a story the press will eat up," Claudia said. Though she didn't think it right that the man that had taken the pornographic pictures of Suzi and had almost caused her death should be mourned as a hero.

"Then it's done," Snelling said.

* * *

"You girls look good in my clothes," Suzi said and Joey laughed.

Nina was swimming in a pair of Levi's cinched up like a little boy wearing his big brother's clothes, but she did look good in the oversized, black Rolling Stones T-Shirt. Very hip. Joey also had on faded Levi's, but they fit her like a glove, so did the New York Yankees T-Shirt.

"So what happens now?" Suzi said. "I mean with you guys, are you going home, back to Brazil and South Africa?"

"Not me," Nina said. "I'm staying here, I just decided. All our lives me and Joana, that's my best friend, have dreamed of coming to America. I'm here now and I'm going to send for her. We're never going back, never looking back. She clutched her backpack. I've got it all planned, we're going to open up a little Brazilian restaurant somewhere by the ocean and kick butt." She paused. "I said it right, didn't I, *kick butt?*"

"You said it right," Suzi said. Then, "And you Joey Ryder, what are you going to do with your million dollars?"

"Mick had this wonderful sailboat called *Satisfaction*. I guess she's mine now, so I'm gonna bank the money and live off the interest as I sail her around the world."

"What?" Suzi grabbed Joey's arm. "You want company?"

THE BOOTLEG PRESS CATALOG

RAGGED MAN, by Jack Priest
ISBN: 0974524603
   Unknown to Rick Gordon, he brought an ancient aboriginal horror home from the Australian desert. Now his friends are dying and Rick is getting the blame.

DESPERATION MOON, by Ken Douglas
ISBN: 0974524611
   Sara Hackett must save two little girls from dangerous kidnappers, but she doesn't have the money to pay the ransom.

SCORPION, by Jack Stewart
ISBN: 097452462X
   DEA agent Bill Broxton must protect the Prime Minister of Trinidad from an assassin, but he doesn't know the killer is his fiancée.

DEAD RINGER, by Ken Douglas
ISBN: 0974524638
   Maggie Nesbitt steps out of her dull life and into her dead twin's, and now the man that killed her sister is after Maggie.

GECKO, by Jack Priest
ISBN: 0974524646
   Jim Monday must rescue his wife from an evil worse than death before the Gecko horror of Maori legend kills them both.

RUNNING SCARED, by Ken Douglas
ISBN: 0974524654
   Joey Sapphire's husband blackmailed and now is out to kill the president's daughter and only Joey can save the young woman.

NIGHT WITCH, by Jack Priest
ISBN: 0974524662
A vampire like creature followed Carolina's father back from the Caribbean and now it is terrorizing her. She and her friend Arty are only children, but they must fight this creature themselves or die.

HURRICANE, by Jack Stewart
ISBN: 0974524670
Julie Tanaka flees Trinidad on her sailboat after the death of her husband, but the boat has a drug lord's money aboard and DEA agent Bill Broxton must get to her first or she is dead.

TANGERINE DREAM, by Ken Douglas and Jack Stewart
ISBN: 0974524689
Seagoing writer and gourmet chef Captain Katie Osborne said of this book, "Incest, death, tragedy, betrayal and teenage homosexual love, I don't know how, but somehow it all works. I was up all night reading."

DIAMOND SKY, by Ken Douglas and Jack Stewart
ISBN: 0974524697
The Russian Mafia is after Beth Shannon. Their diamonds have been stolen and they think she knows where they are. She does, only she doesn't know it.

TAHITIAN AFFAIR: A ROMANCE, by Dee Lighton
ISBN: 0976277905
In Tahiti on vacation Angie meets Luke, a single-handed sailor, who is trying to forget Suzi, the love of his life. He is the perfect man, dashing, good looking, caring and kind. She is in love and it looks like her story will have a fairytale ending. Then Suzi shows up and she wants her man back.

BOOKS ARE BETTER THAN T.V.

THE BOOTLEG PRESS STORY

We at Bootleg Press are a small group of writers who were brought together by pen and sea. We have all been members of either the St. Martin or Trinidad Cruising Writer's Groups in the Caribbean.

We share our thoughts, plot ideas, villains and heroes. That's why you'll see some borrowed characters, both minor and major, cross from one author's book to another's.

Also, you'll see a few similar scenes that seem to jump from one author's pages to another's. That's because both authors have collaborated on the scene and—both liking how it worked out—both decided to use it.

At what point does an author's idea truly become his own? That's a good question, but rest assured in the rare occasions where you may discover similar scenes in Bootleg Press Books, that it is not stealing. Writing is a solitary art, but sometimes it is possible to share the load.

Book writing is hard, but book selling is harder. We think our books are as good as any you'll find out there, but breaking into the New York publishing market is tough, especially if you live far away from the Big Apple.

So, we've all either sold or put our boats on the hard, pooled our money and started our own company. We bought cars and loaded our trunks with books. We call on small independent bookstores ourselves, as we are our own distributors. But the few of us cannot possibly reach the whole world, however we are trying, so if you don't see our books in your local bookstore yet, remember you can always order them from the big guys online.

Thank you from everyone at Bootleg Books for reading and please remember, Books are better than T.V.

KEN DOUGLAS & VESTA IRENE
WANGARAI, NEW ZEALAND

Made in the USA